PRAISE FOR BE

"This cute, quirky, and adorably sweet romance hit all the right notes of tender, funny, and downright charming. Add in hilarious family dynamics (I adore Zach's mom) and you're set for another excellent story by Becca."

PEPPER BASHAM, author of *Authentically, Izzy* and *Positively, Penelope* on *Love in Tandem*

"A charming rom-com filled with unique twists and turns, *Love in Tandem* is sure to bring a smile to readers looking for a lighthearted romance. With unique characters and a fabulous opposites-attract dynamic, this is a sweet escape into an adventure in love, second chances, and holding on to what's most important in life."

REBEKAH MILLET, award-winning author of *Julia Monroe Begins Again*

"Sometimes the bumpiest rides lead to the most serendipitous of finish lines. A sweet tale of misadventure and unexpected romance."

NICOLE DEESE, *Christy Award–winning author* on *Love in Tandem*

"*Love in Tandem* sparkles with summer fun. I enjoyed the premise, the characters, and the humor on every single page. It's the perfect beach read."

ANGELA RUTH STRONG, author of *Hero Debut*

"*Love in Tandem* was everything I hoped for. Becca Kinzer knows how to deliver characters I immediately care about and put them in a situation I had to know more about. Not to mention she delivers on humor, swoony heart-stopping moments, and a happily ever after that still makes me grin long after reaching the end (and reading the author's note). *Love in Tandem* is one for the Top Ten lists."

TONI SHILOH, award-winning author of *In Search of a Prince*

"A charming rom-com. . . . This lighthearted jaunt checks all the boxes readers will expect."

PUBLISHERS WEEKLY on *Dear Henry, Love Edith*

"A rom-com treat for readers to devour. Simultaneously a sweet romance with the perfect amount of heat and laugh-out-loud comedy with a surprising dose of depth, *Dear Henry, Love Edith* is a witty and heartfelt gift from the first word to the last."

BETHANY TURNER, author of *Plot Twist* and *The Do-Over*

"Rarely have I read a romance with such sparkling personality. Everything about Kinzer's vibrant voice and freshly told love story tugged at my heartstrings and widened my smile. Fans of Katherine Reay and Pepper Basham will be enchanted."

RACHEL McMILLAN, author of *The Mozart Code* and the Three Quarter Time series on *Dear Henry, Love Edith*

"A lovely debut by Kinzer that had me cheering for the unlikely, and yet so perfect, pair, Edith and Henry."

MELISSA FERGUSON, author of *Meet Me in the Margins* and *Famous for a Living* on *Dear Henry, Love Edith*

LOVE IN TANDEM

LOVE IN TANDEM

BECCA KINZER

A NOVEL

Tyndale House Publishers
Carol Stream, Illinois

Visit Tyndale online at tyndale.com.

Visit Becca Kinzer's website at beccakinzer.com.

Love in Tandem

Cover designed by Libby Dykstra

Edited by Kathryn S. Olson

Published in association with the literary agency of Gardner Literary LLC, gardner-literary.com.

For information about special discounts for bulk purchases, please contact Tyndale House Publishers at csresponse@tyndale.com, or call 1-855-277-9400.

Library of Congress Cataloging-in-Publication Data

A catalog record for this book is available from the Library of Congress.

ISBN 978-1-4964-6612-9

Printed in the United States of America

30 29 28 27 26 25 24
7 6 5 4 3 2 1

Mom and Dad, this one's for you.

Love you always.

1

It's a terrible thing when a teacher survives an entire school year only to die the first minute of summer vacation.

"Whatcha doing, Miss Carter?"

"Don't move," Charlotte whispered to whichever first grader had spoken. Or maybe it was a second grader. Up until middle school, they all sounded the same. Like little mice helping Cinderella prepare for the ball.

"Are you playing statues?" the nameless child squeaked.

"Not exactly." Charlotte puckered her lips and blew a soft breath without moving a muscle. "There's a bee."

"Where?"

Hovering an inch away from Charlotte's face. What did the kid mean *where*?

"Oh. Now I see him. He's about to land on your nose. Are you trying to get him to land on your nose?"

Must be Nash. She glimpsed a mop of brown curls in her peripheral vision, and of all the O'Mally siblings, he was the most inquisitive. Or troublesome when one wasn't in the mood for inquisitive. "I'm trying to get him to fly away."

"Want me to help?"

Definitely Nash. And definitely *not.* Nash's attempts to "help" often led to blood, tears, and a trip to the nurse's office—or principal's, depending on the type of help involved. "I'm okay, Nash. Really. You can go."

The final bell had rung, and children everywhere bubbled across the schoolyard full of summer excitement. Teachers too. She couldn't be sure, but a conga line might have formed on the way to the bus stop with Ty Zemeckis, the principal, leading the way.

"Want me to shoo it away for you?" Nash persisted.

"Nope. No need to make it mad." Charlotte exhaled another breath, hoping to mimic a gentle breeze that would carry the bee far, far away.

"I got stung once. It wasn't that bad."

It was when you were deathly allergic to bees. Or possibly deathly allergic to bees. Ever since the terrible night Miranda Woods babysat for Charlotte years ago and showed her the terrible movie *My Girl*, which ended with a young boy's terrible death from bee stings, Charlotte had resolved to never find out.

Charlotte's eyes crossed as the bee flitted in front of her nose. She should have boycotted field day. Told Ty she'd pass out popsicles inside the cafeteria. Scrub toilets. Clean gum from beneath desks. Anything but referee three-legged races and kickball tournaments in a field full of flower-pollinating assassins.

Thankfully this slayer must have grown bored buzzing around her head. It flew off, leaving Charlotte to live another day. *Whew.*

She spun for the brick school building, ready to pack up her meager belongings, maybe do a little conga dance of her own, then rush over to

Mucho Mucho Queso. She couldn't wait to see the look of surprise on her parents' faces when she handed them a check for two thousand—

Smack!

Charlotte's head flung back, and pain exploded in her nose. A gush of warm fluid sprayed from each nostril.

"Did I scare off the bee, Miss Carter?" Nash—of course it was Nash—chased after the basketball he'd thrown. He lifted it from the crater-size pothole it'd bounced into, then pointed at Charlotte's face. "Uh-oh."

Yeah, uh-oh. She pinched the bridge of her nose while Nash's face crumpled into tears and the ball dropped from his hands. A few tears leaked from Charlotte as well. Mercy, that hurt.

"I—I'm sorry," he whimpered. "Do I have to go to the principal's office?"

And drag this day out any longer? Heck no. "Lucky for you, Nash, the principal's office is closed. Have a great summer," she said in a voice that now sounded like Kermit the Frog with a head cold.

Nash cried harder. "I k-killed you."

Looked like this day was going to drag out a little longer. "No, buddy. I promise. This wasn't your fault." And honestly, it wasn't. Things like this always happened when Charlotte spent more than fifteen minutes in the wild. And a schoolyard full of crazed children and lethal flying insects most definitely qualified as the wild.

"Shh. There, there." She patted his back. Or at least that was the intent. Unable to see with her head tipped back, she groped the air until she found his hair and settled for petting him like a puppy. "I get nosebleeds all the time."

If *all the time* meant *first time ever*. And in situations involving sobbing children on the last day of school, it did. "It's probably nasal allergies. I used nasal spray the other day. Probably made my nasal passages dry. All that nasal constriction."

She didn't know why she was rambling to a nine-year-old, let alone using the word *nasal* on repeat, but if it dried his tears and distracted from the sensation that fire sparklers were lit inside her nose, she'd go with it.

"Hey, did you know there's a musician named Kenny G who can breathe in through his nasal passages as he blows air out his mouth at the same time?"

"Circ-circ-circular breathing. You told us about that in music class."

"I did?" She risked looking down.

Nash nodded.

"And you remembered?"

Nash nodded again, a half-smile breaking through his freckled face.

Well, how about that? Maybe she'd taught these kids a thing or two after all, despite the music department's abysmal resources and her part-time hours. Just think what she could teach them next year when she had actual instruments. An actual classroom. Actual support.

Part of her still couldn't believe the school board had relented, agreeing to forego reconstruction on the middle school's decrepit parking lot to provide a full-time music teaching position that included a band program. The hours she'd poured into applying for grants had paid off. Between the school board's decision and the promised grant money for all new instruments, Charlotte's dream of a thriving music program was finally taking root.

Take that, Benjamin Bryant.

Charlotte shook her head. Stop. After two years, she doubted her ex-fiancé gave her more than a passing thought. Besides, her desire for a successful music program had nothing to do with him.

Okay, ninety-four percent nothing to do with him. Six percent might still be a little hung up on proving Ben's decision to call off their wedding had been a mistake. His decision to give up on her had been a mistake.

Charlotte squeezed Nash's shoulder as she gently probed her nose and did a little sniff test. The bleeding had stopped. "Who knows? Maybe you'll learn how to circular breathe someday. Have you thought about which instrument you'll choose next school year?"

Nash grinned without a trace of tears. "The trumpet. Or maybe the trombone. Something I can blow real hard in. Then maybe I can help you blow away all the bees."

Charlotte laughed, even though it made her nose throb. "I like how you think, Nash," she shouted as he ran to catch up with his two older brothers, who were waving at him to hurry up.

Charlotte hustled into the school building before anything else thwarted her first moments of summer freedom. Locker doors slammed and shoes squeaked amongst the chatter of giddiness. Charlotte turned a blind eye to the gaggle of girls running to exit the building. Any other day, she'd have told them to slow down. Today, it was all she could do not to crack a whip and yell "Hee-yah!"

Slipping into the classroom she shared with the school nurse, the volunteer librarian, and, whenever he was bored, the school custodian, she pulled the door shut and leaned against it with a long sigh. Then a smile. A giggle. Oh, what the heck—she started to dance.

Somewhere after the fourth or fifth *cha-cha* around the folding table that served as her desk, a throat cleared from the doorway.

Charlotte gasped and spun. "Ty. I mean, Mr. Zemeckis. I mean—" Considering at one time he'd been friends with her older brother and used to torment her with wet willies and wedgies, it was weird knowing how to address him as her principal.

She slugged his upper arm. "You sneaky punk, I didn't hear you come in." School was out for the summer. She'd call him whatever she wanted.

"Ow." He rubbed his skinny arm with mock pain. "Well, maybe if you weren't so busy butchering the lyrics to a Gloria Estefan song. *Come chickabonka, baby, something 'bout a conga?*"

"I'm fairly certain that's how it goes."

The corners of Ty's eyes crinkled behind his glasses. "I suppose you can sing whatever you want on the last day of school." His smile dimmed as he took in the blood spatters on her shirt. "What happened there?"

"Nash."

"Don't tell me any more. I'm off duty until August."

Charlotte waited for the humor to return to his eyes. It didn't. Instead he spent the next several seconds tugging on his ear as he glanced around the box-shaped classroom to where a plastic human skeleton missing two ribs hung next to a narrow bookshelf crammed with tattered books. Then he pulled out one of the student's chairs so he could fold his lanky frame into the seat and spend another eternity rubbing his forehead.

She heaved a deep sigh. "Look, I know what this is about, and I really don't want to talk about it."

Ty's brow wrinkled in confusion. "How did you hear?"

"Ben's mom told me. We ran into each other at the farmers market a few weeks ago. I got so flustered trying to prove I wasn't flustered at the news, I bought fifty-three dollars' worth of fresh spinach, which made me all the more flustered because I hate spinach and she knows I hate spinach, so somehow in all the flusterment I concocted an imaginary friend who loves spinach, whom I may have suggested wasn't imaginary but rather special and perhaps male."

Behind his glasses, Ty's wide eyes blinked like a befuddled owl's. "What are you talking about?"

Now it was Charlotte's turn to blink and ponder. "Ben's wedding this weekend. What are *you* talking about?"

Ty gripped the back of his neck with a groan. "Now I feel even worse. I totally forgot this weekend was Ben's wedding. Why would he get married this weekend? Isn't this practically the same weekend two years ago that you were supposed to—"

"Hey, remember that moment forty seconds ago when I said I didn't want to talk about it?"

"Right. Sorry. I just really wish I had better news to give you right now."

If it wasn't about Ben's wedding, what sort of bad news could it possibly— *Oh no*. Charlotte sucked in a breath and palmed her stomach. "Please don't tell me this is about Will." Her brother had been released from prison over a year ago. If he'd gotten arrested again . . .

"This isn't about Will," Ty said, standing with a grimace. "It's about the music program. We lost the grant."

"What?" Ty may as well have hurled another basketball at her face. "No," she breathed out, leaning against her desk table for support. It slid half a foot away from her.

Ty grabbed the edge before it scooched any further. "I'm sorry. This isn't how I wanted the last day of school to end for you."

"I don't understand." Charlotte lowered the folding table onto its side, needing something to do other than pound the tile floor in a tantrum. She kicked one of the metal legs. "How did we lose the grant? I thought everything had been approved."

"So did I, and I suppose there's a tiny chance it might turn out okay, but I got an email a few days ago warning me the foundation who offered the grant money is under investigation." He took over with the table legs when it became clear Charlotte cared more about kicking than folding. "And unfortunately, the head of the school board has already been in contact, saying if the grant isn't coming through, they don't see the point in pouring money into a full-time music program when we have so many other pressing needs."

"Like what?"

Ty propped the folded table against the wall with a pained smile. "Where do I even begin? A better library for starters."

"*Phhht*. As if students need books to learn."

Ty's lips tugged in a grin. But Charlotte wasn't trying to be funny. "Our town already has a library. What our town doesn't have is a band. Studies show that children who—"

Ty lifted his palms. "I know what the studies show, Professor Harold Hill, and I'm on your side. I want a thriving music program as much as you. But our town doesn't have the funds to support one right now. Especially at the grade school level."

"Which is why I applied for the grant."

"Which is why I'm talking to you now, so we can develop a backup plan."

Charlotte tossed the battered music theory textbook she'd been using the past couple of years into a cardboard box along with a ukulele, two drumsticks, a brown plastic recorder, and the toy harmonica she'd confiscated from Nash the first day of school. She swung her guitar case over her shoulder, picked up the box, and forced herself to take a deep breath. This wasn't Ty's fault. The least she could do was hear him out. "What sort of backup plan?"

He stood in the doorway. "Did you happen to read the front-page article in the newspaper yesterday?"

"Our town still has a newspaper?"

"I'll take that as a no." Gripping the doorframe, he leaned forward and lowered his voice as if the walls had ears. "A. P. Hopkins is dying."

"Uh-huh." Hardly a shocking revelation. Seemed about every seven years, the recluse millionaire claimed to be dying.

"No, I think he's for real this time," Ty said, obviously sensing her skepticism. "If you'd read the article, you'd understand. There was a whole different feel to it. Like he was truly saying goodbye and wanting to go out with a final hurrah. And you'll never guess what his final hurrah is."

"A town music program?" Hope fluttered in her chest.

"A new twenty-mile bike path."

Hope splattered at her feet. "How's that supposed to help anything?"

Charlotte didn't mean to sound insensitive. Certainly, she would miss A. P. Hopkins. Not that she'd ever met him. Not that anyone had ever really met him. But how could she not miss the crazy philanthropist who offered sporadic donations and kept life interesting in her otherwise ho-hum, small Illinois town?

Just once though, she wished he'd invest his money in something that wasn't geared toward athletics. Something the town actually needed. *Something like a stinking music program.*

"Listen." Ty grabbed the box from her arms and set it on the ground as if he were afraid whatever he said next might tempt her to throw the box at him. "The bike path isn't the exciting part."

And now he was using the same tone parents used when telling their kids about an "exciting" trip to the dentist's office.

"The exciting part is . . ." He nudged the box further away with his foot. "Well, you know how every time he offers a big donation, he includes some sort of challenge to go with it just for fun? Like the treasure hunt he sponsored when he paid to remodel the high school football stadium years ago? Remember? The winner got ten grand."

"Of course I remember. Sophia nearly dug up our parents' entire backyard, convinced the funny shaped tree in his clue was our tree because of the giant knot that always reminded her of our great-uncle Benny's nose."

"Exactly. Well, the treasure part. I'm not familiar with your great-uncle Benny's nose."

"Let's just say she wasn't wrong. So what's the special challenge this time?" *Wait.* She clasped her hands together as if in prayer. "Oh, please tell me it's another pie-eating contest, like when he put in the sand volleyball courts. I came so close to winning that one, and I was only eight at the time. You know how much pie I could put down now that my job's on the line?"

Ty pointed his finger at her. "Yes. See? That's what I'm talking about. That's the fire we need. The eye of the tiger."

"Before you go into one of your Sylvester Stallone impressions, would you please just tell me what the challenge is? Is it pie?"

"Probably not pie. To be honest, Hopkins didn't offer many details. He just said the challenge would be something physical and require a lot of time outdoors." He gave her two thumbs up. "Right up your alley though, eh?"

Charlotte stared at him for a beat, then scooped up the box. He flinched as if she were going to fling it at his head. Which she probably would if she thought she could afford to lose any more instruments. "Skydiving into snake-infested jungles so some recluse lunatic who probably isn't even dying can get a laugh watching me torture myself like I'm in one of those dreadful *Saw* movies is not up my alley."

"That's what you got from the words *physical* and *time outdoors*?"

"Out of my way." Charlotte elbowed him in the gut on her way past. If she wasn't in a hurry to meet her parents for half-price margaritas, she'd kick him in the shins for getting her hopes up.

"Wait," he called after her. "Don't you even want to hear what the prize is?"

Charlotte clipped down the hallway, tossing her words over her shoulder. "Why does it matter if I'm not going to do it? Besides, you know I hate competitions. Unless it involves pie. Maybe cheesecake," she added under her breath.

"Twenty-five thousand dollars."

Her feet stuttered. Paused. Slowly turned. "How much did you say?"

He dug his hands into his pockets, leaning forward with that secretive tone again. "You heard me. And you wouldn't be competing with anyone. Hopkins said this time he's only choosing one couple to participate. All they have to do is complete the challenge on time, and he'll give them a prize of twenty-five thousand dollars. He said it should be enough to cover the cost of a nice wedding."

"Hold on. Back up. Wedding? *Couple?*"

Ty cleared his throat. "Yeah, so apparently the whole point of this challenge—other than winning oodles of money—is to put some couple through better or worse and see how it affects their relationship. On a side note, you haven't started dating anybody recently, have you? Because that would certainly make this backup plan a lot more feasible. If Krista and I weren't leaving for vacation next week, I'd try entering us."

Charlotte adjusted the box, half-wondering if she could hit him from this distance with the recorder. What was wrong with him? Nothing about this challenge should make anyone think of Charlotte Carter. *Nothing.*

"Look, Ty, I know you mean well—" truly the only reason she wasn't throwing the recorder at him right now— "but I'm sure I can figure out ways to raise money for the music program that don't involve dismembered limbs or death. Or being in a relationship."

She resumed her march for the exit. "I'll stick to the usual fundraisers, thank you. Maybe this year we can even do one of those kiss-the-pig contests. Which shade of lipstick do you prefer?"

"I'd buy tickets for that," Mrs. Scott shouted from her second-grade classroom.

"Charlotte—" Ty's voice snagged her a few steps from the door. "I don't think fundraisers are going to keep you afloat this time. I think . . . I think you need to start considering other options."

The weight of her box doubled. Other options? In a town the size of a guitar pick, how many options did he think she had when it came to teaching music and staying close to her family? There *weren't* other options. Especially for a single gal nowhere close to being one half of a couple.

She adjusted her grip on the box. Bailey Springs, Illinois, might not seem like much to outsiders—or insiders if she was being honest. But Bailey Springs was her home. Her life. Her future. Why would she have this burning desire to get a music program running in this town if she wasn't meant to see it through? Somehow, someway, she would make it happen. *Take that, Benjamin Bryant.*

Forcing a smile, she pressed her back against the door. "I get your concern, but I'm sure it's going to be okay."

"How can you say that?"

"Because sometimes you don't need a giant budget. Sometimes you just need a little faith." She shoved through the door and spun before Ty saw her smile falter. Before he saw that after years of struggling to catch a break in her hometown, her faith was beginning to develop more cracks and potholes than the school parking lot.

Especially when the voice of doubt grew louder in her ear. A voice that sounded an awful lot like Benjamin Bryant. *Take that, Charlotte Carter.*

2

Charlotte spotted her parents' silver Dodge pickup in Mucho Mucho Queso's parking lot. Hopefully, singing the chorus to George Michael's "Faith" the entire four-minute ride over had erased all evidence of weeping and wailing the previous ten minutes. And if it hadn't, she'd blame Nash's basketball.

With a deep breath, Charlotte climbed out of her car, then double-checked her purse for the envelope she'd made sure to place there this morning. Today might officially go down on her calendar as the stupidest, most disappointing-est day of the year, but at least she could still make this a great day for her parents.

A lively song with Spanish lyrics and the warm scent of Mexican spices greeted Charlotte at the entrance. The owner, Nita, waved and pointed to where her parents were already seated in a booth beneath a painted canvas of a giant bull squaring off with a matador.

At four-thirty in the afternoon, the restaurant wasn't busy, part of the reason Charlotte had chosen this time. The other part definitely had to do with the half-price margaritas.

Charlotte slid into the vinyl booth across from her parents, and they both immediately frowned.

"What's wrong?" her mom asked.

"Does she know?" her dad murmured.

"Know what?" Charlotte said.

"You look like you've been crying."

"Is that blood?" Dad asked.

Charlotte dipped her gaze to her shirt, deflecting Mom's statement. "Nash hit me in the face with a basketball. In a way, it was very endearing. Where's Sophia?"

Charlotte had promised Sophia she wouldn't give Mom and Dad the money without her. *"Just because I'm a broke college student and can't afford to chip in a single cent doesn't mean part of this gift isn't from me."* Who was Charlotte to argue with that logic?

"She's talking to Rick." Mom pointed to where their church's youth minister sat at a table with his very pregnant wife and toddler daughter. "He's probably asking if she can help chaperone the youth group's canoe trip. I heard they were looking for more volunteers."

Charlotte shuddered. "Better her than me."

Mom smirked. "Pretty sure Rick crossed you off that list with a Sharpie when I told him about the time you pepper-sprayed a park ranger during our one and only camping trip."

"He should have identified himself better. I thought he was a bear."

"Clearing his throat outside of the tent. Yes. We remember." Mom tugged her sweater further over her shoulders. Her dark hair had grown back in, albeit more gray, and she'd regained all her weight, but the battle with cancer seemed to have staked permanent claim over her ability to stay warm. Charlotte wouldn't be surprised if she was wearing three additional layers beneath her cardigan and button-down denim shirt, making her look closer to fifty-seven rather than forty-seven.

"Well?" Dad rubbed his hands together, his lifelong career as a mechanic evident in the grease stains on his fingers. "Does it feel good? Another school year under your belt?"

Charlotte reached for a chip, debating how much to divulge. Might as well get it out there. "It didn't end like I hoped it would."

"Because of the basketball?" Dad said.

That actually made Charlotte laugh. "No. I wish. More like because the grant money may not come through." She was still clinging to hope that somehow the whole thing would fix itself by the end of next week.

Mom straightened. Dad stopped rubbing his hands. "Oh no."

"What does that mean for you?" They both spoke at the same time.

Sophia plopped into the open space next to Charlotte, her large gold hoop earrings, dangly bracelets, and sparkled headscarf somehow cute and trendy. If Charlotte attempted the same accessories, she'd look like Captain Jack Sparrow's love child with a fortune teller.

"What does *what* mean for you?" Sophia said. "And why does everyone look like someone died? I was only gone for a minute. Oh wait. Is it because of what weekend this is?"

"Is that why you were crying?" Mom asked, then elbowed Dad in the side when he whispered, "What weekend is this?"

"You guys, I'm fine. I know this weekend is Ben's wedding and all, but it's been two years. I'm completely over him. His name doesn't even cross my mind." *Except for six percent of the time.* Charlotte fisted her napkin, wishing she could strangle her conscience for always being so nitpicky about the truth.

Fine. Six percent of the time Ben's image might breeze through her mind. But that didn't mean she was hung up on the guy. She wasn't. At all. She'd moved on. *She had.*

So why were her parents and Sophia looking at her like she hadn't?

"I wasn't going to say anything, but I actually have plans to see someone this weekend," Charlotte blurted out before her conscience could stop her.

It wasn't *technically* a lie. Charlotte did plan on seeing someone. The fact that someone was Frankie Avalon and Charlotte planned on seeing him on her living room flat screen as she worked her way through her favorite Beach Party movies shouldn't matter, should it?

Based on the hopeful gleam in her mom's eyes, the wariness in her dad's, and the skeptical squint in Sophia's, it probably did matter.

Charlotte smoothed her napkin on the table in her best nonchalant manner. "Who knows if it'll lead to anything serious. He's just a friend. An old friend." *Who may not even still be alive.* "I probably shouldn't have mentioned it."

She *definitely* shouldn't have mentioned it. What was wrong with her? First, making up a special friend who loved spinach for Ben's mom, and now pretending to date Frankie Avalon in front of her family? Maybe Ben's wedding this weekend was getting to her more than she wanted to admit.

"Well, I'm glad you did say something." Mom smiled and lifted a hand to wave goodbye to Rick and his family as they headed out the door. "I feel better knowing you won't be sitting at home this weekend by yourself. Especially after hearing your grant money's not coming through."

"No grant money?" Nita appeared with a tray of waters and more salsa. *"Eso es terrible. Todos esos instrumentos!"*

"*Might* not be coming through," Charlotte tried reassuring Nita. Tried reassuring everyone. "I have faith everything's going to turn out fine." *Sort of.*

"So Ty's not worried?" Dad said after Nita had taken their orders and performed the sign of the cross while murmuring what Charlotte assumed were prayers imploring all the saints above to save the music program. Oh, how she loved Nita.

Charlotte thought of Ty's slumped shoulders. His defeated expression. His words of warning. "Oh, you know Ty. He always has a backup plan."

Not necessarily a feasible backup plan. But she wasn't about to mention the article in the paper. Knowing Sophia, she'd latch on to the ridiculous contest with a stranglehold until she figured out a way to rope Charlotte into it.

"Anyway," Charlotte said, swiping her hand as if the whole possibility of not having a job next school year and watching her entire dream explode in flames on the second anniversary of getting jilted at the altar was nothing but a pesky fly. "Let's talk about something else."

"Like the youth group's canoe trip." Sophia gripped Charlotte's wrist, a habit of hers whenever she wanted a favor. "Can you do it? Please? Rick said he's desperate. It's only a day trip, no camping."

"Me?" Had her sister lost her mind? Sophia should know no amount of desperation would force Charlotte to step foot in a canoe. And she should definitely know better than to grab Charlotte's wrist when she had a chip full of salsa halfway to her mouth. "Why can't you do it?"

"My summer job at the hospital starts this evening, and I don't know any of my coworkers well enough to ask for a trade. C'mon, Charlotte. You could take your guitar and play churchy campfire music when they reach the end. It's totally your thing."

Charlotte shook Sophia's hand off, flinging salsa onto her shirt in the process. It matched the blood splatters, at least. "Canoes and campfires are not my thing. Mom, tell her that's not my thing."

Mom shrugged. "It's really not her thing."

Sophia folded her arms and collapsed against the back of the booth. "Fine. Don't help. Don't play songs about Jesus. Let dozens of teenagers potentially lose their souls because you're unwilling to participate in something that's 'not your thing.'"

Charlotte blotted her shirt with a napkin. "Now that we've got that matter settled, Sophia and I have a surprise for you."

Sophia perked up in her seat, dozens of teenagers' souls apparently forgotten for the moment.

"Surprise?" Dad said. "I thought we were just here for the half-price margaritas." Mom playfully bumped his shoulder as Charlotte pulled the envelope out of her purse and slid it across the mosaic tabletop.

Mom's and Dad's smiles both disappeared.

"What's that?" Dad asked, eyeing the white envelope the same way he tended to eye Charlotte's attempts at a new recipe. Little optimism, ample suspicion.

"Some money I've—" Sophia's pointy elbow jabbed Charlotte's side—"*we've* been setting aside for you."

Her parents stared at the envelope, neither of them reaching for it. Mariachi music blasted overhead for what felt like an eternity before Mom cleared her throat and tugged the check from the envelope. She sucked in a breath, then showed it to Dad.

"Consider it a late anniversary present," Charlotte said.

"You can finally take a vacation," Sophia added.

Dad pulled out his reading glasses from his front shirt pocket. As soon as he looked at the check, he shoved it back in the envelope and handed it across the table. "Char, we're not taking your money."

"Our money," Sophia whispered.

"You're not taking anything," Charlotte said, trying to hand it back to him. "We're giving it to you. C'mon, when's the last time you guys took a vacation?" Probably not since a dozen years ago when it became clear camping wasn't Charlotte's thing.

Of course, between paying off steep medical bills from mom's cancer, trying to help put their kids through college, hiring a lawyer for Will, and losing several deposits from Charlotte's last-minute canceled wedding, it's not as if her parents had been in a good place to take a nice long vacation since then either.

Dad still put in sixty-plus hours a week at the shop, Mom worked her part-time secretary position at the church in addition to cleaning homes, and neither breathed a word of saving for retirement.

They needed a vacation. They deserved a vacation. Which was why

Charlotte had scrimped and saved these past couple of years to give them that vacation.

So why weren't they the least bit thrilled to take a vacation?

"Please," Charlotte said, sliding the envelope toward them. "I owe you." The guilt from all those lost deposits from the wedding two years ago weighed heavy on her conscience.

Mom's warm palm covered Charlotte's hand. "You don't owe us anything. Things happen. It's okay. We're okay."

Dad tapped his fingers on Mom's hand. "If anything, you should be saving this money for your music program. Or fixing up your house. Didn't you say the plumbing's still giving you trouble? Or why not go back to school and get a four-year degree?"

"All right. I get it." Charlotte should have known Dad would never accept a check flat-out. She should have purchased a nonrefundable vacation package.

Sophia slapped her hand over Dad's, her bracelets jingling and trapping all their hands beneath hers. When they looked at her in surprise, she said, "What? I was feeling left out."

Charlotte fixed her gaze on Mom. "Will you at least consider taking a break this summer even if you don't want to accept my money?"

"Our money," Sophia whispered.

"You look exhausted," Charlotte added. "You can't try and tell me you don't need a break."

Mom slid her hand out, and Dad did the same. "We'll see," Mom said.

"We're working through some issues," Dad said.

"Maybe once things slow down a bit," Mom added quickly, then smiled when Nita appeared with a tray full of drinks. "Ah. Perfect timing."

Nita sprang forth before Charlotte could ask her parents to elaborate about what *issues* they were working through. She glanced at

Sophia, who'd gone quiet, probably feeling as confused and concerned as Charlotte. Did this have something to do with Will? Nobody had heard a word from him since his release. Were they holding out to make sure he landed on his feet?

She swiped the rim of her glass and licked the salt grains from her finger. Or were they holding out to see if *she* ever landed on her feet?

Charlotte slid the envelope back into her purse. Nothing today was turning out like it was supposed to. Nothing for years had turned out like it was supposed to.

All the more reason she needed her music program to thrive.

3

Zach adjusted his phone and raised his voice to be heard over the rush of traffic on the interstate and the squealing hiss of a semitruck slowing to a stop in the parking lot. "Guess where I am right now."

"Standing on top of Mount Kilimanjaro," his friend Rick responded over what sounded like a mariachi band playing in the background.

"Guess again."

"Dodging poison dart arrows in a South American jungle."

"Guess again."

"Wrestling alligators in the Everglades?"

"Close." Zach ran a squeegee over a splatter of bugs on his Jeep's windshield. "I'm getting gas at a Piggly Wiggly in Tennessee."

"What a coincidence. I'm getting gas at a Mexican restaurant in Illinois. Hey, can I call you back in a minute?"

"If you promise not to tell any more jokes like that."

"Who says that was a joke?"

Zach grinned and pocketed his phone, then lifted one windshield wiper after the other to scrub away the dirt from his recent Appalachian excursion. Nice to know Rick's humor hadn't changed since the one semester they roomed together in college. The only semester Zach had gone to college. Didn't take a diploma for Zach to learn what he already knew—he didn't belong inside a classroom any more than Rick belonged center stage at a comedy club on open mic night.

Nah, let his brother Ben earn the degrees and climb the corporate ladder like their father. All Zach had ever wanted was space. Air. Mountain trails. Snowy peaks. Rushing rivers. Starry skies. And hopefully someday the love of a woman who shared the same outdoorsy, venturous soul as he did. Which apparently would never be Shannon.

If the Dear John letter inside his back pocket wasn't enough to convince him, the engagement ring on her finger ought to do it. Why he still kept her letter, he didn't know. Could have burned it in any one of the campfires he'd built over the past year.

He attacked a stubborn splotch of bug juice on the upper corner of his windshield. Would have burned it last night if he hadn't written the address for the wedding rehearsal on it.

His phone rang, and Zach swiped it out of his pocket.

"Sorry," Rick said, soon as Zach answered. "We're just finishing up at Mucho Mucho. I swear this baby is going to come out wearing a sombrero. All Kate's wanted for the past three weeks is Nita's salsa. She literally drank it straight out of a to-go cup two nights ago. It was revolting. And by revolting, I of course mean the sexiest thing I've ever seen." Rick's voice grew louder as he was obviously including his pregnant wife in on the conversation. "It's Zach," he stage-whispered.

"Hi, Zach," Kate said.

"Hi, Zach," a teeny, high-pitched voice echoed.

"Did you hear Ryleigh?" Rick said, the adoration for his little girl evident.

"I did. Tell them both hi for me." Zach dropped the squeegee into the bucket of cleaning fluid and climbed into his Jeep. Last time he'd seen Ryleigh, she'd been a drooly baby who liked to coo. Based on the chatter he heard in the background, her vocabulary skills had come a long way since then.

"So hey, man," Rick said. "What's going on? I thought you were working some sort of gig in New Zealand, acting as a personal travel guide for a group of ritzy *Lord of the Rings* fanatics or something." The lively music disappeared, and Zach guessed they had walked outside the restaurant and were getting into their minivan.

"Yeah, that didn't exactly pan out like I'd hoped. I sort of got fired less than two minutes after I got hired."

Rick groaned. "Please don't tell me it had anything to do with a girl."

"Why would you automatically think it had something to do with a girl?"

"Because I remember all too well how girls get around you. They take one look at your man bun and mountain-climbing physique and go googly-eyed."

Zach squinted against the sun, ignoring the two college-aged girls who had smiled at him earlier on their way into the gas station and were now crossing back to their car, waving and giggling with packages of Funyuns and Swedish Fish in their hands.

So maybe Rick had a point. And maybe part of the reason he got fired did have something to do with a girl. But not the way Rick imagined. Zach hadn't even so much as looked at a girl since Shannon.

Unfortunately the man who'd hired Zach to take his family backpacking through New Zealand had a teenage daughter who'd done plenty of looking when she was introduced to Zach in their living room. The moment she'd sidled up to Zach, fluttered her lashes, and inquired about the sleeping arrangements during the trip, her father had escorted Zach to the door.

Zach shoved his key into the lock cylinder, half hoping his Jeep wouldn't start just so he'd have an excuse not to make it back to Illinois.

Ornery thing started up first try. "For the record, I cut off my beautiful locks a year ago right after Shannon dumped me."

Rick gasped. "Like Keri Russell in *Felicity*?"

"Yes. Maybe. Who?"

"Don't act like you don't know what I'm talking about."

"Don't act like it's normal for any man to know what you're talking about."

"Don't act like it's normal for any man to refer to his hair as 'beautiful locks.'"

"You're only saying that 'cuz you're bald. The point is, I'm tired of googly-eyes. I don't want googly-eyes. Googly-eyes cost me big. Not only did I lose out on a big chunk of cash this summer, I lost out on a valid excuse to miss my brother's stupid wedding."

"Forgot that was this weekend. And for the record, I'm pretty sure your mom wouldn't have considered anything other than death a valid excuse to miss your brother's stupid wedding. Didn't you agree to be the best man?"

"Only to prove to everybody how supportive I am of this stupid wedding. Hey, don't you usually do some sort of canoe trip with the youth group about this time?"

"Dude, you can't miss your brother's wedding."

"What time do we leave?"

Rick laughed. "It's actually not until Monday. It's only a day trip, so we're leaving at the butt crack of dawn. But I'm sure you've got things going on all weekend with the wedding that you are absolutely not missing."

Zach ran a hand over his short beard. "I've got the rehearsal dinner tomorrow tonight, the wedding Saturday, but nothing past Sunday." Other than a family brunch he'd love to avoid. "C'mon, man. I love canoe trips. Plus you know the butt crack of dawn is my thing."

"If ever you had a thing, it certainly is that. Well, I mean, if you're sure then."

"As sure as a heart attack."

"Don't think the expression works like that, but I'll take it. The good Lord knows I can always use an extra set of eyes when it comes to teenagers. Usually Sophia Carter tags along, but she's got a work conflict. I'm about to the point of begging Charlotte, if that tells you something."

Zach gripped the steering wheel and stared out the front window. "Charlotte? As in . . ." He almost said *Ben's Charlotte*. But she wasn't *Ben's Charlotte* anymore, was she? Hadn't been for two years. Not since his brother had called off the wedding. "So she's still around, is she?"

Dumb question. Of course, she was still around. Half the reason her relationship with his brother didn't work out was because she refused to leave Bailey Springs. The other half of the reason was because his brother was an idiot.

And now that idiot was marrying Shannon instead.

Rick must not have heard his question about Charlotte. Sounded like he and Kate had entered a serious debate about how much salsa consumption it took to kill a person. "You are not going back inside for more," Rick said.

A truck tooted its horn behind Zach, a line of vehicles starting to form. Zach flipped down his visor. "I've got to hit the road. I'll talk to you later and we can work out the details for the trip."

"Awesome. Thanks again. And hey man, have fun at the wedding."

Zach ended the call with a grunt. Rick might as well have told him to have fun wrestling alligators in the Everglades.

4

No sooner had Charlotte closed the front door to her yellow bungalow house full of charm—or in need of renovation, if one didn't find stained carpets, bad plumbing, and outdated appliances particularly charming—than Sophia burst through the door behind her, flinging a purse, shoes, scarf, and possibly an earring across the small entryway.

"Spill it," Sophia said, slamming the door shut.

Charlotte's cat, Patches, leapt from the couch and fled down the hallway in a blur of gray, no doubt seeking sanctuary beneath Charlotte's bed.

"I thought you had to get to work," Charlotte said, watching her sister rush past.

"Not until I hear about this mystery person you're supposedly seeing this weekend." Sophia started stripping off clothes on her way to the bathroom, leaving the door open as she talked. "Does he by any chance go by the name Frankie?"

"How'd you know?"

"Please, I'm not only a master amateur sleuth who's watched every season of *Psych* at least seven times, I'm your sister. I know your coping mechanisms whenever you get stressed. Now, speaking of stressed, we need to make a plan before it's too late. Right now. Today." Fabric rustled and her jeans sailed out the door. Next came her T-shirt.

Charlotte scooped them from the floor. "Nope. Not today. I'm officially starting a heartbreak sabbatical, and I refuse to make plans or think about anything to do with my job until next week."

"Job? Who said anything about your job?" Sophia jutted halfway through the doorway, buttoning up a white long-sleeve collared shirt. "I'm talking about Mom and Dad. Didn't you hear them? They're having issues, Charlotte. *Issues.* Everybody knows in married life that's code talk for divorce."

Oh, for Pete's sake. Charlotte loved her sister, but the girl could find more drama reading a coffee maker manual than most people found watching an entire season of *The Real Housewives.* "I promise you Mom and Dad aren't getting a divorce. They're fine."

Sophia sped out of the bathroom, tucking her white shirt into black slacks as she jammed on one black shoe after the other. "If they're fine, why were they acting so weird, huh? Admit it, something was off. Mom hardly touched her food. Dad couldn't stop rubbing his hands together. You saw it. I saw it. I'm telling you, we need to do an intervention."

Charlotte folded her arms and leaned against the back of the couch. No way did she believe for one second her parents were contemplating divorce. But she couldn't deny they had been acting a little weird, especially about the whole money issue. All right, she'd humor her sister. "What sort of intervention?"

"Something big. Something Hayley Mills–like."

And now she was done humoring her sister. "Not sure *The Parent Trap* should be our guiding light when it comes to marital issues."

"Well, what do you suggest then?" Sophia grabbed her giant tote bag of a purse and began shoving the wreckage of her tornado costume change into it. "Have you even thought about what a divorce would mean for us? Who are we going to spend our Christmases with? What, one of us goes to Mom's and the other goes to Dad's? Dad doesn't know how to cook. I don't want to eat takeout on Christmas. And I don't want to split the day between parents. I want to stay in my pajamas all day. Don't you want to stay in your pajamas all day?"

"Of course I want to stay in my pajamas all day."

"Then we need to do something for the sake of our pajamas if nothing else."

Charlotte opened the door, ready to end this ridiculous conversation. She had enough on her plate without catering to her sister's delusions. "Sophia, I'm just going to be straight with you. My job is not as stable as I made it sound. If I don't focus on figuring out how to raise enough money for an entire music program before August, I'm going to have to search for a job somewhere else. Do you know how hard it will be to find a music teaching position I'm qualified for? I only have my associate's degree. I was lucky to even get a part-time job here. If I lose it, I'll either need to go back for more schooling, which I can't afford, or move to some remote town in the middle of Wyoming where I'll get snowed in every winter and never make it home for Christmas at all."

Sophia hitched her bag onto her shoulder. "Have you considered bingo? I overheard Arlene at church say she made four hundred dollars in one night. Of course, I think she said something about losing eight hundred the previous week."

Charlotte held the door wider. "Don't you need to get to work and save some lives?"

Sophia glanced at her Mickey Mouse watch, a Christmas gift Will gave her years ago that she still wore every day. "I do. Though I'd hardly call delivering meal trays to patients with no appetites lifesaving work." She sighed and grabbed Charlotte's wrist. "Promise to keep thinking about how to save Mom and Dad's marriage, and I'll keep thinking about how to raise money for your music program. Deal?"

"As long as your ideas don't involve lottery tickets or slot machines." Though the idea of spending another summer swamped in fundraisers made Charlotte consider the idea of betting on horse racing.

Adjusting her tote on her shoulder, Sophia headed to the door. "Too bad you and Frankie Avalon aren't a real item. I hear A. P. Hopkins is offering a bunch of money to a couple who can complete some sort of challenge in ten days. Sounds like a crock if you ask me. But hey, so is your relationship with Frankie. So maybe it's the perfect solution." She winked and pulled Charlotte into a hug. "Hang in there, Sis. We'll figure something out."

Charlotte smiled and waved her sister off the front porch. "Of course we will."

If only Charlotte had the faintest idea where to begin.

5

Zach should have let his beard grow out until he looked like Tom Hanks's character in *Cast Away*. Then maybe shaving it off would have taken all weekend instead of five minutes. At this rate he wasn't going to miss a single second of his brother's wedding rehearsal dinner.

He ran a razor down the left side of his face even though he'd already shaved it smooth three swipes ago.

"You're planning to punch Ben in the middle of the ceremony, aren't you?" a voice spoke from behind him. "I can see it in your eyes."

"Mom." Zach spun from the sink, his razor in one hand, shaving cream in the other. "You can't just come waltzing into a restroom unannounced."

"We're in the church nursery bathroom. In the basement," she added as if that made any difference. Then she rolled her eyes and made a dramatic show of knocking on the door. "Yoo-hoo! Zip up your diapers. Concerned mother of the groom entering the premises." Her singsong voice bounced off the walls covered with cartoonish animals entering Noah's ark. "Better?"

He turned back to the mirror, meeting her reflection past his shoulder with a begrudging smile. So maybe he'd overreacted. Maybe he was a little tense. Maybe he'd purposely planned his itinerary so he'd arrive at his brother's wedding rehearsal last minute with his duffel bag in tow and in need of a quick shave, precisely to avoid a conversation like this.

How's New Zealand working out? It's not.

What's next on the horizon? No idea.

Think you'll ever be ready to tie the knot? Tried that. Didn't take. She's actually marrying my brother now, but thanks for the reminder.

"Please, Zach." Mom leaned against the doorjamb.

"Please what?" Zach bounced another glance off her in the mirror, then sighed. "Fine. I solemnly swear I will not punch Ben in the middle of his wedding ceremony." He swiped the razor down his cheek and tapped it against the edge of the sink. "I'll wait until the middle of the reception."

His mom lunged forward and jabbed his rib cage. *"Oof,"* Zach wheezed dramatically.

"Sometimes I wish you *would* just punch him. That way I'd know it was over and done. Right now it feels like . . . I don't know, a storm is on the horizon, and I'm one of the barnyard animals getting all twitchy about it."

Zach scraped the blades across his chin. "You're not the only one acting twitchy. I overheard Shannon's mother grilling the organist about whether her rheumatoid arthritis was going to hinder her performance of the wedding march. I swear that woman couldn't be any edgier if she were dangling from a mountain cliff by one finger."

"Why do you think I'm hiding down here with you?"

Zach rinsed off his razor. "Is that what we're doing?"

"Of course that's what we're doing. Who shaves five minutes before a wedding rehearsal? Now give me that." She grabbed the razor out of his hand and tilted his chin. "I always loved shaving your father's face. The first time I did it was on our honeymoon."

"This is starting to get weird."

"Quiet or I'll slit your throat."

"Did I say weird? I meant creepy."

Her eyes nearly disappeared in her plump smile as she glided the razor over his cheeks with swift strokes. "I've been missing him a lot this week. I mean I always miss him, but . . ."

"Yeah, I know." Zach missed him too. Every day. His dad had been gone a little over two years, and since then, nothing seemed to have gone right. First Ben's broken engagement to Charlotte. Then a little later Zach's whirlwind romance with Shannon that ended with a letter and a *no*.

Now Ben and Shannon's wedding.

"He loved Charlotte," Mom said, taking another swipe down his cheek. "Not that he wouldn't have loved Shannon, had he had the chance to meet her. I mean, it's Shannon. How can you not love Shannon?"

Zach grunted. That was the worst part. Shannon had to be one of the sweetest women on the planet. Even her Dear John letter was sweet. Probably why he could never work up the heart to burn it.

As much as he wanted to hold a grudge that she'd fallen in love with his brother, he couldn't. Blasted woman was too darn remorseful about the whole thing, apologizing and begging for forgiveness until he couldn't take it anymore. Shoot, she'd even sent him a text the other week about some amazing job opportunity she'd gone out of her way to secure just for him.

He never responded. But he did promise to come back for the wedding as Ben's best man to prove to her and everyone it was all water under the bridge. And it was. Mostly.

"Shannon's certainly a special gal," Zach said.

"Oh, she's wonderful, even if her mother is a bit . . . well. Anyway." Mom shrugged and rinsed off his razor. "All I'm saying is your father had a special connection with Charlotte. I think it was the music. Your dad played bass guitar in a band back in his younger days. They were terrible."

She handed back the razor. "You better finish. Now that I think about it, I tended to cut your father's face quite a bit. So?" She fiddled with the cross pendant on her necklace. "Have you two talked about it at least?"

"Talked to who about what?"

Her exasperated sigh said she wasn't falling for his nonchalant routine. "Ben stole your girlfriend from beneath your nose and is marrying her tomorrow. Seems like the type of thing you should probably discuss. You're not only his brother, you're his best man. Oh no, you're not planning to sabotage him in your speech, are you?"

"Mom . . ." Zach made quick work of finishing his shave. "What Shannon and I had, it wasn't real." He knew that now. Would have been nice to know that before he made an idiot of himself by asking her to elope to Alaska with him last year, but hey. Live and learn, right?

"I just don't want there to be any underlying resentment. That's the type of stuff that builds up over time. Soon you'll be making excuses for why you can't come home for Christmas. Next, the cousins won't be allowed to play together."

"What cousins? What are you talking about?" He dug a tie out of his duffel bag and slung it around his neck. Before he could cross one side over the other his mother's fingers were taking over.

"Yours and Ben's future kids. Don't you remember that documentary about the Sherman brothers? They wrote all that wonderful *Mary Poppins* music together, but their kids grew up estranged from their own cousins. It was so sad. I wept for days."

"Mom, I say this with all the love in my heart. You've lost your marbles."

She tightened his tie. "Fine. Be that way. Say everything's fine. Say you don't care Ben is marrying the love of your life."

"Shannon was never the love of my life." Again, knowledge he wished he'd discovered a bit sooner.

"You can't stand there and tell me you don't have any feelings for her."

"Of course I have feelings for her. She's lovely. For Ben. Not me. I don't know how many times I have to tell you I'm happy for Ben." Or at least he hoped to be. Someday. When he didn't find his perfect brother quite so annoying.

"I'd still feel better if you punched him. Or at least had a date for the wedding. I hate to think of you sitting on the sidelines while everyone's dancing and having a great time tomorrow."

Zach loosened his tie. "Who says I don't have a date?"

His mother's eyes lit up. She grabbed his tie and yanked him closer. "Who is she? Do I know her? Is she pretty? Is she nice? Is she the one?"

Zach slid his arm around his mom's shoulders as he snatched his duffel bag from a changing table and guided her out of the nursery. He flipped off the lights as they entered the hallway. "The only hint I'll give you for now is you do know her. And I happen to think she's adorable."

"Ohhh." Mom clapped a hand over her heart. "I love her already. You should have invited her to the rehearsal dinner. It would have given me an excuse to avoid Shannon's mother. Not that I don't like Joanne. I do. She's just a lot. In fact, Shannon's entire family is a lot. Sometimes I wish Charlotte and Ben had worked out for more reasons than one, and if you tell anyone I said that, I'll cut you with that shaving razor."

"My lips are sealed." Zach escorted his mom up the stairs to the main foyer. "And don't worry," he said, leaning down to her ear. "I'll make sure my date sits next to you throughout the entire dinner tonight."

"So she is coming? That's so exciting. Why didn't you say something sooner? I can't wait to see who it is."

"I think you two will find you have a lot in common."

"They do say boys often marry women who remind them of their mother." She winked and sped down the foyer with a new lightness in her footsteps.

Zach rubbed a palm over his smooth-shaven face, hiding a smile. His mom was going to kill him when she found out his date was Darla, the three-year-old flower girl. Maddy, her mom, was the photographer for the wedding and a good friend of the family. He'd promised Darla a dance at the wedding reception tomorrow. That counted as dating material, right?

Okay, so maybe he shouldn't have played it up so much.

But hey, if he had to suffer through a front row seat to his older brother's success and eternal happiness with the sweetest woman on the planet, the least Zach could do was have a little fun in the meantime.

6

How anyone maintained the will to live when they'd reached the point of pureed salad was a true medical mystery. Sophia Carter wrinkled her nose at the glob of green goo on the corner of the patient's food tray and adjusted her hair net. She didn't even want to imagine what lay dead and buried beneath the lid to the main dish.

The front pocket of Sophia's kitchen uniform buzzed. Looking up and down the bustling hallway, she dug out her phone and glanced at her screen.

A message from Charlotte.

Mom and Dad aren't getting a divorce! Now stop the crazy and get back to work!

Sophia huffed, about to tap a speedy reply along the lines of **You want to stop the crazy? How about you stop acting like you're in a romantic relationship with Frankie Avalon!** when a patient wearing a hospital gown and blue pants strolled past, pushing an IV pole.

Sophia dropped her phone back into her apron pocket. She'd deal with her sister's delusions later. Right now she had a job to do.

"Room service," she called out, balancing the tray in one hand, knocking with the other.

Not the most glamorous of jobs, delivering food trays in a hospital, but as a broke college student who'd put off finding a summer job until the last minute, Sophia had to take what she could get. Which meant part-time hours and the occasional whiff of pureed roadkill at a hospital thirty minutes from Bailey Springs.

She waited a beat, then cracked open the door. "Room service?"

"Cake," a warbled voice said back.

Sophia pushed the door further and stepped into the room. "No cake, I'm afraid. But there is a brownie. Kind of." It had been blended into pulp, but chocolate was chocolate, right? Certainly more appealing than the salad.

As her eyes adjusted to the dark—goodness, talk about depressing—Sophia fumbled her way to a bedside stand and set down the tray. "Can I help you set up your food tray, ma'am?" From what Sophia had gathered, most of the patients on this floor were here because of a stroke.

"Cake."

"Brownie, remember? You didn't order any—"

"Cake!" A hand, small and fierce, latched onto Sophia's forearm.

"Oh my," Sophia muttered back, not sure how an old woman could possess such supernatural strength. The stroke obviously hadn't affected her motor skills. Sophia tried peeling the woman's skeletal fingers off her wrist, certain a pair of police cuffs would be easier to remove.

"Cake," the patient whispered, leaning forward with the same fire in her eyes that Sophia's mother had whenever they played the game Password and she was trying to get Dad to guess the right answer using only one-word clues.

"You're not talking about preferring a different dessert here, are you?"

The patient shook her head back and forth, her gaze peering straight into Sophia's soul. Wow. Who knew delivering food trays could be so intense?

Well, this patient had gotten the right kitchen staff worker. Sophia loved intense.

Sophia read the patient's name on the whiteboard hanging beneath the mounted television. "Okay, Melba. You don't mind if I call you Melba, do you? Since you're currently cutting off all circulation in my right hand, it just feels like maybe we should be on a first-name basis. I'm Sophia."

"Cake!"

"Okay, we'll skip the formalities. Is there anything else you can tell me? I'm excellent at riddles."

"Cake."

"Besides that." At least in Password, if you didn't guess the correct answer, you got another one-word clue.

Melba's eyes scrunched shut. The flickering light from the television revealed the frustration puckered all over her pruny little face.

Sophia glanced to the hallway. She still needed to deliver more trays. Maybe this was a waste of time. Maybe this lady just liked cake.

"Date."

Sophia's head snapped back to Melba. A different word. Hallelujah. Let the other patients' trays go cold. This woman needed her.

"Okay, now we're getting somewhere. Cake. Date. Cake date. Cake date?"

Melba nodded in the same frenzied manner Mom did whenever Dad grew closer to the right answer. Too bad Sophia felt nowhere close to the right answer. "I'm sorry. I'm just not getting—"

"Cake girl," Melba interrupted, then knocked her fist against her forehead. "Ohhhh," she muttered. "Cake. Cake girl. No. Cake girl."

"Wait. You're not talking about that new place in Davenport, are you?" Some of Sophia's friends at college had mentioned the trendy new restaurant with the killer cheesecake. It wasn't called Cake Girl though. It was something like . . . "Cake Lassies?" Sophia mumbled.

Melba lunged forward.

"The place with the amazing cheesecake, right?"

Melba grinned like a maniac, her head bouncing up and down.

"Were you supposed to go there or something?"

Melba released her death grip and clasped her hands together as if in prayer, eyes closed. The relief smoothed out half her wrinkles, shaving a good ten years off her face. She could almost pass for an eighty-year-old woman now.

If this had been Sophia's parents, they would have been hooting and hollering and doing some sort of jig over their cleverness. Well, back when they used to play games together. Back before they started heading for divorce.

"Don't worry, Melba. I'll make sure whoever you were meeting gets notified you're not going to make it tonight." Must have been someone special. "Can you tell me the name?"

"Organ," Melba blurted.

Okay. They'd quit while they were ahead. Sophia patted Melba's hands. "I'll see if I can get your emergency contact number from one of the nurses. I'll take care of this. I promise. You don't have to worry about a thing. Except maybe that pureed salad."

Melba motioned Sophia closer, patted her softly on the cheek with a smile, and rested her head on the pillow with a contented sigh.

And then, right in front of Sophia's eyes, Melba died.

7

Charlotte held a DVD in each hand. "Well, Patches? What'll it be? *Beach Party* or *Beach Blanket Bingo* to start?"

Patches tapped the DVD on the right. "*Beach Blanket Bingo.* Good choice." Charlotte might have nudged the movie in the direction of his gray paw, but this was no time for analyzing feline semantics. This was no time for analyzing anything.

Not her parents' weird behavior. Not her job situation. Not what was supposed to have taken place at this time two years ago. Definitely not what was taking place tomorrow.

She started the movie and flopped onto the couch, where Patches made quick work of snuggling onto her lap. If anything could lift her spirits, it was her favorite movies and the world's best cat and most devoted friend. Who was now sinking his teeth into her unsuspecting hand.

"Ouch!" Charlotte shoved Patches off her lap. So much for world's best cat and most devoted friend. "Can you just set aside your split-personality issues for one evening?"

He sprawled across the carpet and began licking one of his hind legs. She took that as a no.

With a sigh, Charlotte focused her attention back on the movie. After Sophia left earlier, Charlotte had decided to buckle down and come up with a plan.

And right now the plan included keeping the curtains closed while she binged movies and brownies until she came out of her sugar coma sometime next week and forced herself to come up with a real plan.

Her phone chimed next to her on the couch. Sophia.

CALL! Emergency! SOS! Mayday!!!!

Charlotte paused the movie and dialed Sophia. "What's wrong? Is it Mom and Dad?" Maybe they *were* getting a divorce.

"Not them," Sophia answered, breathless. "Melba. One second she was saying, 'Cake, cake, cake,' then the next second she croaked. Just like that."

"What are you talking about? Who's Melba?"

"A patient. I delivered her food tray to her, and now she's dead."

"Goodness, what was on that food tray?"

"You don't want to know. But that wasn't the reason. She didn't even touch the food. She just . . . died."

"Well, you do work in a hospital. I suppose it's expected that some people are going to die."

"Now you sound like the nurses." Sophia altered her voice into a patronizing tone. "'Oh, honey, she was a hundred years old and a do not resuscitate. She lived a good life. It's fine.'"

"Was she really a hundred years old?"

"Ninety-five, but that's not the point. The point is, she gave me a message right before she died, and I promised her I would take care of it, but none of the nurses here want to help me take care of it. 'Oh honey,'" she transitioned back into a voice Charlotte was certain nurses never used, "'people say weird things sometimes after a stroke. Just deliver your food trays and we'll take care of the rest.'"

"That honestly doesn't sound like bad advice. Where are you right now, by the way?"

"Hiding in a stairwell next to the radiology department. Listen, Charlotte, you weren't there. Have you ever had a dying person squeeze the life out of your hand and ask for one final favor? Have you? Have you?"

"Well, no, but—"

"Then you have no idea what it feels like to know you, and you alone, are the only one who can see this final favor through."

"Wowzer, what did this woman ask you to do?"

"She asked me to drive to a restaurant, Cake Lassies I think it's called, and inform whoever's waiting for her that she will be unable to make it, but to remain stalwart, for she is in a much better place, having already moved on to her final reward."

"Goodness, she said all that?"

"Well, technically she said, 'Cake cake cake, date, cake girl, organ.' But I've read a lot of Agatha Christie novels and watched Mom and Dad play Password for years. I know what she meant. And I promised her I would take care of it."

"Okay then, take care of it."

"I can't take care of it. My shift doesn't end for another two hours. I need you to take care of it."

"Me? What happened to 'you and you alone are the only one who can see this favor through?' I didn't make any promises to hundred-year-old dead ladies. Besides, I'm on a heartbreak sabbatical this weekend. I'm not going anywhere. And even if I were, I'm certainly not going anywhere tonight. I've already put my pajamas on and started watching *Beach Blanket Bingo.*"

"Charlotte, you of all people should be jumping at an opportunity like this. What if she was supposed to be meeting her long-lost love?

What if the man waiting for her is the Frankie Avalon to her Annette Funicello? C'mon, Char, this is the cheesy romantic drivel you live for."

"If by *cheesy romantic drivel*, you mean *wonderfully orchestrated masterpiece*." Charlotte let her head sink against the top of the couch and stared at the ceiling. She supposed she could put on a real shirt for the sake of true love. "Where is this restaurant again?"

"Downtown Davenport."

"You want me to drive all the way to Iowa for this?"

"You act like it's a million miles away and not just over the bridge."

"And you act like it's not a thirty-minute drive just to get to that bridge." Ugh. This endeavor required more than a real shirt. She was going to have to put on real pants.

As if reading her mind, Sophia piped up. "Wear something nice. I've heard it's a nice restaurant."

"What's that matter? I'm not staying."

"Would you want someone delivering a message of doom to you in yoga pants and a hoodie? Put on a dress. It'll soften the blow."

This was getting ridiculous. "I hate driving into the Quad Cities. There's always construction."

"Yeah, but there's also always Whitey's Ice Cream to consider."

Good point. For Whitey's she might even be willing to put on Spanx if it came down to it. "Fine. What's this lady's name again? Mabel?"

"Melba. Melba Clark. Just look for an old man who looks like he's waiting for the love of his life to arrive, and kindly relay the news that she's dead. Then maybe pick up a cheesecake before you leave. I think it's what Melba would have wanted."

"Anything for Melba."

8

Zach followed the map directions on his phone over the bridge until he reached Cake Lassies' parking lot in downtown Davenport, Iowa. The Mississippi River snaked a dark path a few blocks down. Zach removed his tie and undid the top button of his shirt, eyeing the towering brick building that housed both a hotel and the world's best cheesecake, apparently.

So far so good. Between Shannon's boisterous family, a sick-to-her stomach maid of honor, and everyone's focused attention on the happy couple, Zach had managed to remain far from the spotlight throughout the entire rehearsal.

Now to make it through dinner. Thankfully his secret weapon should be arriving any minute. Little Darla's dimples could knock the socks off anyone. So long as he stayed glued to her side, he'd be fine.

She'd hopefully distract Ben and Shannon from attempting any more awkward apologies. Hopefully distract Mom from trying to set him up with the widowed arthritic organist if his surprise date didn't work out. And most importantly, distract Zach from thinking about what a mess his life was going to be if he didn't figure out what to do with it soon.

He supposed there was always Joe's Tavern in Montana. His buddy Joe had left a message just the other day to give him a call. Serving drinks and breaking up bar fights wasn't exactly on Zach's bucket list of employment opportunities, but he was going to need some sort of income to tide him over now that the New Zealand gig was a bust.

"Zachary, you devil!" His mother's voice drew his attention as soon as he stepped into the lobby's marbled foyer. She bent over with a laugh, then raced toward him with further giggles.

Ah, see? Darla had that way about her. She could charm a teenager into handing over a smartphone. "I take it my date is here."

His mom's arms circled around him, her face smacking into his chest. "Oh, this has got to be the best weekend of my life." She lifted her face to the cathedral-like ceiling. "Patrick, I'm ready to join you. Our boys are going to be fine. Tell Jesus to get another room ready. I'm coming soon."

Okay, even for Darla this was quite the reaction. "So, you're not mad?"

"Mad? Why would I be mad? I've been praying for this moment every day for the past two years. Okay, technically I prayed about it for Ben. But this is even better."

"What exactly is this moment? And how is it better?"

She dragged him by the hand into the restaurant. He barely had time to register the glass display of cheesecake up front, the colorful wall murals in the dining area, and the woman who appeared to be consoling a group of teary-eyed customers next to a piano before his mom twirled to face him.

"Stop playing stupid. You and Charlotte! Oh, I can't wait to tell everyone. Talk about a surprise." She smacked him on the arm. "I should have known when she mentioned the spinach. You always were my little Popeye, weren't you? But I can't believe you guys kept it such a secret.

Especially since Ben and Shannon have clearly moved on from the two of you."

Zach's mouth opened, probably with the intent to form words. Words along the lines of *huh*? But all the words stuck in his throat. Because sure enough, there stood Charlotte. Next to the cheesecake display. Wearing a blue knockout dress.

How he'd missed her on the first sweep of the room, he didn't know.

Before he could say anything, his mom tugged him closer to Charlotte and joined their hands together. Her hand felt small. Soft. Out of reflex, he squeezed it. Then for some reason, didn't let go.

Maybe because his mother's voice had thickened with tears. "Your father would've been so happy about this." She looked back and forth between Zach and Charlotte. "He loved you like a daughter, you know. The same way I do. Oh, this is so . . . I just can't . . . a bit awkward I suppose . . . your brother after all . . . and you and Shannon . . . but maybe . . ."

She continued speaking in stilted sentence fragments while Zach stared at Charlotte. Her knockout dress. Her flushed cheeks. Her shell-shocked gaze. Her knockout dress. What in the world was she doing here?

"Could you just give us a minute?" Zach asked when it became clear his mother was never going to stop rambling and Charlotte was never going to explain anything so long as his mother kept rambling.

"Of course." His mom motioned like she was locking her lips up and throwing away the key. "I'll let you two be the ones to tell everyone. Just don't take too long. This is still Ben and Shannon's special weekend. Let's not keep them waiting. Or try to trump them, okay? Even though . . ." She grinned and nodded her head like a rabid bobblehead doll. "This sort of does. Shh. I didn't say that."

With a giddy squeal, she pumped her fist before rushing down a narrow hallway. A chalkboard sign with the words *Wedding Rehearsal Dinner* and an arrow pointed after her.

Without a word, Zach dragged Charlotte out of the restaurant in the same manner his mother had dragged him inside less than two minutes ago. When they reached a quiet spot next to a giant fern and a door marked *Utility Closet*, Zach released her hand. "Okay, out with it. What is going on?"

Charlotte took a shaky breath.

Then another shaky breath.

"I have something to tell you, and I'm not really sure how to say it," she said after two more shaky breaths.

Zach hadn't seen Charlotte in two years. Not since Ben had dumped her. Not since she'd wept in Zach's arms and he'd awkwardly patted her on the back because he didn't know what else to do with an attractive crying woman clinging to his torso. Well, other than kiss her.

Which come to think of it, he might have. A little bit. Just on the temple. Nothing serious. But come on, *she was crying*. Zach never could stand to see a girl cry. Especially not a girl like Charlotte. He'd known her forever. She was fun. Sweet. A little cuckoo at times, but hey, a person could have worse faults. And unfortunately, she did. She never wanted to leave Illinois.

Zach couldn't completely blame his brother for breaking off their engagement. But he could blame him for waiting until the last minute to do it. That was a jerk move. So of course Zach had felt the need to console the poor girl when he stumbled upon her bawling her brains out.

But since then, Zach hadn't given that night a second thought.

But . . . *Oh no*. What if Charlotte had given it a second thought? What if she'd given it third and fourth thoughts? Did she . . . Did she have feelings for Zach? Is that why she was here? Had she been harboring some sort of unbridled passion for him ever since that night he consoled her with awkward back pats and unserious kisses in an empty church sanctuary?

Of course. Why else would she be here? Why else would she have led his mother to believe they were a couple? She loved him. What other explanation could there be?

She lifted her gaze, her blue eyes holding his in captivity as she wet her lips, no doubt in anticipation of all the serious kisses she expected to receive after confessing her eternal love for him. "Zach . . ."

He wet his lips. Not in preparation for anything. They were just feeling a little chapped.

"Melba Clark is dead. I'm so sorry. Bye."

Then she spun, opened the door behind her, and disappeared inside the utility closet.

9

Charlotte never should have changed out of her pajamas.

If she'd left them on, it would've prevented this moment—standing inside a utility closet, clutching a broom handle with one hand and frantically searching for a light switch with the other, while one of the most ruggedly handsome men on earth, who just so happened to be her ex-fiancé's brother, politely knocked on the door, inquiring whether she'd lost her mind.

And she had. Oh goodness, she had.

Charlotte gave up on finding a light switch and leaned her forehead against the door. "Just a moment, please."

Yes. A moment. A long moment. A moment to figure out how she'd gone from anticipating a pajama-clad *Beach Blanket Bingo* evening to standing inside a utility closet thirty miles away wearing not only a fancy dress, but the heavy cloak of humiliation. And Spanx!

. . . ✦ . . .

TWENTY MINUTES EARLIER

"Excuse me," Charlotte said to a short waitress with purple highlights carrying a tray full of beverages above her shoulder.

"One moment," the waitress said without slowing her stride.

Charlotte blew out a breath and watched the waitress disappear down a narrow hallway where a chalkboard sign with an arrow pointed to a *Wedding Rehearsal Dinner*, apparently. She took a step further into the restaurant, her gaze connecting with the long rows of cheesecake displayed behind glass. Oh, she was definitely grabbing one of those on the way out.

Wooden floorboards creaked beneath her shifting weight. The restaurant, connected to a hotel, had an industrial feel to it. Brick walls. Piped ceilings. Scuffed floors. Live music floated through the air from a piano player wearing a fedora and a sultry-sounding vocalist in a black dress. Nice.

"I assume you're here for one of the parties." The waitress returned and glanced at a tablet on the hostess stand. "Wedding or birthday?"

"Oh. I don't know exactly."

The waitress glanced up from the tablet, impatience written all over her petite features. "We're booked for the evening. If you don't have a reservation or you're not here with one of the parties—"

"I am. I think. I mean—" Charlotte twisted her fingers together. "I'm here because of an elderly lady." The song ended and a polite round of applause interrupted anything else Charlotte might have tried saying if she could've figured out what to say.

"Follow me." The waitress motioned to Charlotte while speaking to a couple who had entered behind her. "Birthday party to the right. Wedding party down the hall. Otherwise I'll be back in a moment."

The waitress marched to the right, leaving Charlotte no choice but to run after her. Another song started up. Something familiar but

Charlotte couldn't place it. The waitress led Charlotte to a long table near the front, close to the piano, where an elderly gentleman sat in a gray suit with a red carnation in his top buttonhole. The waitress motioned to the table. "I'll take drink orders when the rest of your party gets here."

"Oh, but I'm not—" Either the waitress didn't hear or didn't care. Charlotte had a guess as to which. Either way, she disappeared, leaving Charlotte alone with a man who appeared even more perplexed.

"Hi," Charlotte began, not sure whether to take a seat and introduce herself or blurt out the news and head straight for the cheesecake. "I'm Charlotte." She pulled out a chair, deciding some good old-fashioned manners might be the best starting point to lead into a conversation about death.

"What's that?" the man said, cupping his ear and leaning over the table toward her.

"I said my name is Charlotte," she spoke up to be heard over the music. Maybe having this conversation right next to the piano wasn't a great idea.

He frowned, shaking his head and leaning closer, his red carnation butting into the salt and pepper shakers.

She leaned forward and tried again. If they continued this game, they'd be touching noses in a minute. "I'm Charlotte."

"Charlotte?"

"Charlotte," she confirmed. "And I'm here because of Melba Clark."

He leaned back, a grin spreading across his face. Her words must have landed this time. He pointed to the empty chair with red and white Happy Birthday balloons tied to it and winked. "Me too."

Oh dear. Was this Melba's birthday party? No wonder she kept talking about cake. Charlotte adjusted her dress, regretting the fact she couldn't fit into it anymore without Spanx. This situation was uncomfortable enough without the inability to take a full breath added into the mix.

He must have picked up on her discomfort. His smile faded. "You okay, dear?"

Charlotte shook her head. "I'm afraid I have some bad news about Melba."

He frowned and shook his head, cupping his ear again. "What's that, dear?"

"Melba," Charlotte said, trying to speak loudly and enunciate over the music. "I'm sorry to have to tell you this, but she passed away today."

"What?"

"Melba passed away today."

"What?"

"Melba's dead," Charlotte shouted one moment after the song drew to an abrupt end.

This time there was no applause. Probably because everyone in the dining area, including the piano player and singer, had swiveled their gazes to Charlotte. She tried to ignore them and keep her attention focused on the poor old man who was staring back at her with his mouth gaping and tears building on the lower rims of his eyes.

All in all, he seemed to be handling the news quite well.

Charlotte cleared her throat and slid back her chair, needing to escape before the tears breached new territory. Like his cheeks. "I'm sorry. So sorry. If it helps, I know she died in peace."

That did it. Two fat drops overflowed from his eyes, splashing in what began a synchronized diving contest of tears onto the table. Oh shoot. Was there anything worse than watching a grown man cry? Charlotte grabbed a napkin and handed it to him, then yanked one off the table for herself. "I'm sure she was wonderful."

"The best," he whimpered back as they both dabbed their eyes.

"Did she have a favorite song?" She looked to the musicians, who still appeared unsure how to proceed. "Perhaps we can play something in her honor."

Charlotte emptied out the sugar packet holder on the table and shoved a ten-dollar bill into it as she placed it on top of the piano. "Name a song. Anything. I'm sure they can play it."

"We actually only know about five songs," the piano player whispered.

"Well, she did always seem a bit partial to Frank Sinatra," the old man said.

"Perfect." One glance at the piano player's blank expression told Charlotte that wasn't one of the five songs. "Oh c'mon, you're wearing a fedora. How can you not know at least one Frank Sinatra song?"

The singer shrugged. "We're more into slowed down versions of Led Zeppelin songs."

Charlotte rolled her eyes. "Scoot over. I'll play." She hovered her fingers over the keys, then after one chord, rose to her feet and said, "So I actually don't know many Frank Sinatra songs either. But I do happen to know Nat King Cole's 'Smile'?"

The old man blew his nose in a long honking sound, and Charlotte took that as permission to proceed. By the end of the first verse, the singer had googled the lyrics and taken back her microphone. A good thing since Charlotte was too busy crying. Why was a song about smiling so sad?

Halfway through the second verse, a woman's voice sounded through the sobbing. "Dad? What's wrong? Why are you crying?"

"Maple's dead. They're playing her favorite song."

"Maple's not dead. I just saw her when I went by the house to pick up Mom after her hair appointment. And what makes you think Maple has a favorite song? She's a dog, for crying out loud." The tall lean woman pointed to a short elderly woman standing next to her. "I told you Dad was getting dementia. Didn't I tell you he was getting dementia?"

Another thin woman who looked similar enough to be the first woman's sister started to whimper. "They're going to have to move in with me, aren't they?"

Now the elderly woman started to cry. "But I like where we live."

Charlotte rose from the piano bench. "Excuse me. I think there's been a minor misunderstanding here. I thought this table was reserved for Melba Clark." Charlotte frowned at the old man. "Why did you tell me you were here for Melba Clark?" Maybe he did have the beginning stages of dementia.

He rose from his chair. "No, you said you were here for the marble cake, and I said I was too. My wife always gets marble cake for her birthday. Then you told me Maple was dead."

"Not Maple," Charlotte said. "Melba."

"Who's Melba?" he asked.

More family members had trickled in by now to join the dinner party. "Why's everybody crying?" one of the men asked.

"Did somebody die?" a little girl asked.

"Melba," the elderly man said.

By the fifth *who's Melba?* Charlotte was certain of two things. One, she'd told the wrong group of people about Melba. Two, she was going to murder Sophia the next time she saw her.

Charlotte slipped another ten into the tip jar. "Is 'Happy Birthday' one of the five songs you know?" Then she dodged for the nearest exit.

And she might have made it too. But dang it if that glimpse of cheesecake didn't catch her eye. Make her pause. Make her think about Melba and the fact she still hadn't completed her mission.

And in that pause, she heard a voice. The same voice she'd run into at the farmers market next to the spinach stand two weeks ago. And boy, was it a happy voice. A voice so happy and excited she didn't have the heart to correct it. Hadn't there been enough tears for one evening?

So when the voice said, "You must be Zach's surprise date," Charlotte did as Nat King Cole suggested.

She smiled.

10

Knuckles rapped on the door, followed by the low timbre of Zach's voice slipping through the crack. "Think you're ready to come out now?"

No. Never. "Just finishing up a few things." Charlotte tripped over a mop bucket as a long handle hit her on the back of the head. "Okay. Think I'm all done now."

She opened the door and stepped out of the dark closet, smoothing her dress against her hips. "I actually didn't mean to go in there."

Zach's lips quirked in a smile. "No, I didn't figure you did."

Sweet mercy. How could someone she'd known all her life and never felt one iota of attraction toward in the past suddenly look more appealing than chocolate peanut butter cheesecake? "Well. Good seeing you again, Zach. I think I'll head out now. Maybe try using a real exit this time."

She made it two steps before his hand circled her elbow and spun her against his chest. And what a chest it was. Zach clearly still wore his outdoorsman's physique beneath all that buttoned-down starch.

"Hold it. Just where on earth do you think you're going?"

"Home. Where I should have been this whole time."

"Uh, I don't think so, pilgrim. Not until you explain to me why you told my mom we were a couple."

"I never told her that. And if that was supposed to be some sort of John Wayne impression, it stunk."

"Well, you sure didn't correct her either. And I'll have you know, *pilgrim*, my John Wayne impression is world-renowned."

"I was too busy thinking about Melba Clark and cheesecake to correct your mother. And clearly the rest of the world has never seen a John Wayne movie."

"We'll argue that point later. Who the heck is Melba Clark?"

Oh, she really was going to kill Sophia. "Are you saying Melba isn't with your group either?"

"I thought you said she was dead."

"She is dead. But she was supposed to be meeting someone here tonight for a party. And not a birthday party, I can tell you that much."

"The name sounds vaguely familiar. Maybe she's on Shannon's side of the family."

"Great. You mind passing the message along? Let them know she died in peace." Charlotte tried for the second time to slip past Zach. For the second time, his hand snagged her back to his side.

"Hold it. You can't just show up, make my mom think we're together, then expect me to inform everyone we're not and some lady named Melba died in peace."

"But you just said it so beautifully. I couldn't have said it better myself if I tried. And trust me, I've tried."

"Well, get ready to try again. I haven't seen my mom that happy since before my dad—" His voice caught, and he swallowed. "It's been a while. Please help me explain to her what's happening here. Especially since I'm still very confused about what's happening here."

"You're not the only one. Last I heard you were off wrestling grizzly bears in Alaska. Or was it hobbits in New Zealand? What are you doing here?"

Zach pointed to the restaurant. "Didn't you hear a word my mom said?"

"I heard words. None of them coherent."

"I'm back for Ben's wedding."

Ben's wedding. Of course. He was back for Ben's wedding. Charlotte nodded as the words pinged inside her brain without sticking any sort of landing. Ben's wedding. Oh my goodness. *Ben's wedding.*

She sucked in a breath and grabbed the front of Zach's shirt. "You mean he's here?" She jerked away and spun toward the restaurant. "That rehearsal dinner sign is for Ben's wedding?"

"I thought you knew."

"How would I have known?" But now that she knew— "I have to go."

"Charlotte, wait."

This time she made it five steps before he stopped her. "No, Zach. Please. I have to get out of here. I can't face your brother. I already feel like an idiot."

"Trust me when I say I understand your feelings exactly. I don't want to be here either. But listen . . ." Zach gripped both of her shoulders with a gentle squeeze, crouching down a bit to meet her gaze at eye level. "You know my mother adores you. I don't know why she got it into her head that we were a couple, but we need to tell her we're not, and it might not sting as much coming from both of us. Please?"

He would have the nerve to be attractive and say please and bring his mother into this. How could Charlotte say no to a woman who still owned a corner of her heart? "Fine. For your mother's sake. But I'm not going back into the restaurant."

His eyes narrowed as if he didn't trust her not to bolt. "How about if you wait right outside that room they reserved for the rehearsal dinner?"

Charlotte folded her arms. "To the cheesecake stand. No further."

"This is my mother, Charlotte."

She huffed. "Fine. Hallway, next to the bathrooms. Final offer."

"Deal." He escorted her to the chalkboard sign with the arrow. "Wait here. I'll be back in a minute."

She nodded. The sooner the better. A quick word with Zach's mother, then she could finally be out the door and back to her heartbreak sabbatical. With any luck she'd have time to pick up some cheesecake and make it home to finish the first movie, maybe start the second, before it got too late.

A scream broke off her trail of thoughts right before the door to the women's restroom banged open, nearly hitting Charlotte's face. She jumped a step back.

"I told you not to choose one of the Minelli cousins to be your maid of honor." A tall, dark-haired, attractive middle-aged woman wearing a plum dress strode out of the bathroom. "They're notorious pukers whenever they're pregnant. And goodness knows, they're always pregnant."

A dreadful retching sound punctuated the statement, followed by the flush of a toilet. Charlotte winced, hoping Zach hurried back with his mom. Especially when a younger, shorter woman wearing a cute strapless dress stepped into the hallway, and Charlotte realized she knew her.

It was Shannon. Oh goodness. *It was Shannon.* Zach's girlfriend. Or apparently, Zach's ex-girlfriend. Charlotte recognized her from a picture Zach posted on social media right before he deleted all his accounts and Charlotte had heard through the grapevine they'd split up.

Wait, so that's who Ben was marrying? Shannon? No wonder Zach didn't want to be here. And how had Charlotte not heard *this* through the grapevine?

"Momma, it's going to be fine," Shannon said, a weight of fatigue in her voice Charlotte would have to be deaf not to hear. Which apparently her mother was, because she prattled on without missing a beat.

"This is exactly why I said you needed more than one person in your bridal party. At least then you would have had a backup. Now you have nobody."

"We were just trying to keep things simple."

"Simple my foot. Look at the mess we're in. What about your friend Taylor? I bet she could fit into the dress okay."

"She's in Germany for her job. I already told you that."

"Valerie?"

"Tore her ACL playing volleyball last week. I already told you *that*."

"What about that one friend you used to have? The two of you were always so close. What was her name? Marci . . . Margo . . ."

"Monica?"

"That's it," she said, snapping her fingers.

"She moved away when I was ten."

"Well, you should have stayed in touch. She had such beautiful auburn hair. Would have gone great with your wedding colors." Another terrible retching sound echoed out from the bathroom. "Good night," Shannon's mother muttered. "What are we going to do? Tie a barf bag around her neck for the ceremony? Nobody will even be able to hear your vows over that sound."

"I'm sure it'll be fine, Momma."

"And I'm sure it won't. Isn't there anybody else you can ask?"

"Not at such short notice. Lorelai's grandmother isn't doing well, so she's out of town, and Staci can only make it for the reception. And I'd rather not ask any of the other Minelli cousins because they're all—"

"Too fat. Yes, I know."

"Pregnant, Momma," Shannon said with a patient reprimand in her tone. "Not fat."

"Goodness, this is a dilemma. A real dilemma. You need at least one person to stand up front with you. What are we doing to do? I tried warning you a short engagement would lead to trouble. We haven't had time to plan anything."

The way Shannon's mom carried on made Charlotte feel a new wave of gratitude for her own parents. And maybe a slice of pity for Shannon.

"This wedding is going to be a disaster if we don't figure something out. I'm making some calls right now. Maybe there's a place we can rent a maid of honor by the hour. These days, anything's possible." Shannon's mother spun, nearly colliding into Charlotte. "Oh, sorry. We're blocking the bathroom, aren't we?"

Shannon pulled her mom close to the wall, a kind but tired smile aimed at Charlotte. "Don't mind us. We love carrying out personal conversations whenever we can trap unwilling participants into listening."

Charlotte smiled. "Hardly heard anything." A muffled dry heave slipped through the crack of the door. "Except maybe that."

"Do we know you?" The mother's eyes assessed Charlotte up and down. "You look familiar."

"You do," Shannon agreed before her eyes widened and she sucked in a giant breath. "Oh my goodness. You're Charlotte."

"Who's Charlotte?" Shannon's mother asked, gaze narrowing like a hungry hawk.

"Nobody." Charlotte swallowed, feeling all too much like a scared bunny. What was taking Zach so long?

"Charlotte is Ben's . . ." Shannon swallowed, appearing to fumble for the right words as her cheeks flushed red. "Uh, you remember, Momma. She's Ben's . . ." Shannon began chewing her lower lip, eyes full of apology.

"Ben's what?"

"Nothing," Charlotte said. "I'm Ben's nothing. I'm actually here with Zach. Well, I mean, I'm waiting for Zach. We're not—"

"Oh, Charlotte!" Zach's mother interrupted, rushing down the hallway. "There you are, my dear. And I see you three are talking. That's good. Why make it awkward when we can just celebrate that it's good news, right?"

"I'm afraid I don't know what you're talking about." Shannon's mother raked Charlotte up and down with that predatory gaze once again. Charlotte's spine stiffened as if she were trying to hide behind a thin tree.

"Oh, so she didn't tell you?" Zach's mom clapped her hands together in anticipation. "Joanne, allow me to introduce you to—"

Charlotte only now realized what was happening. She rushed forward from the invisible tree to stop Zach's mother from continuing. But Charlotte had forgotten how Zach's mother could talk faster than an auctioneer on a caffeine high when she got excited.

"—Zach's date, Charlotte. They're a couple. Isn't that a wonderful surprise? An answer to prayer if you ask me."

Shannon gasped and clasped her hands together. "You and Zach are together? Really? Oh, I can't tell you how happy that makes me. I mean it. Truly. I feel like a huge weight has finally been lifted."

"I'm sorry. I still feel like I'm missing something," Joanne said. "Who are you?"

Shannon slid a friendly arm around Charlotte's waist. "Charlotte, Momma. *The* Charlotte. Ben's Charlotte. Except now she's Zach's Charlotte. Isn't that great? Everything's working out like it was supposed to."

Charlotte's mind had gotten stuck like mud on *the* Charlotte. She could hardly pull it out of the slop to *Ben's* Charlotte. Let alone *Zach's* Charlotte.

"You know what this means, don't you?" Shannon said, jumping up and down. Her mother started jumping up and down too. Most concerning was when Zach's mother joined the trampoline of excitement.

"Uh, hey guys," Zach's voice broke into the chaos. "What's going on here?"

"We're celebrating the good news," Shannon said.

"What good news?" Zach's left eyebrow quirked up as he slanted Charlotte a look. "I sure hope this isn't how they're taking the news about Melba."

The women were shouting and squealing too much to hear Zach. "She's going to be the maid of honor!" Shannon and her mother yelled, while Zach's mom screamed something about future grandbabies.

"Uh, whoa—" Zach made a time-out sign. "I don't know what's happened in the past two minutes, but Charlotte can't be the maid of honor."

"Sure she can," Joanne said, looking Charlotte up and down with an approving nod. "She is the perfect size for that dress. I can tell just looking at her. Unless . . ." She wrapped an arm around Charlotte's shoulders and leaned close with a whisper. "You're not pregnant, are you?"

"Momma," Shannon scolded her, obviously hearing the whisper.

"Of course I'm not," Charlotte whispered back in a low breath.

Everyone seemed to breathe a sigh of relief, including Zach. Charlotte could have punched him. She would have, if Joanne didn't have a death grip on one hand while Shannon clung to her other, both of them talking in nonstop rapid-fire sentences.

"Want us to all get along."

"Doctor's already upped my medications twice."

"Practically sisters."

"This close to having myself committed."

All the while, Zach's mother hugged Zach and stared at Charlotte with a teary smile as if she were the prodigal child returned home at long last. Oh boy.

Charlotte inhaled a deep, shaky breath. Somebody needed to tell them. The truth. Soon. Somebody like Zach. Not her. It was his family, after all. "Uh, Zach? Now might be a good time to mention . . ."

"Mention what?"

And there he was. At the end of the hallway. Benjamin Bryant. Dressed to kill. Not a hair out of place. The picture of perfection. The epitome of success. Everything Charlotte wasn't.

His gaze swept up and down the length of Charlotte, and she'd never been more grateful for Spanx in all her life, even if the look in Ben's dark eyes tilted more toward pity than appreciation.

"What's going on?" he asked after Shannon, her mother, and his mother had all tried answering him at the same time. And now they were all trying to answer him again, only louder.

Zach shoved his hands in his pockets and hung his head for a long breath before lifting it.

He'd cut his hair! That's what it was. He'd gotten rid of the man bun. No wonder she found him attractive now. She hated man buns. Had Zach always been this attractive beneath all that hair? Or was it the glimpse of vulnerability she found so attractive?

"Hey, everyone," Zach spoke up over the crazed voices, finally silencing them. "I hate to be the wet blanket here, but I've got some bad news. As far as Charlotte being the maid of honor, she is—"

"Honored," Charlotte blurted out, squeezing Shannon's and her mother's hands to draw their attention away from Zach, who was now looking at her like she'd just smacked him in the face with one of the cheesecakes. "Completely honored. Zach and I would love nothing more than to share your special day with you." Especially if it knocked the look of pity off Ben's face.

"So what's the bad news then?" Joanne asked.

"Nothing. Everything's good. Oh wait." Charlotte sucked in a breath. The whole reason she was here. "Do you know Melba Clark?" This time she was going to get it right.

Joanne nodded. "Of course. Known her for years."

Still holding their hands, Charlotte offered a gentle squeeze. "I'm sorry to have to tell you this, but Melba died earlier today. My sister happened to be with her at the time, so I know for certain she wasn't in any pain, she died very peacefully, and she died with all of you on her heart. This wedding meant a lot to her. It was the last thing she spoke of."

Shannon exchanged a look with her mom. "Who's Melba?"

Joanne snorted. "Oh, she's that lady I was telling you about who shows up to every wedding in the county whether she has an invite or not. She usually tries sitting in the front row with the family. It wouldn't have surprised me one bit if she showed up tonight hoping to snag a piece of the cheesecake."

Charlotte slowly released their hands. "I'm sorry. Are you saying you weren't all that close to her?"

Joanne shrugged. "Not really. Her family all lives out in Oregon. They tried getting her to move out closer to them years ago, but she's always claimed the best wedding cake is here. Speaking of cake, let's get back to the rehearsal dinner. Now that the maid of honor crisis is solved, I've discovered I have quite the appetite."

"Oh, me too, Joanne. Me too." Zach's mother waved for Charlotte and Zach to follow. "Come on, you two lovebirds. No stealing kisses in the hallway."

"Ha ha, stealing kisses, that's funny. Can I have a word with you?" Not waiting for an answer, Charlotte grabbed Zach by the arm and yanked him down the hallway, back to the front of the restaurant and out into the parking lot. Then began slugging him as hard as she could on each bicep. Which wasn't hard enough.

Because it didn't stop him from laughing and saying, "You might be the only person I know who can screw up a situation more than I can."

Charlotte punched him again. This time because he was right.

11

Zach couldn't have orchestrated a better date for his brother's wedding if he'd tried. Move over, Darla. Take that dimpled grin and irresistible cutie-pie charm elsewhere. Zach had a new flame in town. A flame who was somewhere in the tenth round with his left bicep.

"Why are you punching me? You're the one who agreed to be the maid of honor."

"I'm punching you . . . because I can't very well . . . punch your brother . . . can I?" Charlotte dropped her fists to her waist.

"I don't know. My mom was all for it a little bit ago. Are you seriously winded? That was less than thirty seconds of exertion."

A breeze tugged a lock of hair from her ponytail. She swiped it from her eyes. "It was at least a full minute, and I can't believe they didn't care one bit about Melba."

"Of course they did. Didn't you see the look of horror on everyone's faces once they realized how much leftover cake they were going to have now that Melba's not coming?" He took the next punch with a laugh. "Aw, come on. It won't be that bad, will it? Wearing a pretty dress and being my date for one day?"

"You could have spoken up at any point, you know."

"Uh, pretty sure I did speak up and got promptly interrupted." He altered his voice to a false soprano. "I would be honored. Completely honored."

"Well, what was I supposed to say with Shannon looking all happy and her mother looking all scary? Not to mention Ben looking all handsome. I panicked."

"Okay, first off, my brother is not handsome. He's boring. And you're way better off without him."

"Yeah, well I'd feel a lot better if he believed that too."

"So make him believe it tomorrow when you show up as my hot date."

"Saying I do show up as your respectable date, what do you get out of this?"

"Uh, hello. Ben's marrying my ex-girlfriend in case you've forgotten. It'd be nice to spend one entire day where nobody looks at me like I'm on the verge of jumping off a bridge because my brother stole the love of my life even though I've told them at least five hundred times she's not the love of my life and if they call her the love of my life one more time then I will be tempted to jump off the nearest bridge, which won't do me any favors because I'm an excellent swimmer and will make it to shore without any difficulty."

"Wowzer. One day from all that, huh?"

Zach smiled. "Give or take." The wind continued to play with Charlotte's hair. He brushed another strand behind her ear as if that were the most natural thing in the world. But it was Charlotte. Being around her had always felt natural. Like being around a favorite sister he loved to tease. "We should probably head back inside before they think we're out here necking."

"Necking? Seriously? Are we filming an episode of Happy Days all of a sudden?"

Okay, maybe sister wasn't the right description for Charlotte. Maybe it was more like being around a favorite friend he loved to flirt with. "Well, what would you call it?"

"Nothing. Because we're not doing it. Rule number one—no necking. Rule number two—I don't know. What are the rules here? What's the plan? Saying we do make it through tomorrow, what happens after that?"

"After that, well, I say we take a hard look at rule number one and consider revising it." He blocked her punch. "I'm kidding. Who says we need rules? All we have to do is get through tomorrow. It'll be fine."

"Will it?"

"Sure. Later on I'll tell Mom we're better off as just friends. Trust me. Everything's going to be fine."

"The more you say it's going to be fine, the more worried I get."

"It's one day. What could go wrong?"

"If it's anything like today, I'm wondering what can go right?" Charlotte covered her mouth as a giant yawn overtook her. "Oh wow. Who knew subterfuge and boxing could be so exhausting? I'm going to double-check the details for tomorrow, then call it a night."

Zach dug his hands into his pockets to keep from fixing her hair again. "Why don't you head on home? I can text you the details."

"Nah, it's no problem."

"You sure? You really don't have to—"

"I'm going back inside to get cheesecake, okay? I already know the details. I have no intention of speaking to anyone. I'm exhausted, it's been a weird day, and I just want some cheesecake."

Zach lifted his palms. He knew better than to keep a woman waiting for cheesecake. "Just a heads-up, I think I heard my mom say something about shooting photos before the wedding, so we'll need to get there plenty early."

"I'm not going to be in them, am I?" She sucked in a breath. "I'm the maid of honor. I'm going to be in the photos."

"Pretty sure Mom will want you in the family photos too, just so you know."

"This is a bad idea, isn't it?"

Probably. But for some reason, Zach couldn't help thinking how this bad idea felt so good. Maybe because he was already picturing the reception when he'd get to dance with her. In front of Ben. Ha!

His elation plummeted with the next gust of wind. What was wrong with him? Why would Ben care if Zach danced with Charlotte? Ben had dumped Charlotte. Maybe this was a bad idea. "Look, if you don't want to do this, I understand."

"Oh no. Don't pin this on me. I'm committed. If you want to back out—"

"I don't want to back out."

"Then why are we still having this conversation when I could have purchased an entire cheesecake by now?"

"Calm down, pilgrim."

She plugged her ears. "This is definitely a bad idea," she muttered as she headed back toward the restaurant.

"Everything's going to be fine," Zach hollered, looking forward to his brother's wedding for the first time ever.

12

One day. One little square on the calendar. That was all. Charlotte could do this. She could help an annoyingly nice woman with an overly intense mother have a beautiful wedding day with Charlotte's stupidly handsome ex-fiancé. She could. That's why she was here. For them. Not for herself.

Oh, definitely not for herself. If she were living for herself, Charlotte would be at home right now watching *Muscle Beach Party* as she devoured the last of the enormous slice of cheesecake she'd brought home last night after leaving Cake Night, or whatever the place was called.

She would not be here. Holding a bouquet of pink peonies. Forcing her cheeks into a smile as a blushing bride walked down the aisle toward the man Charlotte was supposed to have married two years ago.

Oh my goodness, what was she doing here?

Charlotte inhaled a steadying breath, then made the mistake of glancing at Ben. Dopey-eyed, handsome Ben.

All the air rushed out of her. This was not at all how she had intended to spend her heartbreak sabbatical. At her ex-fiancé's wedding. *In* her ex-fiancé's wedding.

Forcing another breath in, she fixed her gaze on the peonies. *Just get through it.* She'd already made it through the photo session from hell where Zach's mother had insisted on roughly two thousand pictures of Charlotte and Zach since the bride and groom wouldn't be doing their photos until after the wedding. If Charlotte had made it through that, surely she could make it through this.

"Love is patient, love is kind," the minister began.

Charlotte closed her eyes. She didn't know if she could make it through this.

Somehow, twenty minutes later, she had. The processional march began. With trembling fingers, she met Zach in the center of the aisle and looped her hand around his solid bicep. Unable to meet anyone's gaze, she focused on the white paper rolled down the center aisle, covered in flower petals.

Two more hours. Maybe three. That's all. Then back to Frankie and Annette. She could stop pretending to be enamored with Zach. Worse, he could stop pretending to be enamored with her. That was the more troubling aspect of this whole scenario. During the photo shoot, the way he looked at her sometimes, she could almost feel as if he weren't pretending.

And it messed with her head. Made her start thinking about things. Things like those weird kisses they kinda sorta shared two years ago in a sanctuary similar to this one.

Which was a terrible thing to think about. Because then it also made her think about how embarrassed she'd felt afterward, blubbering against his shoulder the way she had. The only reason he kinda sorta kissed her was to stop her snot bubbles, no doubt.

"Don't go far. We're going to get some more photos before we head to the reception," the cheery photographer informed Charlotte and Zach as soon as they stepped out of the sanctuary.

Wonderful. More photos. "Can't wait," Charlotte mumbled. She dropped her hand from Zach's arm and stepped to the side as Shannon, Ben, and their families gathered to form a receiving line. May as well go touch up her makeup while she had time to kill.

Zach grabbed her hand. "Where're you going? The receiving line is this way."

"So? I'm not family."

"You certainly are today, dear," Zach's mother said from behind her. She dabbed her eyes with a lacy handkerchief. "What a beautiful wedding. Wasn't that a beautiful wedding? Oh, I can't get over how beautiful it was. I couldn't have dreamed up a lovelier day. Ben and Shannon, married. You and Zach, together. Oh I'm so happy. So so happy."

She squeezed Charlotte's hand and tugged her next to Zach. "Now you two just stand here and smile. That's right. And keep Darla from pulling her dress over her head if you can. Perfect. Oh, Ethel honey, you made it, I'm so glad." She darted over to clasp an elderly woman's hand with both of her own, hobnobbing and gabbing her way through the line better than any politician running for office.

Charlotte stood next to Zach and kept the little girl from lifting her frilly dress over her face and exposing her tights, which turned into a full-time job once the little girl decided pulling her dress over her head was a fun game. Especially when Zach lifted her over his shoulder, exposing her white-tighted bottom for all the world to see.

Charlotte couldn't help laughing at Darla's delighted squeals. Or smiling at the way Zach shook hands and greeted those who passed through the line as if there weren't a giggling, squirming girl slung over his shoulder. No denying, he'd make a good father someday.

What?

Charlotte flinched. Where had that thought come from? Since

graduating high school, Zach hadn't stayed in one place any better than Darla stood still in the receiving line. What sort of father material was that?

"You okay?" Darla's shiny white shoes nearly clobbered Charlotte in the head as Zach twisted to face her.

"I'm fine. Just having weird thoughts about—" *You.* "The bathroom."

"The bathroom? Really?"

"Yes, just . . . you know, haven't used it in a while. That's weird. You know what? I'm going to go use it now."

He lowered Darla. "Mind taking her with you? I don't know a lot about little girls, but I'm guessing they have little bladders. I'm half scared she's going to pee down my neck every time she giggles."

Darla giggled and Charlotte reached for her hand. "Come on, princess. Let's take care of business. Be back in a jiffy."

Turned out that taking care of business with a little girl in tights takes longer than a jiffy. By the time they made it out of the bathroom, all the wedding guests must have made their way through the receiving line because everyone had disappeared. Everyone but Zach's mother.

She rushed toward Charlotte with a huge smile. "Oh, there you are. You just missed them."

"Missed who?"

"Your parents. But that's okay. You'll see them at the reception."

"I'm sorry, what? What—I don't—my parents? *What?*" She must have been squishing Darla's hand. The little girl tugged it free with a frown, then immediately lifted her dress over her head with a giggle.

"Your mother and father, dear," Zach's mom said with a laugh. "I called them after the rehearsal dinner last night and invited them. I couldn't help myself. I knew there'd be plenty of food. Plus, with you not only being Zach's date but the maid of honor, it seemed appropriate. But oh goodness, was your mother surprised. She had no idea you and Zach were an item either." She waved a scolding finger with mock indignation. "You two shouldn't keep these types of secrets from your mothers."

"Right. Secrets. Bad." Charlotte hurried to the glass doors, hoping to catch a glimpse of her parents. Maybe if she could explain things to them right now, before things went any further . . . "Did you say they were just here?"

"Oh, but they're gone now. I sent them on to the reception. And don't worry. I pulled a few strings with the seating arrangements. They'll be sitting with me. You know," she said, gathering Charlotte's hands inside hers, "after what Ben did to you, I could hardly bring myself to look either of your parents in the eye these past two years. Oh, I know they didn't hold a grudge—your parents are too good of people for that sort of nonsense—but all the same, I just can't tell you how wonderful it is to feel like we've made amends. And it's all because of you and Zach."

After another fierce squeeze, she released Charlotte's hands and disappeared out the door. Wow, Charlotte really needed to get to her parents before this got any worse. She started for the door, then remembered her purse. Which was somewhere. Where? She spun in a circle.

"Looking for this?" The photographer stepped out of the sanctuary holding Charlotte's purse in one hand, her camera in the other. "Cute purse."

"Thank you."

"No problem. And thanks for keeping an eye on Darla. Did Zach tell you? We're driving to the railroad tracks on the south end of town to get some more photos before the reception."

"Oh. Um, do you need me for those? Sounds like bride and groom photos." Charlotte really needed to get to her parents and explain. Preferably before Zach's mom put any more ideas into their heads.

"Shannon thought it'd be fun to include you and Zach in a few of them as well."

"Did she?" Of course she did.

"Ready?" Zach appeared next to her side. "It might be a good idea if we drive separately. Ben and Shannon can't stop making out. I don't think they'll notice if we're not with them."

Charlotte grabbed Zach by his suit jacket. "This is a disaster."

"Okay, fine. We can ride with them."

"Not Ben and Shannon. You and me. And my parents. My parents, Zach. My mom and dad. My parents."

"I know what the word *parents* means."

"Well, did you know they were here for the wedding? Did you know they're on their way to the reception?" The church custodian, who had started to clean up the sanctuary, sent them a concerned look. Charlotte lowered her voice and pretended she was swiping lint off Zach's suit. "Your mom invited my parents. Now they think we're together. What are we going to do, huh? What are we going to do? What are we going to do?"

"First, we're going to stop repeating the same question over and over." Zach's palm slid around her back, giving her a gentle push to the door. "Next, we're going to drive out to the railroad tracks, smile, and finish getting photos for Ben and Shannon. Then, last but not least, we'll wait for a train to run over us before we have to explain anything."

Charlotte elbowed Zach in the gut. "I'm serious. After everything my mom and dad have been through, especially this past year with Will, they don't deserve another disappointment."

Zach stiffened. "What's going on with your brother? I heard he was out of prison."

"He is. But you wouldn't know it based on the distance he keeps from us." Charlotte sighed, not wanting to go into the problems with her brother at this minute. Especially since it was no secret Zach and her brother had never gotten along. They stepped outside the church and made their way to her vehicle. "My parents aside, your mom is so happy. I don't want to ruin this day for her."

"Don't worry about my mom. When we get to the reception, just pull your parents aside and explain. They've always been reasonable people. I don't think they're going to get upset over a little misunderstanding.

Shoot, they'll probably be relieved we're not really together. Want me to drive?"

She handed him her keys, then allowed him to open the passenger's side door for her, so she could maneuver into her seat without messing up her dress.

Zach was right. Her parents were reasonable people.

Which is why she had no earthly idea how to explain to them why she was serving as the maid of honor in her ex-fiancé's wedding and pretending to date his brother.

Because what reasonable explanation did she have?

13

Zach had never served as best man before, but he had the feeling hiding behind a dumpster as he prayed for the redemption of his soul was not on his list of wedding duties.

He swatted a fly away from his head, the stench of spoiled garbage ripe despite the cooled evening temps.

How had he gotten here? He paced back and forth. Well, he knew how he'd gotten here. He'd burst out the back exit of the reception hall and hooked an immediate right. But how had he gotten *here*? To this moment? When his liar liar pants should have been on fire.

Not his lips.

. . . ♦ . . .

TWENTY MINUTES EARLIER

Zach scooped a spoonful of peanuts into his hand, then reached for a cup of punch. He'd shed his tuxedo jacket as soon as they'd arrived from their photo session on the tracks, but the packed reception hall was heated with dancing guests to a point that no amount of shedding could compensate for.

Oh well. Zach had made it through his speech, the dinner, and the bridal party dance. The rest of the reception could take place in a sauna for all he cared. The worst was over. Right?

Zach wolfed the peanuts, then chugged the punch, making up for lost calories. Between nerves wound tighter than the organ player's perm and the sight of his glowing mother seated next to Charlotte's parents throughout the entire reception, he'd struggled to clean half his dinner plate.

He gulped down another cup of punch, hoping Charlotte had set her parents straight by now. He'd deal with his own mom later.

A Michael Bublé song started up as he reached for a piece of wedding cake.

"How do you have an appetite?" Charlotte appeared next to his side, talking low. "My stomach has been in knots all day."

"Did you get a chance to talk to your parents?"

She shook her head as she grabbed a fork and helped herself to a bite of his cake. "Every time I get near them," she said around a mouthful, "your mother swoops in and goes on and on about how thrilled she is we're together."

She started for another bite, and Zach lifted his plate out of reach. "I thought your stomach was in knots."

"I'm stress eating."

"Stress eat your own cake."

"My stomach is in too many knots to stress eat my own cake. Will you do it?"

"Do what? Speak to your parents? No way." He gave up on keeping his plate out of reach. They dueled for the last bites of cake until it was finished.

"Well, somebody's got to tell them."

Zach pointed his fork over Charlotte's shoulder. "How about your sister?"

"Sophia? She's not here." Charlotte spun to where Zach pointed, then spun back to face him. "Oh my word. My sister. She's here."

"She sure is." Zach handed Charlotte another piece of cake before she started eating off some innocent bystander's plate. She shoved half of it into her mouth, then said something that was probably meant to be "I need to tell her what's going on" even though it sounded more like "I need a ten-pound watermelon" before she handed Zach back the plate and darted for her sister.

"Hey, we need to talk." Ben's voice, low in Zach's ear.

Michael Bublé finished singing and the "Chicken Dance" started up next.

"Honey, get out here," Shannon shouted from the dance floor where she was surrounded by guests of all ages.

Zach forced a bright smile as he finished off the other half of Charlotte's cake and tossed it into a trash can next to the dessert table. "Better get out there. Sounds like your song."

Ben waved to his wife. "Be right there," he shouted back, then met Zach's gaze. "Look, I've kept my mouth shut up until now because all I wanted was for Shannon to have a nice wedding without any drama. But don't think for a second I don't know what this is really about."

"C'mon, Ben." Darla grabbed his hand and tugged him toward the dance floor. "Shanny says you have to dance like a chicken." She dropped his hand and showed him her version of the moves. "You too, Zach. C'mon."

Zach lifted an eyebrow in challenge and tilted his head toward the dance floor. "Shall we?"

They sidestepped to the edge of the wooden dance floor and began flapping their elbows.

"No way you and Charlotte are really a couple. I bet you can't even name one thing you have in common," Ben said, hips twisting back and forth.

"We both love John Wayne." Zach clapped his hands, figuring it was true. Who didn't love John Wayne?

"Name another thing."

"Cheesecake."

They linked elbows and spun from partner to partner until they were facing each other again and making talky motions with their hands. They locked gazes, and Zach wasn't sure whether they were having a staring contest or a chicken dance-off, but either way he refused to lose.

And apparently so did Ben. "John Wayne and cheesecake. You really expect me to believe that?"

"I don't know why you wouldn't. It's John Wayne and cheesecake."

"I know what this is really about."

Zach clapped his hands. "Great. Mind filling me in?"

"This is about me kissing Shannon."

Zach rolled his eyes. "She's your wife. Pretty sure there's going to be more than kissing going on."

Ben glanced around, then stepped closer to Zach. "I'm not talking about today. I'm talking about the week before I was supposed to marry Charlotte. Are you telling me you really didn't know?"

Zach stopped dancing. What? He ran through the timeline in his head. Ben's almost-but-not-quite wedding to Charlotte was two summers ago. Zach didn't meet Shannon until later that winter at a ski resort. In the all the time they dated, she never said anything about already knowing Ben. *Kissing Ben.*

But boy, did some of the things in her breakup letter make a whole lot more sense now. "Does Charlotte know?"

"I never told her. I didn't want to hurt her."

"So you just dumped her at the altar instead."

Ben rubbed the back of his neck as the song ended and guests shuffled around them for a break. "Look, I'm not proud of how I handled any of that. Dad had just died, I had all these new responsibilities at his company, and I was a mess. But that doesn't mean I didn't care about Charlotte. I hate that I hurt her, and I hate that you're going to hurt her too. So whatever you think you're doing with her, just stop. Okay?"

"What if I'm not ready to stop?"

Ben's jaw ticked. Maybe their mom was right. Maybe they just needed to punch each other and get whatever this was between them over and done. Because Zach didn't even know why it mattered so much to prove his brother was wrong about his relationship with Charlotte. Especially since his brother was absolutely right about his relationship with Charlotte.

Ben stepped closer and lowered his voice for Zach's ears only. "Would you be ready to walk away for ten thousand dollars?"

Zach jerked back as if his brother really had punched him. "Wow. Bribery. Keeping it classy, I see."

Ben at least had the decency to look chagrined. "I didn't mean it that way. I meant the job Shannon texted you about last week. The retreat center in Northern California? What if I gave you ten thousand just to help get you out there and settled? Come on, Zach. You know this job is too perfect an opportunity to pass up."

Hmmm. Zach probably should have read that text message a little closer. He shook his head with a nonchalant shrug. "Remind me of the details again?"

"I knew you didn't read Shannon's message." With a growl Ben tugged Zach off the dance floor, away from any listening ears. "Shannon's uncle has a buddy who used to be some hotshot attorney in LA for a bunch of years until he retired. Now he owns this retreat center. It has tons of outdoor activities. Kayaking, hiking, camping, zip-lining, all that stuff you love. But he needs someone to work as the guide-slash-expert for the equipment, itinerary, tours, I don't know what else. All I know is it sounds perfect for you, pays well, and you're as good as hired if you want it thanks to Shannon. So I don't know what you're doing playing around like you're dating Charlotte when we both know she's never going anywhere, let alone California. Ditch the girl and take the job already."

"And if I don't?" Good grief, maybe Zach loved John Wayne a little too much. Instead of jumping all over this job opportunity—that honestly did sound perfect for him—he couldn't keep himself from standing like the Duke and adding *pilgrim* to the end of every sentence in his head.

But man, did his brother have a way of making him want to defend the Alamo even if it was a lost cause. And right now, Zach's Alamo was Charlotte.

Before Ben could respond to Zach's standoff, Shannon was at his side telling him they needed to go say hi to some of the guests, and Charlotte was at Zach's side whispering, "Things are getting out of hand."

She could say that again.

A slow Ella Fitzgerald song began to play.

"You okay?" Charlotte touched his hand. "You're shaking."

No. Zach wasn't okay. He tugged Charlotte close and lowered his mouth next to her ear. "Dance with me. Please. Before I do something crazy." Like punch his brother in the kisser right in the middle of his wedding reception.

Ben just always had to flaunt his success around, didn't he? He couldn't just tell Zach about the job. He had to throw in the ten grand too. Tossing the amount around like it was nothing more than a Tootsie Roll at a parade. Zach didn't want Ben's money any more than he wanted a Tootsie Roll. He wanted . . . well, right now he didn't know what he wanted. Except maybe to keep dancing with Charlotte.

Zach pulled her closer, dropping his cheek to the top of her hair. Man, she smelled good. And the way she nestled in his arms, he couldn't help thinking he must not smell that bad either.

Everybody has their kryptonite, and "The Nearness of You" must be his. Every romantic cell in his body buzzed to life while Charlotte continued nuzzling closer. Wow, it felt good holding a woman in his arms. Pretending his brother's words hadn't hit him square in the chest. Pretending this woman in his arms was the real deal.

Too bad the woman in his arms didn't seem to be on the same page. Before the song ended, she pushed away from his chest. "I—I can't do this."

"Dance? I thought you were doing pretty well."

"No, *this*." She waved a hand back and forth between them, backing away. "It's too . . ."

"What?" Much? Weird? Real?

"Complicated." She punched his arm. "Life was so much simpler when you had a bun."

Before Zach could question what in the world that meant, a blur of red crashed into them. "Sorry," Sophia said when Zach had to grab Charlotte to keep the two of them from toppling over. "Forgot to put on my brakes. I'm so excited. Zach's mom just offered our parents her time-share. You have to convince them to take it, Charlotte. Come on. Hurry. You too, Zach."

Sure enough, when they reached the table, Zach's mom was doing her best to convince Charlotte's parents to travel down to North Carolina. "It's a beautiful sea cottage right along a sleepy beachfront. I feel so guilty not using it. Patrick loved it, and we always had the best time. But it hurts too much going there without him. And yet, at the same time, I just can't bring myself to let it go. I hate that it sits empty four weeks every summer. Honestly, it'd do my heart a world of good to know it was getting used."

"You hear that, Mom?" Sophia said. "You'd be doing her a world of good."

"And it's free," Zach added, which apparently wasn't the right thing to add. Charlotte elbowed him on one side and Sophia elbowed him on the other. "What?" he whispered. Was he the only one hurting for money these days?

"I don't know," Charlotte's mom said, tugging her shawl further over her shoulders. "That's such a generous offer, but it doesn't feel right. Not for free. That's the type of thing you do . . . well, for family."

"But you are practically family. Or you will be, right?" His mother covered her mouth, shooting Zach an apologetic look. "Or am I speaking out of turn?"

Of course that would be the moment Ben arrived at the table. Zach felt every gaze, especially Ben's, swivel in his direction. He cleared his throat. "Uh . . ." He looked to Charlotte. "No?"

She gave a slight nod of agreement.

"No," he said again with more confidence. "You're not speaking out of turn. I mean, look at us. We're together. We're a couple. We're . . . you know . . ." He patted Charlotte on the head. "Serious."

Her parents didn't appear convinced. Probably because he continued patting their daughter's head in an attempt to make it seem like the natural thing to do anytime a man was serious about a woman.

"I don't know," Mrs. Carter said, shooting a hesitant look at her husband. He shrugged and looked down at his grease-stained hands.

Sophia lunged forward. "Mom, if they weren't really a couple, do you think Charlotte would have agreed to chaperone the youth group canoe trip with Zach?"

Both of Charlotte's parents' heads snapped up. "She did?"

"I did?" Charlotte said before Zach slid his palm from the top of her head down over her mouth.

"But Charlotte hates canoeing." Mrs. Carter looked at Charlotte. "Honey, you hate canoeing."

"But she obviously cares for Zach," Sophia said.

"Oh, she cares a great deal," Zach said, meeting Ben's doubtful expression with his biggest grin as Charlotte tugged his hand away from her mouth, then didn't seem to know what to do with his hand, which really, neither did he.

"But hey, if you think that's crazy, get this," Charlotte said as they continued some sort of weird thumb war with their intertwined fingers. "Zach agreed to help me raise money for the new band instruments this summer."

"Oh my," his mother said. "Things must be serious. Zach loathes fundraisers."

"Zach certainly does," Zach said with forced cheeriness. He disentangled his fingers from Charlotte's and ran his palm up and down her arm as if warming her up. "Honey, I think you misremembered what I agreed to though. I thought we agreed I would simply help you try to stir up some donations this week."

"Well, that was before the canoe trip came into effect, *shnookums.* Once I agreed to that, you then decided it was only fair to help me with at least five fundraising events this summer."

"Five? Is that what I decided?"

"Oh yes, you were very emphatic."

Fine. Be that way. Zach smiled, running both hands up and down her arms now. "Ah. Now I remember. We did have that conversation. It was right after I had asked you if we could extend the canoe trip into our own little camping trip, and you said yes."

Charlotte cocked her head. "I don't—"

Zach pulled her in for a hug, pressing his cheek next to hers. "Isn't she the best? She knows how much I love spending time out in nature. When I told her the canoe trip was only one day, she said, 'Why not stay longer and camp out for a couple of nights? That way we can have a little time, just the two of us.'"

Charlotte leaned far enough back to pinch his cheek. "And then this beautiful lug said, 'Two nights together won't be enough time to satisfy me. I'm helping you with every single fundraiser all summer long.' Remember that?" She patted him lovingly on the cheek. Or at least that's probably what she intended. His cheek burned from the smack she actually gave him.

Ben cleared his throat. "What about California, Zach? Seems like if you and Charlotte were serious, you would want to at least mention *the amazing job opportunity* you received that only a fool would turn down. You might want to at least get her take on it before you promise a summer of fundraisers."

Zach's knuckles had never itched so bad to knock the smirk off his brother's face as they did in this moment. A warning bell deep in his gut warned him to walk away before he relieved the itch.

Too bad he'd never been good at listening to that warning bell. Probably why he did something even stupider. "I don't need her take on it. You know why?" *Pilgrim.* "Because you're right. Only a fool would turn it down. Which is why I guess you should consider me a fool in love."

Zach wrapped an arm around Charlotte's waist and dipped her into the type of kiss a man gives a woman before he goes off to war. But when the kiss was finished, rather than go off to war, Zach excused himself amidst the cheering and applause, ran for the back exit, and hid behind a dumpster.

14

"Charlotte, wait!" Sophia's high heels clacked across the parking lot faster than a woman ought to be able to run in high heels. Certainly faster than Charlotte. Sophia circled around her and blocked Charlotte's path. "Where are you going?"

"Home. The moon. Anywhere but back in there." Charlotte pointed to the reception hall where a loud bass beat hummed.

"What about Zach?"

"What *about* Zach?"

Sophia folded her arms in the red dress that on closer inspection looked a lot like one of Charlotte's. Had her sister raided her closet? "You don't think it's going to look a little strange that right after you two practically confess your eternal love, you peel out of the parking lot and he disappears behind a dumpster? And really, a dumpster? Who runs and hides behind a dumpster?"

"People who can't find utility closets."

Sophia squeezed Charlotte's wrist. "Think about mom and dad."

"Right now I'd rather think about fleeing the country."

"Charlotte . . ." Sophia tugged her away from her car. "You're being ridiculous."

"I'm being ridiculous? *I'm* being ridiculous? If anyone is to blame for being ridiculous, it's you and your pathetic sleuthing skills. You're to blame for all this." Charlotte altered her voice into a high-pitched squeal. "'Oh, what if she's meeting the love of her life? What if he's the Frankie to her Annette?' *Bah.* You know why Melba said 'Cake, cake, cake'? It's because she loved cake, cake, cake. That's it. She didn't even have an invitation to the wedding. And now look at the mess you've put me in."

Charlotte attempted to get into her car, but Sophia blocked the door. "Oh, I'm sorry. Remind me again of the part where I told you to be Zach's date. Remind me how I coerced you into being the maid of honor in this wedding. Maybe you can jog my memory about when I told you two to make out in front of our parents, because I'm drawing a blank."

Charlotte's shoulders drooped. "Okay, fine. So maybe it's not completely your fault. Zach is obviously to blame as well."

"Charlotte . . ."

"Stop saying *Charlotte* like that."

"Like what?"

"Like Dad does when he thinks I'm being unreasonable."

Sophia's eyes sparkled with mischief. *"Charlotte . . ."* she said again, bringing an unwanted smile to Charlotte's lips. Her sister really did sound just like their dad. Charlotte sighed, leaning against her car next to her sister. The back of her dress would probably get dirty, but that was the least of her worries at this point.

"I don't have time for this. I'm supposed to be figuring out how to keep my job, not dealing with—" she flapped a hand at the reception hall— *"that."*

Sophia's shoulder bumped against hers. "You can't tell me the idea of you and Zach being a couple isn't a tiny bit appealing. He's the epitome of ruggedly handsome, even without the man bun."

"You mean *especially* without the man bun. But it's not real. Our relationship, I mean." His good looks were unfortunately all too real.

"But think of Mom and Dad. North Carolina. The time-share. You saw them. They won't accept this opportunity if they don't think you and Zach are an actual couple. What if this is their only chance?"

"For a vacation?"

"To save their marriage. Remember? *Issues?* They need this time away. And they made it pretty clear they're not going to accept a gift like this from us. Not while we're still struggling to make ends meet."

"I was thinking of picking up a second job."

"With what time? Sounds to me like you'll be too busy working on fundraisers for anything else."

"Ugh. You're right. Two days into summer vacation and it's already a disaster."

"It doesn't have to be. Don't you see? Date Zach a little while longer, and you'll kill thirty birds with one stone. Think about it."

"I am, and now I feel guilty about all these dead birds."

Sophia squeezed Charlotte's wrist. "Stick with me a second. You've been wanting to find a way to repay Mom and Dad, even though it wasn't your fault your wedding got cancelled and they've been trying to tell you for two years that it wasn't your fault."

"I knew going into the week of our wedding that something wasn't right between us. I should have pushed harder for answers. Made him talk."

"None of that matters at this point. What matters is Mom and Dad won't let you repay them, and their marriage is in trouble. This might be our only opportunity to get them away for a while so they can focus on fixing it. Isn't dating a hunky guy worth it for them?"

"Not if I have to go camping for two days. Do you know how long two days is out in the wild?"

"I'm guessing around forty-eight hours."

"An eternity. That's how long it is. I hate camping. There's never a toilet when you need one, and if you do come across one, there's a thousand daddy longlegs waiting to crawl inside your underwear. What if we get lost? What if we run out of water? What if we have to drink urine out of a sack made from snakeskin? I saw that on an episode of one of those *Survivorman* shows. I wanted to gag, vomit, and die all at the same time."

"So see? Everything is going to be fine."

"How did you get 'everything is going to be fine' from anything I just said?"

"Hey, you're the one always telling me to keep the faith, remember?" Sophia slung her arm around Charlotte's shoulders.

Sophia was right. Where was Charlotte's faith? It'd clearly gone out the window along with her honesty. "I don't like that this idea involves lying to Mom and Dad. You know I've never been a good liar. They're going to see through me before they even pack their first bag."

Sophia grabbed Charlotte's hand. "Who says you have to lie? Date Zach. Be a couple. Nobody's saying you have to marry the guy. Just keep dating him until Mom and Dad get down to North Carolina. Surely you can handle being in a casual relationship for that long."

"Assuming he can handle being in any sort of relationship with me. The man did run off and hide behind a dumpster after all."

"Yeah, but that was right after he planted a kiss on you steamy enough to curl even *my* toes."

As if Charlotte needed the reminder.

Zach would have been better off staying behind the dumpster all weekend. What had possessed him to kiss Charlotte like that? And what on earth had possessed her to kiss him back?

Because she had. Oh, she had.

And now all he could think about was kissing her again. And again. Something that was probably frowned upon for chaperones of a church's high school youth group event.

He nudged shut the front door to his mom's house, careful not to wake her. Though after all the excitement of the wedding and Charlotte, not to mention all of Mom's dancing to "Electric Slide" and "Shout" afterward, followed by at least a dozen retellings the next morning at church, Zach doubted she'd wake until sometime midweek.

Zach hefted his camping gear into the back of his Jeep. It was still early, and the sky remained cloaked in a blanket of charcoal gray. He'd promised Rick to get to the church before 6 a.m. so they could begin loading supplies into the back of the van and be on the road by 6:30.

He tried rubbing the sleep from his eyes. Had Charlotte tossed and turned over that kiss as much as he had the past two nights? He hoped so. He hated to think he was the only one reliving their kiss over and over.

When Zach pulled into the back corner of First Christian Church's parking lot, Rick was already shoving a cooler into the van.

"Hey, man." Rick reached out to shake Zach's hand and pull him in for a quick bro hug before he headed into the church storage shed. "Thanks for helping out. I can't believe you were able to convince Charlotte to come along too. Really appreciate that. How was the wedding, by the way?"

Zach rubbed the stubble on his chin as he followed Rick. "Hard to describe."

"Did you at least make it through the day without punching your brother?"

Zach nodded and grabbed a stack of life jackets. "Yeah. Yeah, I did." He wagged his head to the side. "But I didn't quite make it through the day without kissing my brother's ex-fiancée."

Rick whipped around, whacking Zach on the shoulder with a pile of canoe paddles. "You kissed Charlotte?"

Oh, he did more than that. "Some might say we're sort of a couple."

Rick dropped the paddles. "When I said we could really use a female chaperone, I didn't mean you had to seduce the poor woman."

"I didn't seduce anyone." Zach threw an armful of life vests into the van. "I just . . . I don't know. It was a very strange weekend."

"This is Illinois, not Las Vegas. We don't have strange weekends like that. How did you sort of become a couple with a woman you hardly know?"

"I wouldn't say I hardly know her, considering we grew up together, she dated my brother, then nearly became my sister-in-law two years ago."

"And now she's your girlfriend?"

"It's a long story. I'll explain it all later."

Rick pursed his lips, probably wondering if having Zach and Charlotte on this trip was such a blessing after all. Vehicles started pulling into the parking lot, tired teenagers climbing out and grunting quiet greetings to one another.

Zach scanned each arrival, eager to catch a glimpse of Charlotte. Part of him wondered if she'd even show.

After their kiss, or rather, after he'd worked up the courage to come out from behind the dumpster after their kiss, everyone was busy sending Ben and Shannon off with bubbles and noisemakers. He only caught a glimpse of Charlotte before she climbed into a vehicle with her sister and left. But he was pretty sure Sophia had mouthed the words "continue on" to him across the parking lot.

Continue on. What did that mean? Continue on with the canoe trip? The fundraisers? The kissing? *What?*

"Hey." Charlotte's quiet voice interrupted his internal turmoil. He slowly turned to face her. A backpack was slung over one shoulder, her braided hair over the other. The sky had lightened enough for him to see her tired eyes, as if maybe she hadn't slept a whole lot the past couple of nights either. *Hooyah.*

She fiddled with her backpack as if she was nervous. Or maybe disappointed and full of regret over her life decisions this past week, starting with the one that led her to Cake Lassies Friday evening.

But here she was.

"Hey," Zach said, taking her bag from her shoulder. "I'll put this in with my stuff." He motioned his head toward his Jeep, working hard to keep his tone neutral. "I figured we'd drive separate since we're planning to stay longer."

She played with the end of her braid and chewed on her lip. "So we're still going through with that, are we?"

He fought to hold his grin in check. "We wouldn't want anybody thinking what we said the other night wasn't true, would we? But hey, don't worry. I think by the end of Wednesday, you'll discover you don't hate camping as much as you think. Stick with me and you may discover you adore it."

"I find that about as likely as you adoring fundraisers."

Good point. Zach patted her arm. "Let's just take it one day at a time, how about that?" He'd wait until tonight before confessing he had no intention of making her camp out with him for two nights. In fact, it'd be better if she didn't. The only reason he intended to camp out for a couple of nights was to avoid everything. His mom. This town. The memory of that kiss. "Have your parents decided about the time-share yet?"

"They have." She stopped chewing her lip, a genuine smile lifting the corners. "And they're flying down there Wednesday afternoon. Seems once they embraced the idea, they couldn't pack fast enough. Plus they found an amazing deal on a flight."

"Good. I'm glad."

"Me too. I mean, it is the reason I'm doing this." She motioned to the van. "I'm still not really sure why you're making me do this though. Was there seriously nobody else in the world you could get to go on this canoe trip?"

"Is there seriously nobody else in the world you can get to help with your fundraisers?"

"Touché." Charlotte slurped coffee out of her thermos. "Let's get this over with. And by the way, because you've tacked on extra days to this already horrific expedition, I think it only fair to warn you I felt the need to come up with something equally horrifying to compensate for the mental and emotional turmoil this trip is sure to cost me until my dying day and apply it to you in equal shares in regard to my fundraising endeavors."

Zach shook his head. "That's a lot of words to unpack at six in the morning. Not sure I followed all of it."

"I'm going to make you pay."

"That I follow." Zach slipped a worn Chicago Cubs ball cap out from his back pocket and tugged it over his head. "Pretty sure making me spend countless hours selling baked goods and doing car washes will be payment enough."

Charlotte scoffed. "I need big bucks, not pennies. This year I'm thinking outside the box."

"How far outside the box?"

"Pig kissing."

He opened the passenger side door for her. "That idea is totally inside the box. Nobody wants to see that."

"Oh, I'm pretty sure people are always happy to pay good money to see a handsome man smooch a pig. Or wait." She snapped her fingers. "Maybe we give them an option. They can pay said handsome man to either kiss the pig or kiss them."

"Am I said handsome man? I can't tell whether to be flattered or scared."

"It'd be like a pig-kissing booth."

"Scared. I should definitely be scared."

"Now you know how I feel about camping."

"Pretty sure we're not going to run into any pigs out in the woods."

"Yeah, but we may run into spiders."

"And are you planning to kiss them?"

"I'd rather kiss a pig."

"Well then, maybe you should be the one in the pig-kissing booth."

Charlotte smiled at him, and he smiled back. And they might have gone on smiling at each other for a while longer if Rick hadn't walked over, looking down at his phone.

"Uh, guys?" Rick turned the screen to face them. He had the online newspaper site pulled up. Zach had just spotted his name when Rick said, "You're seriously going to try doing this couples challenge?"

16

ARE YOU NUTS?

WHAT WERE YOU THINKING?

I KNOW YOU'RE BEHIND THIS!

THERE WILL BE BLOOD, SOPHIA. BLOOD!

The texts from Charlotte had started before Sophia even got out of bed that morning and had continued at intervals throughout the day, probably whenever Charlotte could find a phone signal. Before she could slide her phone back into her work apron pocket, another text buzzed through.

STOP IGNORING ME!

Fine. Sophia pushed her food cart to the side of the hallway and ducked into a restroom outside a visitor's lounge on the second floor. She tapped her sister's contact number and said, "It's not what it looks like," as soon as Charlotte answered.

"Really? Because it looks like you signed Zach and me up for a challenge that requires riding a tandem bicycle five hundred miles in ten days on something called the Natchez Trace."

Sophia met her own wincing expression in the mirror above the sink. "Okay, it might be what it looks like. But listen, I didn't know all the details at the time. And I certainly didn't think you guys would get picked."

"Then why did you sign us up?"

"I had to. My back was against the wall. Or rather the booth. Either way I had no escape."

"You need to explain yourself better than that."

Sophia sucked in a deep breath and leaned against the bathroom door. "I went to brunch with Mom and Dad after church yesterday, and Ty was there. He pulled up a chair, wanting to know if the rumors were true about you and Zach. Of course I had to tell him yes. I mean, Mom and Dad were sitting right there. But then he started going on and on about that challenge and asking why you and Zach hadn't entered your names yet and pointing out how the deadline was later that afternoon."

She pushed off the door and began pacing. "I tried coming up with some good excuses, I did. But they all sounded flimsy. Especially when everyone knows how much you could use that money. So when Mom and Dad started hitting me with questions too, I panicked. I told them you guys had been so busy with Ben's wedding, you'd probably forgotten. Well, next thing I know everyone's looking at me like I should just go ahead and fill out the application for you."

She yanked a paper towel out of the dispenser, starting to sweat as much now as she had yesterday when she'd received a rapid response to her email. A response that said yes, they qualified—so long as A. P. Hopkins received a short essay on why they were the best couple to be chosen to attempt the challenge.

"You wrote an essay?" Charlotte said once Sophia finished explaining. "About Zach and me? As a couple?"

"Ty helped. He practically dictated the whole thing."

"What did this essay say?"

"We mostly focused on you. And your music program." Sophia inhaled a deep breath, preparing to say the next bit as quickly as possible. Like ripping off a Band-Aid. "And maybe tossed in a sentence or two about everything you sacrificed to help your family when Mom was battling cancer, only for you to get dumped at the altar afterward, which is why we're all so very excited you've met the true love of your life and know without a doubt you two are up for this challenge. And we may have also added a picture of you and Zach kissing at the reception. That was actually Mom's idea."

Sophia held the phone away from her ear just in case. When she didn't hear any screaming, she slowly brought it back and said, "Charlotte? You still there?"

"Why didn't you tell me about this sooner?" Charlotte gritted out in her ear.

"Everything happened so fast. I didn't want to say anything until I came up with a way to fix it first."

"And?"

"I never came up with a way to fix it." Sophia dabbed her forehead. "Hopkins loved the essay and said you were in."

"Sophia!"

There was the scream. She jerked the phone away from her ear for a few seconds, then replaced it. "Listen. Mom and Dad are leaving for North Carolina in two days. Just go along with it until they get down there, okay? Remember. You don't have to complete this challenge. You only have to *attempt* to complete it. Actually—"

She snapped her gaze to the mirror. Of course. That was the answer! Why was she sweating? "Don't you see? This is perfect," she said, tossing her paper towel in the trash. "Fail to complete it, nobody will be surprised. I mean, let's be honest. You. Biking. Outdoors. Not the recipe for success. But if by some crazy miracle you do complete it? Twenty-five thousand dollars, Charlotte. Think about that."

"Right now I'm more consumed with thinking about five hundred miles on a bicycle seat. Let alone sleeping in a tent every night. With Zach. Not sure our relationship has blossomed to the sharing-a-tent status already."

"So take two tents."

"And put them where? I'm serious. How do you pack for a trip like this? How much can we bring? Where does everything go? Do we drag a U-Haul behind us? I don't even know where this Natchez Trace is. How am I supposed to prepare? We don't even have a tandem bicycle."

"You've still got a couple of days. I'm sure we can come up with a tandem bicycle in the meantime. Just eat a PowerBar and stop stressing. We'll figure out where the Natchez Trace is later. I have to go. And hey, aren't you supposed to be on a canoe trip right now?"

"I am. Can't you hear the utter despair and agony in my voice?"

Sophia ended the call. Some questions were better left unanswered.

17

Close to forty-eight hours later, Charlotte sighed, not sure which was more ridiculous—the fact she'd driven thirty miles to stand inside a dressing room at Buddy Boy's Bike Shop so she could prepare for a challenge she didn't want to complete, or the goofy names people were coming up with for the challenge when they decided calling it 'the challenge' wasn't exciting enough.

Charlotte crouched as if sitting on a bike seat, her right elbow banging against the dressing room wall, and shook her head. Nope nope nope.

There was a reason she'd never gone out for the volleyball team in high school. Okay, two reasons. The first was that she stunk at volleyball. But the other reason, the main reason, was she refused to participate in any athletic endeavor that required wearing tiny spandex shorts. Especially an athletic endeavor some were now referring to as the Beloved Biking Bonanza.

Who cared if these biking shorts reached down to her knees? They did not flatter her figure. And if she was expected to ride a tandem bicycle with a man who could make tube socks and a cardboard box look flattering, she'd need something better than this.

Standing, she twisted to look over her shoulder. Good grief, what was with all the rear end padding? As if Charlotte had ever needed additional padding in that department.

"Think those will work?" the bike store clerk, a thin man who probably did benefit from additional padding, asked through the locked door. "We have a couple of other options if you haven't found what you're looking for."

"Oh, I've seen plenty for one day," Charlotte assured him, struggling to get the spandex shorts down her hips.

"What about the bike? Still interested?"

Not for two thousand dollars. Who knew tandem bicycles were so expensive? This one was even marked fifty percent off. Didn't help that it was a top-of-the-line model and, of course, the only one the store had.

"I should probably sleep on it. You know what they say. Don't make big decisions without sleeping on it first."

"Sure. You can take the shorts home to sleep in if that helps."

"No, that's not . . ." Whatever. Fine. "Thanks." Any excuse to get out of this store.

Too bad she hadn't had an excuse to get out of the canoe trip the other day. Or rather, the river, where she'd spent the majority of the canoe trip. Considering the number of times the giddy foursome of teen girls had tipped the canoe trying to ogle Zach, they'd be better off not even bringing a canoe next time.

Not that there'd be a next time for Charlotte. The likelihood of her stepping near a canoe the remainder of her lifetime ranked up there with the chances of her getting these shorts down her thighs without swearing.

"Ugh!" She kicked the black shorts against the door. This was supposed to have been her best summer in ages. Why wasn't anything working out like it was supposed to?

Charlotte reached for her skirt. Okay, maybe some things were working out, considering her parents should be landing in North Carolina any moment. That little detail had turned out better than planned. Almost made the past few days of craziness worth it to hear them so excited about getting away. Especially since she hadn't actually had to go camping two extra nights with Zach.

She slipped back into her skirt—made with breathable cotton, thank you very much—and inhaled a calming breath. All hope was not lost. If things had worked out for her parents, maybe things could still work out for her.

"Faith, girl. Faith," Charlotte whispered to herself as she opened the dressing room door.

The clerk had stepped to the other side of the store and was educating a child about the importance of helmets. He held up one that was cracked and shattered. "See this?" he said. "This would have been the guy's head if he hadn't been wearing his helmet."

"Did he die?" the child asked.

"No. I mean, well yes, technically the person who wore this helmet did die, but not because of the bicycle accident. He had an abdominal aortic aneurysm that ruptured a few years later and—you know what? Don't worry about that. The important part is he didn't die from a head injury."

"What's an abdominal whatever you said?"

"Nothing. Just wear your helmet." The clerk pointed at the shorts in Charlotte's hand. "Ready to take those home for a good snooze?"

She shrugged and handed over her credit card. "Why not?" Made about as much sense as anything else lately.

Her phone pinged with a text message as she slid into her car a few minutes later with her purchase. It was from Sophia.

We did it! Mom & Dad just landed!

Sure enough, another text message pinged through from Mom, saying the same thing. Charlotte texted her mom back with a thumbs-up emoji just as Sophia texted again.

Let's meet at Mucho Mucho to celebrate!

Charlotte clicked her seatbelt in place. She'd worry about finding a bike and squeezing into ridiculously tight shorts later. Right now a giant burrito filled with mucho mucho everything was calling her name. She texted Sophia back.

Meet you in 30.

. . . ✦ . . .

Thirty minutes later Charlotte opened the door to Mucho Mucho and spotted Ty making a beeline for her. "You just missed him," he said, grabbing her hand. "But come with me. I want to show you what we've come up with so far."

"Missed who?"

"Zach, silly girl. Who else?"

Charlotte waved with her free hand to Nita and glanced around for Sophia, all while Ty continued dragging her to a booth where Rick stood, trying to balance four giant Styrofoam cups in his hands. Ty guided Charlotte to one side of the booth, then plopped down on the other.

"Did you tell her?" Rick said, setting the cups back down on the table and stacking one on the other, so he could hold two cups in each hand.

"Not yet. You want to tell her?"

"No. You go ahead," Rick said, motioning to Ty with his chin.

"But it's technically your news. You should be the one to tell her."

"But you're more excited. It'll be better coming from you."

"Will someone just tell me something?" Charlotte blurted.

"We found you a tandem bike," they both said at the same time before Rick continued. "Well, one of the kids in my youth group did. It was just sitting in his grandparents' garage gathering dust, so they said you could have it."

"Isn't that great?" Ty said, bouncing up and down in his seat like a kid on Christmas morning.

"Well . . ." Sure. Great in the sense she didn't have to spend two thousand dollars on a bicycle she didn't want. Not so great in the sense she was one step closer to having to bike five hundred miles on a bicycle she didn't want.

"I better get this salsa home to Kate before she puts a hit out on me." Rick lifted the cups and shot Charlotte a wink. "Good luck, kiddo. We'll be praying for you."

"Thanks." But she had a feeling Ty was going to need those prayers more than she did if she and Zach failed. Ty was still bouncing and rambling about the greatness of it all. She'd never seen him so excited. Might be best to give him a heads-up that she and Zach weren't exactly a do-or-die couple. The chances of them completing this challenge . . .

She cleared her throat. "Listen, Ty, before this goes any further, I need to let you in on something. Zach and I, well, we're—"

"Scared? Of course you are. Who wouldn't be? It's a lot of pressure. That's why I took the liberty of helping you out." He began unfolding a map and spreading it across the table.

"I'm not sure *scared* is the right word I'm looking for in this situation. Maybe more like . . . oh, I don't know, regretful? Because believe me, I get more than anyone how handy twenty-five thousand dollars would be, but—"

"Twenty-five thousand?" Ty looked up from what appeared to be a day-by-day itinerary scrawled across a piece of notebook paper and reached across the table to grip her hand. "No. No, no, no. Didn't you hear? You seriously need to start reading the paper, woman. Hopkins said to make this a more valuable experience, he's decided to add another zero to the prize. We're talking *two hundred fifty thousand dollars*. Why do you think I'm so excited?"

Before she could say anything, he slid the notebook paper in front of her, tapping a bunch of words with his finger. "Now I know this is totally out of your element, and I know Zach's not much of a planner, so I made sure to map everything out for you."

Charlotte stared at the notebook paper full of town names she'd never heard of and mileage distances she rarely covered one day in a car, let alone on a bicycle. "Why does that say Nashville?"

"Because that's where the Natchez Trace starts. And honestly, Hopkins was doing you a favor when he picked it. It's all paved non-commercial highway, so you won't be battling lots of traffic, definitely no semis. The speed limit is 50 miles per hour the entire route, and there's plenty of camping sites along the way, which is good. Save you some money. Plus I hear it's very scenic."

He ran his finger down the map. "Now the Trace only goes around 440 miles, so you'll have to do nearly sixty off the trail to get to the finish line. And technically, yes, the finish is a little further than five hundred miles. But not by much." He tapped a dot on the map. "Tiny little town in Louisiana called Jackson. Now you'll still need to get somewhere you can pick up a rental car and make the drive back, but other than that, it sounds perfect, don't you think?"

Charlotte stared at the notebook paper. The map. The notebook paper. The map. "Pretty sure *perfect* isn't the word I'm looking for in this situation either."

18

Zach's arms burned as he powered through another set of push-ups. They weren't really going to go through with this, were they? He finished the push-ups, then flipped onto his back for rapid crunch repetitions.

He'd be the first to admit his moral compass didn't always point due north, but entering a challenge for couples to win any amount of money when they *weren't really a couple* seemed unethical even by his standards.

They shouldn't do it. Plain and simple. That's all there was to it.

Unless . . . they decided to make some sort of commitment? Maybe be a real couple? The type of couple who kisses?

Jumping up, he grabbed the Nerf Chicago Bulls basketball that went along with the miniature hoop still attached above the door and began pacing the creaky hardwood floors of his childhood bedroom. He tossed the ball from hand to hand.

What was he thinking? They couldn't be a real couple. So what if he was developing weird feelings for Charlotte? She had weird feelings for this town. They weren't compatible. Period.

But for two hundred fifty thousand dollars, mightn't they be the teensiest bit compatible? They both loved John Wayne and cheesecake, after all.

And it's not as if the rules said they had to get married once the challenge was over. Or that they even had to stay together as a couple. They could still go their separate ways. They'd just be going their separate ways after splitting two hundred fifty thousand dollars first.

"All right," he said to the basketball. "If I sink this shot, we should do the challenge."

Zach aimed for the basketball hoop. The ball smacked off the upper doorframe, bounced off a lamp on his desk, and rolled beneath his bed. "You know what? Close enough."

He grabbed the T-shirt he'd shed earlier from his old Star Wars bedspread and slammed it over his head. Enough stalling. He needed to convince Charlotte to do the challenge before either of them spent too much time considering whether it was the right thing to do.

Zach rushed down the stairs, flung open the front door, hurled himself down the porch steps, then screeched to a halt, the top of his body pitching forward.

"Whoa." Strong hands caught him by the shoulders. "Some sort of emergency?"

Yeah, you could say that. Zach was developing weird feelings for a weird woman whose greatest dream was to stay planted in a town Zach had spent his entire adolescence dreaming of escaping. And now that weird woman's estranged ex-convict brother was standing right in front of him.

"What are you doing here?" Zach asked once he'd regained enough balance to take a step back. Zach had known Will for as long as he'd known his own brother. Will and Ben had been inseparable growing up. Occasionally they'd let Zach tag along with them. Mostly they hadn't.

And mostly Zach hadn't cared since he'd never liked Will all that much. Eventually Will started hanging out with a different crowd in high school anyway.

Will dug his hands into his jeans pockets, something different in the stoop of his shoulders from the last time Zach had seen him. A heaviness despite his wiry muscles. He wore a St. Louis Cardinals ball cap low on his forehead, as if trying to stay hidden. He should. This was Chicago Cubs territory. "Your brother called me."

Zach crossed his arms over his chest. "Seems like a man on his honeymoon ought to have better things to do than call up an old friend to shoot the breeze."

"It wasn't exactly a casual conversation." Will shifted his weight from one leg to the other. "Just what do you think you're doing with Charlotte?"

His mom's neighbor, Patty, popped out the front door of her brick ranch house across the street and offered a "Howdy!" as she gathered her mail. Zach lifted a wave in return. "I'm not doing anything with Charlotte," Zach said to Will.

"Heard it was a beautiful wedding," Patty shouted.

"Then what's all this garbage I hear about you two in a relationship?" Will asked at the same time.

"It was!" Zach called to Patty, attempting a polite smile, which proved difficult since he was also trying to intimidate Will with a menacing glare. "You know, I find it interesting you can't be bothered to pay a visit to your own family, but you'll show up at my door with concerns that are none of your business."

"Charlotte is my business. She's my sister."

"Your mom told me about your exciting news," Patty continued. "You and Charlotte! How exciting!"

Good grief, lady. Just take your mail and be gone. Zach lifted his hand again. "Thank you!" he yelled to her. Then, "Maybe you should be paying a visit to her, not me," he said to Will.

"It's not her I have the problem with."

"Think you'll be setting a date soon? I know your mother certainly hopes so," Pesky Patty persisted, lifting up crossed fingers for good measure.

Zach inhaled a deep breath. "We'll see! Got a lot going on right now!" He lowered his voice. "Then what exactly is your problem?"

"You're going to hurt her."

"That's right," the perky pest called back. "The Nuptial Readiness Challenge. Mylanta! That's certainly a lot of money."

"Oh, and you haven't hurt her?" Zach ground out, before, "It certainly is!"

"She's too good for you," Will said.

"She's perfect for you!" Patty called. "Such a doll! Even if you don't complete the challenge, you've landed yourself a prize. Don't let her go now, you hear?" With a final wave of her mail, she disappeared into her house.

Patty was right. Charlotte was a prize. A prize Zach had no business winning if he had zero intentions of sticking around this town. But still. Will had no business dictating their relationship. And neither did Ben. These two annoyed him just as much now as they did when he was a kid.

Zach inhaled a deep breath, his inner John Wayne itching to take over again. "From what I recall, you stopped showing any concern for your family years ago. And from what I hear, you're still doing your best to avoid them. So what's this really about?" *Pilgrim.*

Will tugged the bill of his hat further down, providing Zach a glimpse of a jagged scar running the length of his forearm. Probably a little something he'd received during his prison stint. Zach sighed, a slice of compassion, maybe pity, oozing out of him. As much as Will irked him, he didn't envy whatever he'd been through these past few years.

"I'm just trying to do better now."

"Then maybe you should actually, I don't know, start by seeing your family."

"I have. Some of them." Will squeezed the brim of his baseball hat, turning in a half circle. Zach thought for a second he might leave. But he finished the rotation and dug his hands into his pockets, shoulders hunched as if he were cold. "Look, I know I've been a lousy brother to Charlotte, but that doesn't mean I don't love her. I do. I always have. So please just don't hurt her, okay? That's all I'm asking. You may think you know her better than I do, and maybe you're right, but I know this. She doesn't deserve to get her heart broken again. So don't do it."

Will ambled down the walkway to his car, with a slight limp—something else that was new—then drove around the corner. As soon as he disappeared from view, Zach marched back into the house and slammed the door. Stupid punk. Where did he get off? If anybody was likely to hurt Charlotte again, it was Will. It was Ben. It was *not* Zach. He would never hurt Charlotte.

Would he? *No.* He massaged his temples. He wouldn't.

Would he? He lowered his hands and tapped his head against the door. Shoot. He might. If he spent enough time with her and she started developing similar weird feelings for him.

Shoot. He couldn't risk it. Not when there wasn't any hope for a future between them. They shouldn't do the challenge. That's all there was to it. He'd find another way for Charlotte to save her music program.

In fact, if Ben had been so willing to fork over ten thousand dollars just to get Zach out to California, Ben ought to be willing to donate the same amount to help Charlotte. It wasn't two hundred fifty thousand by any means, but it was better than nothing. And it was the least his brother could do for kissing another woman the week he was supposed to be marrying Charlotte.

Zach pulled out his phone, not caring that his brother was on his honeymoon. They had some issues to resolve once and for all. Including that job in California.

As tempted as Zach was to explore these weird feelings for Charlotte, it was time for him to get on with his life. Definitely time to get out of Illinois.

19

Charlotte stared at her bedroom ceiling as early morning light snuck past the curtains. She didn't care if the prize was enough to save her entire career, she couldn't do it. Who needed two hundred fifty thousand dollars? Not her. She'd stick to the usual fundraisers, thank you very much.

So what if it took up her entire summer and she didn't even scrape together one percent of the amount? Better than riding a tandem bicycle for billions of miles with Zach, wilderness man extraordinaire. He'd probably make them hunt rabbits for dinner every night—if he even showed up. She hadn't seen him in person since the day of the canoe trip. For all she knew, he'd already fled town and forgotten about her.

Some couple they were.

All the more reason to not even entertain the idea of attempting the challenge. She'd find another way to keep her job. Something that didn't involve being in a relationship with zero potential.

Unplugging her phone from the charger next to her bed, she sat up prepared to start searching the internet for new fundraiser ideas when the screen lit up with a FaceTime call.

"Hey, Mom," Charlotte said, after accepting the call. "What are you doing up so early?"

Her mom lifted her wrist and looked at her watch. "Oh, I guess it is still pretty early your time. Sorry. Forgot we're an hour ahead. Why, we've already been out for a walk and finished a crossword puzzle and eaten breakfast at—oh, what was that place called?" She twisted in her seat. "Dan, you remember the name of it?"

"Waffle House," Dad's voice answered from off to the side.

"No."

"Pancake House."

"No."

"Grits House."

"You're not even trying. *Anyway*," she said while Dad continued listing off breakfast items followed by the word *house*. "We just wanted to check in. See how you and Zach were doing. To be honest, when you said you were seeing an old friend, I never in my life would have guessed it was Zach."

Dad leaned into the screen. "We would have guessed Frankie Avalon long before we ever guessed Zach."

"Ha. Frankie Avalon. That's a good one." Charlotte released a strangled laugh as she padded down the hallway to the kitchen to brew up some coffee. Now might be a good time to set the record straight with everyone. Starting with her parents. "You know, it's actually funny you should mention that," she said, opening a cabinet to grab the coffee filters. "Because I have a funny story about it. It's really funny. Super funny. We're all going to laugh. It's about Zach and me. Yeah. So, here's the funny thing. We're not—"

"Berry Nut House," Dad said, snapping his fingers.

"That's it!" Mom twisted to give him a high five. "See, I knew you'd remember." She jumped out of her chair with a whoop and began bumping her hip against his in the weird celebratory dance they used to break into occasionally during the game Password.

Charlotte forgot about the coffee as she stared, uncertain whether to be embarrassed by her parents . . . or envious. She couldn't remember the last time she'd seen them so carefree and happy, Mom whooping and hip bumping, and Dad standing with both fists raised like he'd just taken down the Soviets in *Rocky IV*.

"Sorry," Dad eventually said, taking a seat and tugging Mom onto his lap, so their faces were both in view of the camera. "The sea air is obviously making your mom wacky. I'm trying to keep her under control, but—"

Mom must have done something to him out of camera range. He flinched, she giggled, then they both blushed.

Blushed.

This phone call needed to end. Now.

"So what were you saying about you and Zach?" Dad said after clearing his throat.

"Something funny?" The laugh lines around Mom's eyes deepened as if in anticipation for all the laughter sure to follow.

"Oh, um . . ." Charlotte realized she was pouring coffee grounds all over the countertop and nowhere near the filter. "Whoops," she muttered and began swiping them into the sink.

"Everything okay?" Mom asked.

Not really. "Yep. Just . . ." *Figuring out whether to keep hiding what's really going on in my life right now or not.* Charlotte rinsed off her hand and quickly dried it on a towel hanging from the stove. Looking at their two faces squished together onto the screen, both of them grinning like besotted fools, she slid into a chair and faced the truth.

Which was that she couldn't tell them the truth.

Not yet. Not when they looked so goofy and happy. Charlotte still didn't know what "issues" they'd been working through prior to the trip, but those "issues" sure didn't appear to be weighing them down now.

And she wasn't about to give them a new issue, like the fact she was single and close to being out of a job.

She made a show of twisting to look at the kitchen wall clock. "You know what? Just noticed the time. I'll have to tell you about it later. It's kind of a long story, and there's so much I need to get done today." Like figure out her entire future.

"Right." Mom's eyes lit up. "Your trip starts soon."

"That's what everyone keeps saying," Charlotte said with a smile she hoped didn't look too painful. "I better get moving."

"We understand," Mom said. "Like I said, we just wanted to check in."

"Hey, weren't we going to tell her about—" Dad murmured out of the side of his mouth before Mom cut him off with a swiveled mouth murmur of her own. "Let's wait until after the challenge."

"You know just because you press your lips to the side doesn't mean I can't hear you," Charlotte said. "Is there something you need to tell me?"

"Nope," Mom answered a little too cheerfully. "It can wait."

"You sure?" Dad said, back to the side mouth murmuring. "Because now might be a good time. The doctor said—"

"Take care, sweetie! We'll talk to you after you get back. And hey, even if you don't complete the challenge, we're so proud of you. And we love you so much. We just want you to be happy, okay?" Was Mom tearing up?

Before Charlotte could say anything, like *what the heck did the doctor say*, Dad took the phone, said a quick "Love you, Char, bye," and ended the call.

Charlotte tried dialing them right back. No answer. Then a text came back from her mom.

Headed out for another walk. Such a beautiful day! God is good! No matter what, God is good!

Charlotte stared at her mom's response for the next several minutes, a dreadful thought taking over her mind and churning her gut. Their weird behavior lately . . . working through issues . . . euphoric dancing . . . *"the doctor said"* . . . *"we just want you to be happy"* . . . *"no matter what, God is good"* . . .

No matter what.

There was only one other time Charlotte had seen her mother acting this way. Charlotte set her phone down and dropped her head into her hands, everything clicking into place.

Her mother's cancer was back.

20

"I'm such a punk," Zach murmured, glancing at his phone, unable to believe Charlotte hadn't backed out of the challenge yet. Didn't she realize how much camping and time outdoors it would entail? Of course she did. She had to be freaking out. Which is why he was such a punk.

Soon as he got off the phone yesterday with Ben, Zach could have put Charlotte out of her misery. Not only did Ben agree to donate ten grand to Charlotte's music program, he planned to ask his company board to start a grant in their dad's name as a way to honor their father's memory and also provide new band instruments for Charlotte's school. His brother must be on a honeymoon high or something.

And Zach was a total punk because he'd been keeping all this wonderful information to himself simply to see how long it took Charlotte to break.

Zach thanked the teenager who'd bagged his groceries, then hefted the paper sack into his arms and headed to his Jeep. Charlotte couldn't seriously be thinking of going through with it, could she? Don't get him wrong, the prize amount was a nice chunk of money. People did crazier things for far less.

But this was Charlotte. She'd barely made it through one day of subterfuge at Ben's wedding. No way her little church-going conscience would allow her to carry on a charade like this for a five-hundred-mile bike trip. Not for money. Maybe for cheesecake.

He cracked a smile as he drove the half-dozen blocks from the grocery store to Charlotte's cul-de-sac and parked in front of her small bungalow. The girl certainly did love her cheesecake. Which is why he'd driven all the way to Cake Lassies to pick up a piece of raspberry swirl before hitting the grocery store in town.

He had a feeling that once he told her the good news about Ben's donation and the fact they could end their relationship, she'd be ready to celebrate. Assuming she was home. The driveway sat empty, the inside of the house dark. Maybe she was out with Sophia. He shot off a text and waited a minute for a response. When he didn't get one, he grabbed the slice of cheesecake and walked to the porch, taking a seat on the top step.

A minute later, the door opened behind him. "Why are you sitting on my porch with cheesecake?"

He twisted to find Charlotte on the other side of the screen door. "I didn't think you were here."

"That makes perfect sense then. Carry on." She closed the door.

Zach stood, a smile tugging his lips as she immediately reopened the door and motioned him inside with her head. "I'll get the forks."

Once they were settled on the living room carpet in front of the coffee table with their backs pressed against the couch, the slice of cheesecake between them, Zach pointed his fork at her. "So? Are you ready to say it yet?"

"Say what? Oh." She stabbed a bite and lifted it between them. "You're right. Where are my manners? *Thank you.* I love raspberry cheesecake."

She offered a smile so innocent Zach was tempted to kiss it right off her lips. Instead he stole the cheesecake off her fork, enjoying her startled gasp as much as the sweet creamy texture of the dessert.

"I can't believe you just did that."

"I can't believe you haven't said you're ready to back out of the challenge."

"Why would I say that when I have zero intentions of backing out of anything? Is this your way of saying you're ready to back out, Mr. Iron Man Wilderness Explorer?"

"Why would I say that when I'm Mr. Iron Man Wilderness Explorer?" He popped open his button-down shirt and feigned embarrassment. "Shoot, must have left my costume at home. Well, this is awkward."

He earned a small smile and blush from Charlotte as she tried not to look at his chest but couldn't seem to help herself. "Is that a cross tattoo?"

"What? Oh." So that's what she was looking at. "Yeah. Got it years ago. Before my dad died." He cleared his throat and rebuttoned his shirt, trying to divert her attention. He hadn't meant to expose that one. "So if you're not backing out and I'm not backing out, does that mean we're actually doing this?"

Because *this* was crazy. And not at all the plan. The plan was to come over here and listen to Charlotte back out, so he could surprise her with Ben's offer and look like a hero. Sure, it was Ben's company's money, but Zach had been the one to guilt Ben into convincing the company to hand over that money. And that's the type of heroism a girl might deem worthy of a kiss. Right?

Zach scrunched his eyes shut. Wow. He really needed to stop thinking about kissing Charlotte so much. Maybe once he got out to California, it'd be easier.

"Truth is I need you, Zach."

Zach opened his eyes. Maybe thinking about kissing Charlotte wasn't such a bad idea.

Smashing the last bite of raspberry swirl in the tines of her fork, Charlotte stared at her plate, hopefully unaware that Zach couldn't stop staring at her lips. Especially at the trace of white cheesecake caught in the right corner.

"My mom's cancer is back, and I need you to help me win that money."

All thoughts of kissing fled Zach's mind. "Back? What do you mean *back*? Is she going to be okay? Does she have to start more treatment?" She had looked so good at the wedding. Tired maybe. Concerned, definitely. But Zach had just figured that was because she thought her daughter was in a relationship with him.

Charlotte wiped her lips with a napkin and set her fork on the plate as she rose to her feet. "I don't know all the details yet. I don't want to know all the details yet. Right now I just want to focus on one thing. Completing the challenge. In fact, I'm thinking that's been the whole point of everything that's happened lately. I mean, think about it. It's crazy."

Oh, it was crazy, all right. About as crazy as the look in Charlotte's eyes as she began pacing the living room.

"Us running into each other the way we did," she continued to ramble. "Everyone thinking we're a couple. Then boom, there's this challenge for couples who could win a bunch of money just as my mom's cancer comes back, which I know from experience will take a lot of money to treat. This has all got to be a God thing, right?"

Zach would never claim to be an expert on God things, but he had a little trouble seeing how cancer and misunderstandings were part of those "things."

"What exactly are you saying?" Zach watched Charlotte continue to pace. A gray cat appeared and took advantage of Charlotte's distraction to check out the few remaining crumbs of cheesecake.

"I'm saying I have complete faith that accepting this challenge is the right thing to do."

Zach slid the plate away from the cat's face. He hated to break it to her, but accepting the challenge was the easy part. It was going to take more than faith to actually complete the challenge. Especially since they hadn't prepared for it at all. They were going to have to bike fifty miles a day. At least. Which was easily doable for him. For Charlotte?

"I hope you do realize a trip like this is going to require more than faith. It's going to require stamina."

"I've got stamina."

"Endurance."

"Have it in spades."

"Butt cream."

"I . . . will purchase some immediately." Then, "Hey, get out of that." Charlotte scooped the cat into her arms. "There'll be rules, of course."

"I know. I read over the article at Mucho Mucho yesterday. I have to admit though, I thought there'd be more to it. Sounds like the only real challenge is that we can't bring along any credit cards or phone chargers. Is that it? Am I missing something?"

"You mean other than that little challenge of biking five hundred miles in ten days, which you've already implied is going to require more stamina than I currently possess? No. I think you covered it. But those weren't actually the rules I was talking about. I'm talking about our rules."

"What sort of rules do we need?"

"Well, have you heard some of the names people are calling this challenge?"

Zach couldn't hold back a laugh. "My favorite by far is the Canoodling Couples Challenge."

"That's what I'm talking about. Rule number one is there will be no canoodling during this trip. Canoodling complicates things. And this whole thing is complicated enough as it is."

"Define *canoodling*."

"Kissing and amorous cuddling. I looked it up five minutes before you got here."

"I'm scared to ask what the next rule is." He folded his arms and leaned back against the couch as the cat slunk past him in search of more cheesecake.

"If we do this challenge, we need to be a couple. A real couple. But just for the duration of this trip. We both know a relationship between us would never last in the long run. Which is why there won't be any canoodling."

She tossed the cat three feet away from the coffee table. He landed on his feet, then immediately returned to the cheesecake plate.

"So let me get this straight," Zach said, sliding the plate away from the cat. "You want us to be a real couple. You want us to bike five hundred miles together. But you don't want us to canoodle. What if we just kiss?"

Charlotte laughed, a rush of pink flooding her cheeks. Then her eyes widened and her face paled. "Please tell me you're not serious."

Honestly, Zach didn't know. He just knew those weird feelings he was developing for Charlotte might seriously get him into trouble, so yeah, maybe some ground rules were a good idea. But you know what else was a good idea? Kissing.

"I just don't think we should make any hard rules against it," he said. "I mean, we're going to be out in the wild. Things happen. We may find ourselves in a situation where our only means of survival is to lock lips. You never know."

"I think once was enough."

Once was far from enough. "Fine. But since I know you'll eventually regret that rule, I'll add a clause for your sake." Zach rose to his knees, grabbed the cat and tossed him over his shoulder onto the couch. "You may ask me for one kiss at the time of your choosing, and I will oblige. But just one, Charlotte. I mean it. I know you'll want more. Tons more. Every day. But you only get one. Understand? Are we in agreement?"

Her soft smile contained a perfect blend of sweetness and gratitude. And Zach half wished she'd ask for that kiss now. "Absolute agreement."

"All right. Now that we've got that settled." He lifted one knee as he knelt on the other and reached for her hand. "Charlotte Carter, will you do me the great honor of entering a committed canoodling relationship with me for the next five hundred miles?"

She punched him in the shoulder. "You want to try that again?"

Oh, this was going to be fun. Surely California could wait another ten days.

21

"Ready?" Zach tested the bungee cord wrapped around the camping supplies and duffel bags packed onto the bike trailer the following afternoon. "You know what they say. All journeys begin with a single step. Or pedal rotation, I suppose."

"I don't understand why we're doing this." Charlotte tugged the hem of her bicycle shorts down toward her knees. "I mean I know why we're doing this. I just don't know why we're doing *this*." She swiveled her gaze to where half the town crowded outside Pinky's Pancakes with balloons and noisemakers.

"Well, you know this town. Can't do anything without a hullabaloo." Zach hit Charlotte with his biggest smile, hoping it conveyed more confidence than he felt.

It was hard to be truly confident, considering he and Charlotte had only ridden a tandem bicycle around the block once— without the trailer and additional baggage—before the chain fell off and the front tire caught a flat, which led to discovering further problems and a better realization as to why the bike had been gathering dust in someone's garage. Zach and Charlotte had been forced to buy the only other tandem bicycle available on short notice, the top-of-the-line model at the bike shop that was on sale for two thousand dollars.

Talk about hullabaloo. The trip hadn't even started, and they were strapped for cash.

"Anyway, you know Ty insisted on a big ceremonial send-off. For posterity's sake. Oh—" Zach snapped his fingers. "That reminds me. You packed plenty of butt cream, right? Because you're definitely going to need it for your posterior's sake once we really get going tomorrow."

Sophia let out a loud whistle, cutting off Charlotte's response, as she joined them next to the bike and snapped a photo with her phone. "Looking hot there, Sis. Don't be leaving a trail of broken hearts now."

"Shut it," Charlotte said, now yanking the waistband of her shorts up to the middle of her abdomen. "I'm already chafing. And don't you dare post that picture online."

"If it makes you feel better, biking shorts look way more flattering on you than on Zach." Sophia elbowed Zach with a wink.

Zach worked hard to not adjust his own shorts. He didn't give any thought to wearing them when he was biking by himself, but for some reason, standing here in front of Charlotte and half the town, yeah, he might be chafing too. "Ready to get this show on the road?"

"Yes. Maybe. I don't know. Should I use the bathroom again?"

"Charlotte, we're only biking half a mile." Long enough to appease Ty and make everyone happy, then load up his Jeep to drive down to Nashville, where they were staying overnight at a buddy's place before the real start of their journey tomorrow morning. "Let's just get going. We're already behind schedule."

"I know. I just . . ." She tugged on her shorts. "Do I need a Shewee?"

"What in the world is a Shewee?" Sophia said.

"I don't know, but Arlene said I needed one. Something about it helping me pee like a man in the woods. Do I have to pee like a man in the woods? Why can't I pee like a girl in the woods? I'm not sure I want to pee like a man in the woods. I'm not sure I want to do anything in the woods. Aren't there bears in the woods? I thought the Natchez Trace was a highway. I thought I could do this. I thought—"

"You can do this," Sophia said, pulling Charlotte into a hug tight enough to thankfully squelch her rising hysteria. "Think of your music program. Think of Mom and Dad. Think of anything but your bladder, and you'll be fine."

Charlotte released a whimpering laugh, and some of the nerves Zach didn't realize had been gripping his stomach loosened. Sophia was right. Everything was going to be fine. It was. Especially once they put some distance between them and this town.

As if reaching the same conclusion, Charlotte lifted her shoulders in a deep breath, then blew it out as she turned toward Sophia. "Speaking of Mom and Dad, have you by any chance talked to them recently?"

"Not since they've been in North Carolina. Why?"

Charlotte shrugged nonchalantly. "No reason. Just curious."

Did Sophia not know about their mom's cancer coming back? And was Charlotte not going to tell her? Weren't sisters supposed to share everything?

Rick breezed over with a giant foam finger on his right hand, distracting Zach from overhearing any more of their conversation. "Hey, man. Can't wait to hear all about your trip. I don't know why, but this is so exciting. It's probably how people felt watching Charles Lindbergh prepare to take flight, don't you think?"

"Charles Lindbergh? How old are you?"

"Old enough to remind you that I don't want to hear about any funny business taking place inside that tent. Charlotte's a sweet girl. So don't you be putting the moves on her and making her all googly-eyed and leading her into doing something she'll regret. Got it?" Rick jabbed his foam finger against Zach's chest.

"I'm pretty sure after a full day of sitting on a bicycle seat, Charlotte's going to feel like she's wearing a chastity belt. I don't think you need to worry about googly eyes."

"Good. Glad to hear it. And now that we've got that out of the way—" Rick pressed the foam finger against his brow in a salute. "Good luck. Godspeed. Fare-thee-well. Parting is such sweet sorrow. I will always love you."

"I get the idea," Zach said.

"Last one." Rick lowered his giant finger from one shoulder to the other as if he were knighting Zach with a sword. "May your roads be flat and your bottoms not sore."

"Beautiful."

Rick smiled. "I'll be praying for you, buddy." Then he disappeared back into the crowd.

Charlotte finished saying goodbye to Sophia with a promise to call when they reached the halfway point. "If you don't hear from me, just assume I'm dead and try to move on."

"That's my girl," Sophia said, squeezing Charlotte's hand. "But I'm sure you'll do great. The whole town's praying for you, you know."

Zach settled onto the front seat before Charlotte caught him rolling his eyes. Prayers weren't going to get them anywhere if they never left the parking lot.

Still, that didn't stop him from tossing up one of his own. *Dear Lord, don't let this whole thing be a mistake.*

22

This was a mistake, wasn't it? Sophia spun her Mickey Mouse watch around her wrist, staring out the window next to her booth at Pinky's Pancakes, gaze locked on the empty street corner where Zach's Jeep had turned and disappeared more than thirty minutes ago. The corner she fully expected to see Zach's Jeep return to any minute when Charlotte realized this whole thing was a mistake.

Except Sophia knew her sister. She spun the watch faster, chafing the skin on her wrist. Sophia could stare at the corner all she wanted, but Charlotte wasn't coming back. Not until she'd either completed the challenge or failed. And if she failed . . .

Sophia closed her eyes and tried shaking away the thought of Charlotte even more dejected than she'd been two summers ago. When she'd worked so hard to convince everyone she was fine. But boy, was she *not* fine.

"Need a top-up?" Before waiting for Sophia to reply, a waitress poured coffee into Sophia's mug, then rushed on to the next booth.

Sophia had been drinking hot chocolate, but whatever. She cradled the warm mug in her hands. Mistake, mistake, mistake. Sophia never should have pushed Charlotte into doing the challenge. Not when nobody knew for certain if the prize money was for real.

"What do you mean?" Ty had said when Sophia voiced her concern fifteen minutes ago over a pile of pancakes. "Of course it's for real. When has Hopkins never come through before? He already deposited the funds for the new bike path. The mayor said it arrived a few days ago. Besides, you know how else I know this challenge is for real?" Ty said before he dashed out the door to leave for his vacation. "Because it's Charlotte's last hope."

If Ty had meant for his parting words to bring comfort, he'd failed miserably. Sophia wanted proof. Stressful enough worrying whether Charlotte would be able to complete the five-hundred-mile journey on time. Even worse was imagining her crossing the finish line only to discover it was all for nothing.

Sure, Hopkins had always come through in the past. But nothing about this challenge felt like the ones he'd done in the past. Something about it just didn't sit right. Maybe because this time so much was riding on it. Literally.

Would Charlotte really have to move to find a different job if she didn't win the money?

Sophia didn't even want to think about her parents' shaky marriage—or why Charlotte had asked with a weird expression whether Sophia had talked to them recently. Had they finally admitted to Charlotte they were having marital issues?

They better not try admitting it to Sophia. Divorce was the last thing she could handle right now. In fact, she might want to avoid all conversations with her parents until Charlotte returned. Charlotte had always been Sophia's rock. If their family was falling apart, Sophia needed her rock by her side. All the more reason to make sure this challenge prize money was for real.

So what was she doing sitting here then? Sophia swung her legs out of the booth. Time to stop drinking terrible hot chocolate coffee. Time to track down the recluse A. P. Hopkins and make sure this wasn't a mistake.

23

This was a mistake. A huge mistake. Charlotte didn't know if there had ever been a mistake as big as this. If she had a time machine, she'd be in it right now, twisting the dial back to the moment she'd volunteered to be maid of honor in a wedding she had no business being a part of.

No, before that. The moment she'd let Sophia talk her into stepping foot into that restaurant on a fool's mission.

No. Before that. The moment Ty had told her the grant money had fallen through and her music program was at risk. She'd go back to that moment and tell Ty not to worry because she'd never been all that fond of music in the first place.

Okay, fine. Maybe not that moment. She didn't want to lie. Well, not any more than she already had. So how about a different moment? Like the moment her friend Megan had tried talking her into going out for the cross-country team in junior high, and Charlotte had wrinkled her nose, saying cardio wasn't really her thing.

Yes, if Charlotte could go back to that moment and choose cardio over music, then maybe she wouldn't be stuck in this moment. With a screaming rear end. A pair of burning thighs. A set of gasping lungs. All while pretending they weren't less than four miles past the sign welcoming them onto the Natchez Trace Parkway.

"That waitress . . ." Charlotte tried finishing the sentence. Couldn't. It required too much oxygen. But if she had the oxygen to finish complete sentences, she would have said "wasn't kidding."

When Zach had insisted they eat a hearty breakfast this morning at The Loveless Cafe, a place Charlotte had never heard of but which was apparently famous for its biscuits, their chipper waitress had warned them there'd be lots of hills to conquer this first day. Oh, how Charlotte wished that lady had been kidding.

Hanging her head, Charlotte focused on the pavement gliding beneath the rotation of her feet. *Just keep pedaling. Just keep pedaling.*

After five minutes of hearing Dory's voice from *Finding Nemo* in her head, her own voice took over. *Mistake, mistake, mistake.* Could their bike even stay upright with how slow they were moving? And where was the other side to these hills? Why were they only going up?

All good questions. Another good question—what was really going on with her mom's health? Maybe it wasn't as dire as it sounded. It had been early in the morning. Everything sounds dire before coffee.

"Doing okay back there?" Zach asked over his shoulder. "I know you're not used to this, so we'll take a break early on. Maybe after ten miles."

Ten miles was "early on"? Wonderful. By then, Charlotte would be dead.

"Great," Charlotte said, trying to hide how winded she felt. No need for Zach to get worried. Not when they had over sixty miles to go that day. At least.

Sixty miles. At least.

Oh, mistake, mistake, mistake. The way she felt right now, she'd be lucky to make it another three miles. "Where . . . we stopping . . . the day?"

"Why? Getting tired already?" Zach said with a laugh.

Charlotte attempted to laugh back, but it came out sounding like a wheezy old man on his deathbed.

"Meriwether Lewis Park." He lifted a shoulder. "But we'll see how we're feeling. If we're doing okay, we might want to bike a little further than what Ty planned on the itinerary." He shrugged again. "We'll see what happens."

Charlotte adjusted her position on her seat. Maybe she should have been less consumed with the fit of her shorts the past few days and more concerned with the itinerary. Even though Ty had planned out the entire trip, she had the feeling Zach was the type of person to wing things. Did he know where'd they stay, what they'd eat, if they biked "a little further than what Ty planned"?

Too bad she didn't have enough air to ask. She certainly didn't have enough air to yell at him if she didn't like his answer. Probably better to not know and hope for the best. Like a hotel room. A hot shower. A continental breakfast. She knew their budget was tight, but a girl could always dream.

They pedaled past trees and old-looking fence posts that Charlotte would have normally found scenic and romantic as she daydreamed about what history might have taken place at these spots. But right now all she could think about was her rear end, her thighs, and her need to breathe.

Surely her body would adjust at some point, right? Preferably some point in the next sixty miles?

Zach adjusted the gears as they reached the top of the hill. "We can finally coast for a bit," he said as they started going down.

"Hallelujah." Charlotte breathed out the word, meaning it with every fiber of her being. She stretched her legs out one at a time as they glided down the gentle slope. Or at least what started off as a gentle slope. Their speed kicked up several notches as they continued gliding. Then began racing. Soon flying.

Charlotte squeezed the handlebars until her knuckles turned white, taking note for the first time that she had zero control of the brakes. How fast were they going?

Fast. Very fast. Scary fast.

Her eyes watered against the wind as she held on for dear life, praying their first day wouldn't end with them both in the hospital after leaving half their skin on the pavement. Or worse.

They rounded a curve and the road flattened out in front of them, their speed blissfully slowing down to where they were no longer breaking the sound barrier.

"Hallelujah," she whispered again. Maybe biking uphill wasn't such a bad thing after all. "How fast were we going?"

Zach tapped the speedometer that the store clerk had thrown in for free since they'd bought the top-of-the-line tandem model. "We hit just over thirty miles per hour."

"That's it?"

Zach chuckled. "How fast did you think we went?"

"I don't know. Sixty. Eighty. Fast enough for me to nearly wet my pants."

She didn't have to see his face to know he was smiling. And maybe she was a little bit too. It had been a teensy bit fun. Now that they'd survived.

"Hey, Charlotte," Zach said after a minute or so of silence. "You know, any time you wanted to start pedaling again, that would be great."

"You can tell when I'm not pedaling?" Her feet had been circling on the pedals, but she hadn't been applying any pressure.

"Uh, the fact I'm pedaling for my hundred-and-seventy-pound frame as well as your hundred-and—"

"If you know what's good for you, you will not finish that sentence."

"If you don't want me guessing your weight, you better carry it. Now start pedaling."

Charlotte began pushing the pedals again. A group of motorcyclists approached them from the opposite direction. The lead rider in the group had a woman riding behind him. They both lifted their palms in a subtle wave as they flew past.

Zach and Charlotte waved back in similar fashion. "Bet that guy doesn't make her carry her own weight," Charlotte muttered.

Zach twisted his head to the side. "Tell you what. If we reach a point in our canoodleship where we get matching tattoos and wear leather chaps, then I'll do all the pedaling."

"I'm holding you to that." Charlotte couldn't stop her smile from spreading. Maybe this trip wouldn't be so bad. They'd made it up the first few hills. They didn't die coming down the last one.

Maybe it hadn't been a mistake. Maybe the next four-hundred-plus miles would zip by faster than she thought. The first six hadn't been so bad. What was a couple hundred more?

She adjusted her position on the seat again. Her brain could say whatever it wanted, but her rear end shouted a different opinion. And it ran along the lines of *mistake, mistake, mistake*.

She looked back down to the pavement beneath her rotating feet. "So when did you say our first break was going to be?"

24

Several hours and sixty-nine miles later, they were almost done biking for the day. *Finally.*

Somehow Zach had convinced her to keep going past Meriwether Lewis Park. As much as she hadn't wanted to climb back onto the bike, the promise of better amenities than an out-of-order toilet and better food than peanut butter tortilla sandwiches spurred her on. Or perhaps she'd just been slightly delirious and too exhausted to argue. Who's to say? But at least now they were here. Wherever *here* was.

Charlotte eyed the small town they'd entered after breaking off from the trail. "Where are we going to stay?"

"I'm sure we'll find something."

So far she wasn't seeing a whole lot of "something." A gas station and a bar, that was about it. Searching for where Zach had in mind to spend the night, she leaned forward and asked again. "Where are we going to stay?"

He pointed to the bar. "Let's eat dinner, then we'll figure something out."

Zach steered them to a gravel parking lot where a small, rectangular-shaped bar named The Drink greeted them. Or rather, The Drunk, since someone had altered the sign,turning the *i* into a *u*.

Zach braked at the corner of the bar next to a large front window, where inside an older couple pointed at their tandem bicycle with amused smiles and shaking heads.

Charlotte unclipped her helmet. "I didn't see any place for us to stay."

Zach removed his helmet and ran a palm over his sweaty hair, making it stick up in different directions. "I'm sure we can bunk for the night in that park we passed on the edge of town."

"What park? What are you talking about?"

"The park with the picnic benches."

"The park with the picnic benches buried in a field of overgrown weeds?" Charlotte climbed off the bike and grabbed a post to keep her noodle legs from collapsing. She needed food. Real food. But darn it, she needed shelter too. "You're not serious, are you?"

"We could put our sleeping bags on top of the picnic benches."

Oh, sweet mercy. He was serious. "Zach, there's no way I'm sleeping on those picnic benches. First off, you could barely see the benches because of all the overgrown grass. Do you know how many snakes are living beneath those benches? Millions. By morning they'll be slithering all over us. No way. Uh-uh. Nohow. You need to come up with a better plan. A plan that at least involves a tent."

"I'm not sure there is a better plan in this town."

"Then why did you choose this as our stopping point? Why didn't we stop in the town Ty mentioned near that Meriwether Park place? The one that had a hotel?"

"That place was an hour and a half ago."

"Oh, believe me, my rear end knows exactly how long ago that place was."

"Charlotte, every mile counts if we're going to complete this trip on time. And I thought you wanted some real food."

"I do want some real food."

"Then let's get some real food." He motioned to the bar.

"Because a full stomach will suddenly make me okay with sleeping with reptiles?"

Zach's hand gently wrapped around her wrist. "I will figure something out, okay? Trust me. But first, let's get something to eat."

Charlotte closed her eyes, took a deep breath, then nodded. But only because she was starving. She was still mad at him. And she swore on her grandmother's grave, if he didn't come up with a place besides a couple of weed-infested picnic benches for them to sleep, she was going to bludgeon him to death with the bicycle horn—another addition that came with the bike free of charge.

Following him into the bar, Charlotte bit back a moan as the scent of fried food gripped her stomach with a ferocious squeeze. Okay, maybe shelter could go on the back burner for now. Because whatever she was smelling, she wanted it. All of it. Right after she guzzled a two liter of pop.

The bartender, a man with bright blue eyes and a gray beard down to his chest, nodded at them from behind the bar. Zach nodded back as he led Charlotte to a small dining area with a half dozen square tables. A middle-aged couple nursing two beers and a pepperoni pizza eyed Charlotte and Zach as they settled into their seats. A country song played in the background.

"Shoot," Zach said as soon as they settled into their seats. "I left the money outside. Mind ordering me an orange soda? I'll be right back."

Charlotte ordered their drinks, then wobbled back to her seat, too tired and shaky to stand at the bar and wait. How was she going to make it through another day? How was she going to make it through *nine* more days? What if they couldn't finish? What if they didn't get the money? What if her mom couldn't afford treatment without that money? What if she called Sophia right now and asked her to come pick her up because she was going to fail anyway?

"Aw, come on," a slurred voice said. "Stop looking so glum."

It took Charlotte a moment to realize the voice was speaking to her. A skinny man wearing a flannel button-down shirt and red suspenders stood a few tables away, lifting his mug of beer in her direction. "Don't worry," he said. "Be happy."

Charlotte couldn't tell if his slur came from alcohol or a past stroke. Either way, she offered him a tight smile and hoped he'd go away. She was not in the mood to make friends.

He took two unsteady steps toward her. "That's better," he said.

Was it? She darted a glance out the front window, where Zach squatted next to their bike, rummaging through their bags. What was he doing? *Hurry up, Zach.*

"When you're smiling . . ." Oh, wonderful. Mr. Intoxicated had started to sing.

"Oh, I'm smiling. Yes. Thank you." Charlotte waved a dismissive hand, then gave a few short claps of applause, anything to make him stop.

"When you're smiling . . ." He wasn't stopping.

She searched for Zach. Still outside. And now apparently talking to some dude on a motorcycle. Perfect.

"The whole world . . ." The man had reached her table, holding his mug like a microphone, which he now placed in front of her mouth. "Go ahead. You know it."

"I don't. Not a single word." Charlotte gently pushed the mug away. He forced it right back. "No, really."

"Come on, don't worry, be happy." He made jazz hands and leaned side to side, his beer sloshing over the rim.

"Ope, you're dripping there. I'm actually pretty tired. We've ridden a long way." She had to speak up to be heard over his whistling. "You know what? I think I may need to use the ladies' room." She stood from her chair, grimacing at the muscle aches.

Before the man could say anything, she forced her lips up. "Still smiling. Feeling great. Excuse me." She hobbled past him to the door marked *Gals* and shoved the door shut behind her, locking it and leaning against it.

Why did all her interactions with strangers lately lead to songs about smiling?

Too dehydrated to actually need the bathroom, she waited a couple of minutes, washed her hands, tried not to look at her sweaty reflection in the mirror, and prayed Zach was back at the table by now, ready to deflect further inebriated crooners.

After waiting another minute, Charlotte returned to the table, relieved to see both Zach and their sodas waiting for her. Her singing friend must have forgotten about her. He was chatting it up with the bartender.

She gulped down several long pulls of her Sprite. "Oh wow," she said, wiping her chin. "I don't think I've ever tasted anything so divine."

"Then you haven't tried this orange soda."

"Orange soda. Blech. Speaking of blech, have you figured out what we're going to do about sleeping arrangements tonight?"

"It's been five minutes. You expected me to come up with sleeping arrangements in five minutes?" He tilted his glass toward her. "Well, I did. Because I'm amazing. And since you know that, it makes perfect sense you expected me to come up with those arrangements in five minutes."

"Oh my goodness, I am not in the right frame of mind to deal with you right now."

He chugged his soda and set down his glass with a loud clink. "Do you want to sleep on snake-infested picnic benches or deal with me right now?"

"I'm all ears."

He motioned to the window. "I was talking to one of the locals outside. He, of course, wanted to know what we were up to. I told him and mentioned we needed a place to toss down our tent for the night. He told me I should ask Willie."

"Who's Willie?"

"You don't know Willie? Everybody knows Willie."

Charlotte dropped her chin on her fist, so unamused.

Zach cracked a smile and pointed with his thumb over his shoulder. "Willie owns the bar. I already talked to him, and he said we could use the field out back to put up our tent. He said he doesn't mind if we come in and use the bathroom later if we need to. Bar doesn't close until two in the morning."

The skinny man in suspenders, still at the bar, lifted his mug in a salute. Charlotte half-heartedly lifted her pop in return. "That's Willie?"

"Yup. Nice guy. Isn't this great?"

Charlotte released a bone-weary sigh. Sleeping outside some bar in Hicksville, Tennessee, with Willie the crooner and over four hundred miles between her and the finish line. "Sure. Can't stop smiling."

25

Stomach stuffed with greasy pizza, thirst quenched with orange soda, Charlotte-approved sleeping arrangements made, Zach looked to the dark sky, allowing himself to take his first deep breath of the day. Seventy-five miles. Not bad. Especially considering how neither of them were functioning at full capacity.

After all the craziness of the wedding, the stress of her mom's health, and rushing to get everything prepared for this challenge, he didn't imagine Charlotte had been getting much sleep. He sure hadn't. The memory of their kiss at the wedding reception still kept him awake at odd hours, if he was being honest.

But hopefully tonight neither of them would think about anything except sleep. Then maybe tomorrow they'd both have more energy. The harder they pushed it now, the less pressure they'd have later. And the sooner Zach could get away from Charlotte and these weird feelings. The sooner he could get to California.

The parking lot lights from the bar blotted out any possible star-gazing, but the night remained clear. He wouldn't have to spend his first night on the trail getting drenched, so that was a plus.

While Charlotte had gone back into the bar to use the bathroom once more before they settled in for the night, Zach made quick work of setting up the tent. Now the soft swoosh of footsteps in the grass announced her return.

Clutching a small toiletries kit against her chest, she paused and looked at his sleeping bag spread across the ground outside the tent. Then looked at the tent. Back to his sleeping bag. "You're not sleeping there, are you?"

"Well, yeah. Unless you want me to sleep on those picnic benches three blocks over."

"I want you to sleep in there." She pointed at the tent. "Next to me."

Well, this was certainly unexpected. And certainly not recommended. Not for a man trying to battle weird feelings some might label as attraction. He scrubbed his face, searching for an excuse. Any excuse. "I can't. Rick said—"

"I don't care what Rick said. Rick's not here. But you know who is here? A bar full of Willies who've been drinking away their inhibitions all night long. No way I'm sleeping in that tent all by myself."

"But wouldn't it make more sense for me to sleep outside the tent then? If anybody tried to bother you, they'd have to get past me first."

"What if they tried bothering *you*? Huh? Did you ever think of that? What if they quietly slit your throat and I had no idea, because you're outside the tent and I'm inside the tent? We should have brought a gun."

"Your mom told me about the pepper spray incident with the park ranger. I don't even want to imagine you with a gun. Now get inside the tent and go to sleep. We've got a long day ahead of us tomorrow. We need to cover a lot of ground."

"I'm only getting in the tent if you do. That's the deal."

"I don't recall making any deals about this. The only deals I recall—"

"I don't care what deals we made before we left home. Back there we were on our turf. Now we're on their turf." She jabbed her thumb at the bar. "People do crazy things on their turf. Like slit people's throats. Please, I'm begging you. Sleep next to me. I'm not going to sleep at all unless someone's between me and that zipper."

Zach rubbed his forehead. She was being ridiculous. But honestly, he was so tired he didn't care where he slept. Inside the tent, outside the tent, it didn't matter.

Okay, the scales definitely tipped toward the sleeping-inside-the-tent-right-next-to-Charlotte option. Especially when she whispered, "Please, Zach."

Her quiet plea barely registered over the country music leaking out from the walls of the bar. But it was loud enough for him to know he'd do just about anything for her when she used that soft tone. "Fine. If you think it'll make you more comfortable."

"So much more comfortable." She was already tugging his sleeping bag inside the tent next to hers. "See?" She gave it a pat as she settled on top of her bag. "Isn't that better?"

Much better. Which made it much worse. Zach scrubbed a palm down his face again, this time trying to scrub away thoughts of Charlotte lying next to him. For the second time that day, he prayed he wasn't making a mistake.

"I'm going to use the bathroom." Maybe a few extra minutes to get a hold of himself and think of all the reasons he shouldn't be attracted to Charlotte and take advantage of this opportunity to have the length of his body lying next to the length of hers would do him some good.

After stalling as long as he reasonably could, Zach climbed inside, zipping the tent closed behind him. It took effort not to bump into her as he situated himself into his sleeping bag. "Don't you want to get in your sleeping bag?" Zach asked. "The night's cooling off."

Honky-tonk music continued to drift from the bar. "Nah, I'll get too warm," Charlotte mumbled, right before a yawn snatched her words.

The fabric of her sleeping bag rustled as she stretched, then moaned. "I feel like this has been the longest day of my life."

Yeah, well, Zach already felt like this was turning into the longest night of his life. And here he'd been counting on a good night's rest.

The heat of her body radiated next to him in the close quarters as if she were pressed directly against his side. It sure would be helpful if she climbed into her sleeping bag. "You sure you won't get cold?"

"Mm-hmm," she murmured.

He cleared his throat and turned onto his side, facing away from her. "So tomorrow I'm thinking we get up and eat breakfast, then pack and hit the road no later than eight o'clock. We're probably going to be up against a lot of hills again. So the more time we give ourselves, the better. It'd be great if we do sixty miles. That'd take some of the pressure off the next day. Especially since I heard something about rain. Maybe we should go for another seventy miles tomorrow. That sound okay?"

He waited for a response. When he didn't hear one, he rolled over to face her. Well, he tried rolling over to face her. Little rascal had scooched over to the edge of her bag, curling her body into him.

The steady sound of her breaths told him everything he needed to know. She was dead asleep. And he was definitely in for a long night.

So much for feeling rested.

26

Seriously. Sophia should star in a Hallmark Movies and Mysteries series. Her amateur sleuthing skills were *that* good. In less than two days she'd tracked down the whereabouts of one Andrew Patrick Hopkins, formally known as the eccentric and mysterious A. P. Hopkins.

She had to admit, part of her was a bit disappointed to discover he wasn't Anthony Hopkins, the actor, like she'd always secretly hoped. And another part of her was a little embarrassed to discover she'd dropped off a food tray for him three days ago without realizing it.

Turns out while she was making dozens of phone calls the past two days to discover his full name and home address, he'd been holed up in the oncology unit at the very hospital where she worked. To think she could have asked him about the challenge money and put her mind at ease days ago.

Bounding up the stairwell, Sophia prayed he wasn't sleeping. Her shift started in ten minutes. She'd meant to get to the hospital earlier, but her car had been acting up, making weird noises. The same ones she noticed yesterday and hoped would magically go away on their own.

Suffice it to say, no magic occurred overnight. So she'd driven slower than usual. And that was after she forgot to set her alarm clock, oversleeping a solid forty-six minutes.

Today was not off to a great start. Hopefully her conversation with Mr. Hopkins would turn the tide.

Hustling down the hallway past the nurses station, she glanced at her watch. Eight minutes. Surely enough time to ask a simple question and get a simple answer, then bust it back down to the cafeteria kitchen.

She glanced at her watch again. Seven minutes. Good grief, she'd better pick up the pace. Sophia rounded another hallway corner, then halted. A pretty Indian woman wearing a doctor's white coat and a stethoscope around her neck was talking to a man outside of Mr. Hopkins's room.

"I'm so sorry," she said, patting his arm. "We asked him several times if there was anybody he wanted us to call, and he always said no."

The man's shoulders drooped. He turned his head to the side long enough for Sophia to catch a glimpse and see he was young. And cute—in a Clark Kent sort of way. Not that this was the time to be noticing things like that. Not when it sounded like Mr. Hopkins might be . . .

Oh, please don't be.

The young man removed his dark framed glasses and rubbed his eyes. "No, no. I understand. I'm not blaming you. I just wish he'd let me know sooner. I would have been here. I would've stayed with him. I just hate thinking he was alone when he . . . you know, died."

Sophia winced, wanting to plug her ears. Maybe they were talking about somebody else.

"Mr. Hopkins seemed like a wonderful man," the doctor responded.

Crud.

"And for what it's worth," the doctor continued, patting the young man's arm. "This was how he wanted it. For whatever reason. I assure you, he was completely lucid and in his right mind when he made these decisions. Up until yesterday morning, he was still working on his computer. It wasn't until late last night that his body finally wore out. He slipped into unconsciousness. Knowing his condition was terminal, he'd already made the decision ahead of time not to be resuscitated when he reached that point. That's when we called you."

A high-pitched *beep beep beep* sounded. The doctor pulled her pager out of her pocket and read the message. "Sorry. I need to answer this. But I'll be around if you have any more questions."

She started past him, then turned back. "Oh, I meant to tell you. The nurse overnight said Mr. Hopkins did have one more lucid moment early this morning before he passed away. Long enough for her to tell him we'd called you and that you were coming. She said even though he had a far-off look in his eyes, he nodded like he understood, and said you'd find what you needed at home. Or something to that effect. I'm sorry. I really do have to take this."

"No, I understand. Thank you. Thanks for everything."

The doctor brushed past Sophia with her gaze focused on her pager. The young man remained in the hallway, his gaze pointed down at his Converse sneakers. Poor guy. He looked lost. Now was obviously not the right time to introduce herself and ask whether he knew anything about the money Mr. Hopkins had promised for the challenge.

But at some point she would have to approach him. And considering Charlotte was already beginning day two, that point would have to be sooner rather than later.

Maybe as soon as Sophia finished her shift today.

27

Somehow, miraculously, Charlotte managed to get dressed and out of the tent the second morning of their trip without the use of an oil can. She stretched her arms over her head with a yawn that transitioned into a groan. "I have a whole new level of empathy for the Tin Man. Oh my goodness, it hurts."

"Where?"

"Everywhere. Everything. Even my bladder." She rubbed the sleep from her eyes. "Don't suppose the bar's open."

Zach cracked a grin and pointed over his shoulder. "If you need to use the bathroom, you're going to have to make do with that bush."

"In that case, I'll just hold it forever." Charlotte shot the quiet, locked-up bar a wistful look. How detrimental would it be to her health if she gave her kidneys time off and just sweat out her fluids the remainder of the trip?

"So other than your entire body, including your bladder, being in pain, how'd you sleep?" Zach started disassembling the tent.

"Oh man, I crashed. I don't remember waking up once." Charlotte frowned. So then why did she recall finding herself snuggled tightly against Zach at some point in the night? Probably just a dream. A super nice and cozy dream. "You? Sleep okay?"

He shot her a weird look. Almost like an annoyed smile. "Yeah. Oddly enough I did." His smile turned more genuine. "Probably because nobody slit my throat."

"That does always make for a better night."

After helping Zach roll up the tent and repack the trailer—with lots of grunts, groans, and "Is this what it feels like to be ninety?" exclamations, Charlotte couldn't delay the oncoming torture any more than she could fend off a freight train barreling toward her on the tracks.

Time to get back on the horse. Or in this case, tandem. Though part of her wished it was a horse. A saddle had to be more comfortable than *that*.

She glared at the tiny black seat on the back of the bike, swearing it'd shrunk several inches overnight. "How far did you say we have to go today?"

"It's about sixty miles to Tishomingo State Park. Give or take."

After one more stretch toward her toes, her fingertips barely making it past her knees, Charlotte prayed she'd loosened her muscles enough to climb onto the seat. Prayed the seat would somehow feel like cotton balls. Prayed the next sixty miles wouldn't be as bad as she feared.

The moment her rear end touched the seat, all hope fled.

"Zach?" Charlotte whimpered. "I don't think I can do this."

"You can."

"I feel like I'm sitting on a metal bar."

"Try shifting around."

"It doesn't help. It feels like everything down there is all bruised."

"Once we get moving, it'll get better."

"How?"

"You'll get used to it."

"How?"

"By stopping thinking about it. Now come on. On three. One, two, three."

He didn't give her a choice but to start pedaling with him. They rode out of the parking lot, away from the bar.

"How am I supposed to stop thinking about it when it's all I can think about?" Charlotte asked as they biked the main road out of town. "I already feel like I need a break."

"Tell me a story."

"What?"

"A story. Think of three stories from your childhood, ones you've never told anyone else, and I'll do the same."

Right. Because chewing the fat would distract her from wanting to cry. "I don't know. I can't think of anything."

"I'll go first then."

They climbed a short entrance ramp, the road flattening out once they made it back onto the Trace. No hills for the moment, thank goodness. A row of trees lined each side. If Charlotte weren't so miserable, she might feel a little more grateful for the shade.

"All right, I got one," Zach said. "In second grade, I puked. Right in the middle of class. All down the front of me, all over the floor, everywhere. But here's the crazy thing. I was so quiet about it, the teacher didn't notice. She was sitting at her desk, doing whatever, and didn't realize what'd happened. So all the students were just sitting there, staring at me, like hey, you gonna tell the teacher you puked? And I was sitting there staring at them, like hey, I need a moment to gather my thoughts."

Charlotte waited for him to continue. When they pedaled for another minute and all she heard was the sound of her heavy breathing, she tapped his back. "Well? What happened?"

"The teacher finally noticed. She sent me to the office, and I went home sick."

"That's your story?" Charlotte leaned forward on her handlebars.

"Yeah, that's my story."

"That was lame."

"I didn't say the story had to be amazing. I just said a story from childhood you've never told anyone before."

"Well, I can see why you've never told anyone *that* before. It'd put them to sleep."

"Okay, Charles Dickens, let's hear your story then. At least I came up with one."

"If I'd known the bar was going to be set so low, I would have too. Like oh, I know, that time I ate a peanut-butter-and-jelly sandwich in kindergarten, and I bit off too big of a bite. I had to chew at least ten times before I could swallow. Can't believe I never told anyone that story before."

A spray of water splashed her in the face. "Hey," Charlotte said with a gasp. Zach had lifted his water bottle as if to take a drink, then sprayed it over his shoulder. Charlotte couldn't help but laugh. "Don't blame me when you run out of water later."

She adjusted her position on the seat, realizing she hadn't thought about her sore rear in all the time they'd bantered back and forth. Zach's intention, no doubt.

"So tell me a real story," Charlotte said.

"What? After all the heckling you just gave me?"

"You know heckling is my love language."

He straightened in his seat, cracking his neck side to side. How he could keep his balance without holding the handlebars amazed her. Also made her nervous. "Can you keep one hand on the handlebars at all times, since my life is in your hands when you pull stunts like that?"

"What, stunts like this?" He lifted both hands above his head. "You can't see me, but I've got my eyes closed too."

"You better be joking or I'm going to kill you."

"Then we'll definitely crash."

"Zach!" She smacked him on the back.

"Ooh," he said, lowering his hands to the bar and arching his back like a cat. "Could you do that a little lower and more to the center. And use your nails this time."

"I'm not scratching your back."

"But that's one of the responsibilities of the posterior rider. Everybody knows that. The anterior rider leads and keeps the bike from crashing. The posterior rider keeps the anterior rider comfortable and happy. Didn't we go over this? I could have sworn we went over this."

Charlotte shifted on her seat, the adjustment painful, but slightly more bearable. Maybe she could make it through the day without crying. Or dying. "So . . ." She poked him in the back. "About that next story."

28

Sophia jammed her foot on the gas pedal to make it up the steep hill, not sure who was groaning louder— herself or the car. "Come on, baby, I know you're ready to be put out to pasture, but I can't afford another car right now, so you're just gonna have to keep climbing. You hear me? *Climb.*"

Her car clearly didn't hear her. Or perhaps didn't appreciate her attempts at singing "Climb Ev'ry Mountain" in her best Reverend Mother voice.

So maybe driving straight here after work this afternoon had been a mistake. Maybe she should've figured out what was wrong with her car first. Especially since finding Mr. Hopkins's house required taking the whee-way.

In high school Sophia's friends had nicknamed this back country route *the whee-way* since it had so many rolling hills that made them yell "Whee!" Now it only made Sophia want to yell "Why?"

Why did Mr. Hopkins have to die before she got the chance to talk to him? Why didn't she talk to the cutie-pants Clark Kent guy when she had the chance at the hospital? Why were there so many hills in the second-flattest state in the continent?

"Come on, girl. *You think you can, you think you can* . . . Almost to the top." Of this hill. Sophia didn't have the heart to tell her Little Engine That Could that they had at least two more after this one. From its sputters, Sophia guessed her car already knew.

After several morbid rattles, then one steamy hiss, her car must have given up the ghost. It drifted into deathly silence, leaving Sophia just enough time to steer it to the side of the road before stopping completely.

Well, great. She set the parking brake. At least getting a tow shouldn't be a problem. One of the perks of having a dad who worked at a mechanic's shop. She pretty much had Rusty on speed dial. Or Trusty Rusty as she liked to call him.

Sophia began digging into her purse for her phone, then remembered. She didn't have her phone. In her rush this morning to swing by Charlotte's and feed the cat, she'd forgotten her phone on the kitchen counter.

Okay, maybe not exactly forgotten. Maybe more like purposefully abandoned.

Leaving her phone behind made avoiding conversations with her parents a lot easier. If only it didn't make calling for a tow truck a heap trickier.

Sophia sighed, scanning the empty road and stretch of cornfields surrounding her. The Hopkins house shouldn't be far from here if she remembered the directions correctly. Might as well start walking, right? She wasn't going to find answers—or a ride back to town—just standing here.

About twenty minutes later, Sophia stumbled across a narrow dirt path on the side of the road. On closer inspection, the narrow road appeared to be a long driveway surrounded by overgrown bushes. And embedded in one of those overgrown bushes sat a mailbox with the initials A. P. H.

Funny, she'd never noticed this driveway before. Of course, when you were busy tossing your hands up and yelling "Whee!" it was kind of hard to notice anything.

After hopping over a mud puddle left from a shower sometime overnight, she hustled down the dirt path that eventually opened to a large spread of green acreage where several mature trees graced the property, adding additional charm to the white two-story farmhouse with a wraparound porch.

The driveway curved around the right of the house, ending at a garage. Or maybe a workshop. Whatever it was, the cute Clark Kent guy she'd glimpsed earlier at the hospital emerged from there, tugging at his short dark hair, as a German shepherd bounded along next to him.

The dog noticed her first, immediately changing course to lope toward her with a few quick barks.

"Oh, hi there, big doggie. Friendly doggie, I hope." Sophia held out her hand, letting the dog sniff. His tail kept wagging, so Sophia knelt, their new relationship quickly escalating to kisses and hugs. "Well, aren't you the sweetest thing? Yes you are, yes you are."

"D'Artagnan, down," the man said, snapping his fingers and pointing to the ground. The dog sat, tail still wagging.

"D'Artagnan, huh? Well, where are your other musketeers, buddy? All for one and one for all?" Sophia finally looked up and startled onto her rear end. Oh wow. Yeah. This guy was definitely cute. And oh, sweet mercy, he was wearing a vintage Superman T-shirt. She fought hard not to grin like an idiot.

"Hi." Sophia climbed to her feet and dusted off her rear end. "It's nice to see you again. Not that I've seen you. I mean I have seen you, but you haven't seen me, so I don't know why I said it was nice to see you again. We haven't met. But I did see you earlier today at the hospital. I work there." Oh my goodness, she should have just grinned like an idiot and kept her mouth shut.

Like this guy was doing. Except without the grin.

"Lovely place." Sophia motioned around them. "I love the stone fence. That must have been a lot of work. Those stones look heavy. Especially that dark giant one in the middle. But goodness, very charming. I feel like I've stumbled into a chapter from *The Secret Garden*. Did you ever read that book? I bet you have. I mean, your dog's name is D'Artagnan. Not that that has anything to do with *The Secret Garden*. It just seems like anyone who names their dog after an Alexandre Dumas character would probably be at least somewhat familiar with other classics. Although to be honest, I haven't read either book. I'm more into mysteries. My name's Sophia, by the way."

Sophia stuck out her hand and inhaled a deep breath. Sometimes she amazed herself at how many words she could cram into a nervous situation. Not that she was nervous. Well, maybe a little bit nervous. He *was* awful cute—even if he did look rather rumpled and tired.

"Joshua," he said, shaking her hand with just the right amount of gentleness and firmness. She always believed you could tell a lot about a person by the way they shook your hand. And—she decided at this very moment—the behavior of their pets.

D'Artagnan sat, panting politely next to her feet.

So far Joshua was racking up all sorts of trustworthy and dependable points.

"And um . . . thanks." He waved his free hand to the rock wall. "But this isn't my property. The person who lived here died. That's why I was at the hospital earlier. He appointed me as his financial power of attorney just a few weeks ago. I had no idea he was sick, though. We actually didn't know each other all that well. So now I'm trying to get things straightened out, and . . ." Joshua stared at her, still holding her hand with the perfect amount of pressure as his tired, friendly eyes narrowed with confusion. "I'm sorry, why are you here?"

"Oh. Right. Probably should have started with that." She squeezed his hand with the sort of pressure that hopefully conveyed she wasn't a lunatic. "I came here to ask you about money for the Canoodling

Couples Challenge, but the whee-way killed my car, and I don't have my phone to call Trusty Rusty."

Okay, that might not have been the best I'm-not-a-lunatic-explanation. Poor Joshua appeared even more tired and confused. "I'm sorry, canoodling what?"

She released him from undoubtedly the longest handshake of his life and took a step back. "Do you know if Mr. Hopkins really has the two hundred fifty thousand dollars he talked about in the newspaper?"

Judging by Joshua's blank expression, Sophia wasn't going to get her answer today. "I'm sorry, canoodling what?" he said again.

Nope, definitely not getting her answer today. Sophia explained the challenge as best she could while Joshua leaned down to rub D'Artagnan's side.

"Sorry," he said once she'd finished another lengthy ramble, including how her sister and Zach had been chosen. "I'm a little overwhelmed, trying to figure out burial arrangements and things. Two hundred fifty thousand dollars? Is that what you said? Wow. That's a lot of money. But yeah, I know there's still a ton of paperwork I need to go through, so I'm sure I'll find something about it. I'll get back to you soon."

"Great. Really appreciate that." Sophia started walking away, before remembering she didn't have a working car. "And now I don't suppose I can borrow your phone."

"Because the whee-way killed your car and you need to call Trusty Rusty."

"Exactly."

For the first time, Joshua's lips curved in a slow smile. "Do you ever say anything that makes sense?"

Sophia smiled back. "I'm sure at some point in my life it's happened."

When he handed her his phone, their fingers brushed, shooting a pleasant dip to Sophia's stomach. The same sensation she used to get zipping along these back road hills.

Whee.

29

A wooden sign engraved with the words *Tishomingo State Park* welcomed Charlotte and Zach to a winding road lined with trees. Charlotte breathed a sigh of relief. They did it. They'd made it through their second day.

No, they hadn't biked as many miles as their first day, but they'd biked far enough. Especially since three and a half of those miles had been in the wrong direction, which meant they'd needed to bike those three and a half miles again to reach where they'd started.

For a man who traveled the world, Zach sure had a terrible sense of direction. Unfortunately, hers was even worse. Which is why a fight didn't break out when they realized their mistake. Charlotte just wished they'd realized their mistake sooner. Three and half miles sooner to be exact.

Besides that, though, the day had been a success.

Well, besides that and the late start they got after lunch, which may have been Charlotte's fault. But to be fair, it really did feel like she would never be able to move from that rest area picnic bench again and the best course of action would be for Zach to leave her behind and someday return for her body so he could spread her ashes over the finish line in her memory.

Okay, then there was also the flat tire that took Zach a while to repair—which again, may have been Charlotte's fault since she stumbled away to collapse in the shade and forgot to mention that she'd moved all the bicycle repair tools to a different bag earlier in the morning.

Yes, besides all *that*, the day had been a success.

Pedaling past a vacant ranger station next to a sign listing the park hours and camping fees, Charlotte leaned forward on her handlebars. "Don't we need to pay somebody to stay here?"

Zach shrugged and kept pedaling. "If they want to get paid, they can come find us. I just want to eat, rinse off, and set up our tent for the night."

Our tent. Charlotte pressed her lips together before she said something silly. Something like how nice and appealing those two words sounded together. Obviously the word *tent* should never be considered nice or appealing. Even so, it was nice having someone other than her cat sleeping next to her all night.

She could get used to that. Some day. Down the road. With the right man. A man she could be a couple with for more than ten days. A man who didn't find the word *tent* so nice and appealing.

They pedaled further down the winding path without seeing another camper.

Eventually the road led to a camping area next to a small building and lake. Zach slowed the bike to a stop. "How about somewhere around here? We won't be far from the bathrooms. I know I could definitely use a shower."

The building labeled *Latrine* sat on the edge of a parking lot. One side read *Boys*, the other *Girls*.

Zach climbed off the bike and stretched his back. "Why don't we clean up first? Then after we're cooled off, we can fix some food, relax, and set up the tent."

Charlotte nodded. The lake sparkled. A speck of a man sat on the opposite side in a small boat, probably fishing. "Surprised there aren't more people around." She glanced at the empty parking lot.

Zach shrugged and dug into one of his bags. "The place probably picks up on weekends."

"Good point." Charlotte reached for her own bag. "It's only been two days and I've already lost all track of time in the real world."

"I know. Isn't it great? And don't lie." He hitched his bag over his shoulder and winked. "Your butt's feeling a lot better now, isn't it?"

"I don't think we've reached the point in our relationship where we should be discussing our butts yet. And even if we had, the answer is a hard no."

"You said 'yet,' which leads me to believe you think we'll eventually get to the point in our relationship where butt discussions are allowed."

"Hit the showers, Zach. This discussion is over." Charlotte grabbed her bag, trying not to smile, as she entered her side of the bathroom. Her hindquarters did feel a lot better. Not great. But better. And part of her was also relieved to hear Zach still cracking jokes even though the day hadn't gone according to plan. She couldn't help but think how differently Ben would have responded.

Inside the shower room, she swept a plastic curtain to the side. Water dripped from a leaky showerhead to a dirty tiled floor and trailed to a drain in the center. Not a bubble bath by any means, but better than a spit bath in the sink. Loads better than a Porta-Potty. Or a bush.

She could work with this.

The muted sound of spraying water carried through the thin walls as she started up her own shower. She tried not to think too much about Zach stripping down and getting ready for his shower nearby.

Or how spending time with him these past two days hadn't been completely awful.

Especially when they swapped stories. Stories she hadn't thought of in years. Stories she probably never would have thought of if she hadn't been stuck on a bike, wracking her brain for anything that would take her mind off her out-of-shape body.

She dug her fingers into her hair, massaging her scalp as miles of grime washed down the drain. Had anything ever felt so divine? The tepid water turned to ice. Okay, maybe not quite divine.

Working quickly, she finished her shower, then shut off the water. Wringing her hair with one hand, she reached past the curtain and grabbed the special fast-drying towel Zach had packed for her that was apparently perfect for this sort of trip. She would have preferred something bigger, but it did dry out quickly and covered the important parts at least.

Too bad the humidity from the showers refused to let her get dry no matter how fancy a towel she used. She might as well get dressed and finish air-drying outdoors.

Charlotte dug into her bag in search of clean clothes, shoving aside toiletries as water dripped from her hair next to her bare feet. Where were the clean clothes? She searched another minute, then tipped back her head.

Ugh. She really shouldn't have rearranged things earlier. This wasn't the right bag.

Water sprayed from the other side of the wall. Apparently Zach didn't mind glacial water. Sounded like he was still showering.

She stared at the door separating her from the bike trailer. The bike trailer containing the right bag. Beads of water continued to trail down her skin. She really didn't see any other option here. Not unless she wanted to put on her stinky spandex shorts and sweaty, salt-encrusted biking top just to step a few feet outside and grab the right bag.

She glanced at the wall separating her from Zach. She had time. The bike trailer was seriously no more than a couple of feet from the door. And she knew exactly where her bag was. And nobody else was here. Nobody but a lone fisherman too far off in the distance to see anything.

She tightened her towel around her, wishing for just a few more inches of material to help her feel not quite so exposed. Not that it mattered. She'd be fast. Quicker than lightning. Speedier than a bullet.

She whipped back the curtain and tiptoed across the grimy tiles. The shower was still running from the men's side. See? Plenty of time.

Cracking open the door, she spotted the bag she needed on the trailer. Perfect.

A giddiness bubbled through her, making her giggle. She must look ridiculous. Wet. Half naked. Crazed.

Rushing four steps out the door, she grabbed the bag, double-checked inside, then spun back for the door. And slammed against it. What? She pushed the handle. It wouldn't budge. *What?* She rammed her shoulder against the door. Nothing. Locked.

Only now did she notice the sign taped on the outside of the door. *Keep propped open to avoid getting locked out.*

Ah, so that was the purpose of the little wooden block she'd tripped over on her way inside.

Okay. She willed her heartbeat to slow down. She had her bag. She had her clothes. She'd just get dressed quickly out here. No need to panic.

"Whoa!"

Zach.

Charlotte spun, dropping everything but her towel. Her tiny towel. Her towel that suddenly felt like it had shrunk to the size of a chipmunk's towel. Time to panic. "Don't look at me."

His eyes bugged out of his head. He was definitely looking. "Why are you out here like that?"

"Why are you out here at all?" Charlotte stretched the towel as far as the fabric would allow. "Turn around!"

He held up his hands, spinning away from her. "I didn't see anything. I mean I saw some things. Like your legs. But that's it. Maybe an elbow."

"Shut up and don't move." Charlotte grabbed her bag from the ground, using it to conceal more of her body as she backed away from Zach toward the corner of the shower house. "I mean it. Don't you dare turn around."

"I'm not. I wouldn't."

Her right heel banged against the corner of the building, tripping her off balance. She flailed her arms. Her next step landed on something sharp, slicing into her heel. "Ow," she screamed, followed by "Don't look!" just as her other ankle twisted on a rock.

She yelped. Spun. Then pitched forward into what she really prayed wasn't a patch of poison ivy before she let out another scream.

"So . . . can I look now?"

30

Two hours later the glass doors to the Emergency Department slid open, allowing Zach to step inside, but not without catching a glimpse of his unshaven, disheveled, helmet-haired, deer-in-the-headlights reflection first.

Because . . . *what happened?*

One minute he was stretching his legs, waiting for the park ranger—who apparently had water pressure issues at home—to finish taking his shower, so Zach could take his. The next minute Zach was standing in front of a wet, screaming, wearing-nothing-but-a-towel Charlotte.

Zach rubbed his eyes to scrub the image from his brain.

Nope. Still there. Legs, elbow, and all.

He ignored the quick glances from the only two other people sitting in the small-town ER's waiting room—a heavyset middle-aged woman and a bored-looking teenager who quickly went back to staring at his phone. Zach had just started to sit when a nurse called his name.

"You can come back now. The doctor's all done with her."

The nurse hit a round button on the wall, and Zach followed her past the automatic doors. The nurse pulled back a curtain and spoke to Charlotte. "Your boyfriend's here. Once I find you a wheelchair, you can go."

The nurse let the curtain fall back into place. Zach stared at it for a beat. Then slowly pulled it back and peered inside.

Charlotte lay on a stretcher, her right foot wrapped in a bandage and propped on a pillow. She tugged her blanket up to her neck as he stepped next to her.

He opened his mouth, not sure where to start.

"I don't want to talk about it," Charlotte cut him off.

He closed his mouth. *Ooooh-kay.*

A circle of pink infused her cheeks, and she kept her gaze locked on her foot. His mouth worked, trying to form words. Because they *had* to talk about it, didn't they? They couldn't just pretend none of that had happened. They were in an emergency room, for crying out loud.

He cleared his throat. "What did the doctor say?"

She continued staring at her foot.

"Charlotte, we have to talk about that." He pointed to her foot. "And—" he made a generalized circular motion with his hands toward the rest of her body—"that."

She tugged her blanket further up her chin.

"The poison ivy," Zach said. "Not . . . you know." The fact he'd seen her in nothing but a towel, and even though she'd been completely covered and he hadn't seen anything he shouldn't have, the sight of her in nothing but a towel had affected him more than seeing a woman at the beach, scantily clad in a bikini, ever had.

Yeah, probably best not to discuss that. "What did he say about the poison ivy?" Zach repeated.

Her forehead smoothed out and she seemed to relax the tiniest bit. "They gave me some cream just in case, but so far it seems to be fine.

Maybe a spot or two on my right side. I might be one of the lucky few that's not that allergic."

"And your foot? That was a big piece of broken glass you stepped on. Is it going to heal okay? Are you going to be able to ride? Do we need to call off the rest of the trip?"

"They cleaned it up, put in a few stitches, and gave me a tetanus shot. It's on my heel. I should still be able to bike since I don't put much pressure on that part of my foot when I'm pedaling."

Zach winced. "You sure? Is that what the doctor said? We don't have to—"

"We do." Charlotte jutted out her chin. "We can't stop. Not now. We're halfway there."

"We're not even halfway to halfway there."

"All the more reason we have to keep going then. I'll be fine." She scratched her right side, then seemed to realize what she was doing, and forced herself to stop. "And not another word about this. To anyone. *Ever.*"

The nurse swiped back the curtain and pushed in a wheelchair. She angled it right next to the stretcher. "All right, Charlotte. Here we go." Looking at Zach, she said, "So I'm sure she already told you all this, but she'll need to keep that foot clean and protected and elevated for the next twenty-four hours."

Zach met Charlotte's gaze, and she gave her head a small shake. He rolled his eyes, biting back his words, until they made it out of the emergency room. The moment the doors closed behind him, he leaned around her. "The doctor said it was fine to keep riding, did he? What about keeping your foot elevated?"

"*If possible*, he said. If possible."

Zach shook his head and pulled out his phone. The same Uber driver who'd picked them up from the park, probably the only Uber driver in a thirty-mile radius, arrived in the parking lot. "Everything turn out okay?" the young man asked.

Charlotte pushed herself up from the wheelchair as Zach opened the back door for her. "Two stitches. No biggie."

Zach harrumphed as he shut the door and returned the wheelchair to the entrance. "No biggie," he muttered. He'd see how she felt about that tomorrow after they'd been riding all day and her heel throbbed liked the dickens and she was ready to claw her skin off.

Still, he had to hand it to her. She was taking the pain and discomfort in stride. Much better than the way she'd handled being seen in a towel.

He slammed his eyes shut. *Nope. Don't go there. Erase. Delete. Forget.*

The more he tried to forget, the more he remembered. Maybe it would be better if they did talk about it. "You know, Charlotte—"

"Don't say a word."

"All I was going to say is—"

"I mean it. Nothing."

"But how did you know I was going to talk about—?"

"Because I know that's all you're thinking about."

"That's not true. I mean, not completely true. It's a little bit true. Mostly true. Majority true, but—"

"Zach, I'm serious. I never ever want to speak of that one awful minute again. Got it?"

"Fine. But for the record, it was two and a half glorious minutes."

Charlotte punched him in the arm. "Yeah, about that. Could you have fumbled to get my clothes out of the bag any slower?"

"You were bleeding and yelling at me while you were *half naked*. Be glad I managed to get any clothes out at all." Zach altered his voice into a soprano. "Don't look at me! Close your eyes! Get my clothes! Get that glass out of my foot! What are you looking at? Keep your eyes closed!"

"I said I don't want to talk about it."

The Uber driver adjusted his rearview mirror, shooting them a glance. "Maybe you should talk about it. I'm no expert, but it seems to me a lot of issues never get resolved unless people talk about it."

"Exactly," Zach said.

The driver nodded. "And if I were you, I'd start with the part about being half naked."

"Just drive," Charlotte snapped. "And for the record, Mr. Uber, I have tried talking through issues in the past, and it didn't help. So no thank you. I'm done talking."

"What issues?" Zach said.

"What issues? Are you serious?" Charlotte looked at the Uber driver. "Is he serious, Mr. Uber?"

"It's Jon, actually. And yeah, I'd say he sounds serious."

Charlotte scratched her side, shaking her head. "Gee, I don't know. Maybe like some of the issues Ben and I were starting to have before the wedding. Issues like your father's death. The fact that it led to a complete crisis of faith for him. For you too, if I'm guessing correctly."

"That's an issue, all right," Jon muttered.

"Okay, Mr. Uber, that's enough," Zach said. "And that's not how it all went down."

"How did it all go down?" Jon asked.

"None of your business," Zach said.

"I'll tell you how it all went down." Charlotte leaned forward in her seat and jabbed a thumb at Zach. "This guy's brother here asked me to marry him."

"Congratulations."

"Thanks, man," Zach said. Charlotte smacked him on the arm. "What? I'm just being polite."

"We planned out our wedding, then a month before the big day, his father died."

"Sorry to hear that," Jon said.

Zach dipped his head in acknowledgment, then shifted in his seat. "Maybe we don't need to talk about this."

"See? That's what I'm saying. He's just like his brother. Oh yeah, it's fine to talk about *me* rolling around in humiliation as I bleed to death in a patch of poison ivy, but bring up something personal to *him*, and 'maybe we don't need to talk about this.'"

"First off, I'm nothing like my brother. Secondly, you weren't bleeding to death. As I recall, your exact words were 'Two stitches. No biggie.' So don't make this sound like it's anything remotely equivalent to my father's death. You were embarrassed, that's all."

"Zach, you saw me in nothing but a towel. A very tiny towel."

"Now, we're getting somewhere," Jon said, turning onto the road to the park.

"Shut up, Mr. Uber," Charlotte and Zach both said.

"So what?" Zach flung his palms up. "It wasn't on purpose. It was an accident. And besides, it's just me. Zach. It wasn't like I was some stranger. Besides, you're a beautiful woman. You have nothing to be embarrassed about."

Charlotte seemed to sink into herself. Maybe none of that had come out right. Women were hard to talk to sometimes. You tell them they're beautiful and you get slapped. You tell them they're neurotic and flawed, and they tear up and kiss you.

He braced himself for the slap. Two minutes later as they returned to their camping site, it still hadn't come.

Mr. Uber slowed to a stop in the parking lot. Maybe she was waiting until after they'd gotten out of the car and she had more space to swing her arm before she whapped him across the face.

Nobody said anything, not even Mr. Uber, as they opened the doors and climbed out.

"Hope you work everything out," their driver finally said as he began pulling away. "Good luck with that foot."

Zach watched the car's taillights until they disappeared up the road. Charlotte hadn't moved and he wondered if she was waiting for him to do something. Like carry her. Or at least offer an arm to lean on. He took a step toward her.

"Did it ever occur to you . . ." She spoke so quietly, he had to stop moving to keep the sound of his footsteps from muffling her words. The hoot of an owl echoed from the trees and a flying insect buzzed next to his ears. He held still, waiting. ". . . that I felt the same way?"

The dim yellow security light from the bathroom glowed just enough to reveal the earnestness on her face. "I get that, after your dad's death, Ben felt shaken. In a way, maybe exposed and naked. But it was me, Zach. *Me.* Ben didn't have to hide. Not from me. But that's what he did."

She turned from him, limping as she stepped on the ball of her injured foot to walk. "I think you're more like your brother than you want to admit."

31

It's not that Sophia wanted to appear as a crazy stalker, but when a cute guy holds her sister's future in his hands and promises to call "soon" with news about that future, then lets over twenty-four hours pass without sending any word whatsoever, well . . . What else is a girl to do but sneak back to his house late at night in search of answers?

Sure, there'd been a lovely write-up in the paper today about A. P. Hopkins's life, including his recent donation for the bike path and the couples challenge he issued to go along with it. And sure, learning he'd once been married, then watched that marriage fall apart, shed some light on why he might have issued this particular challenge.

But if everything was all fine and dandy with the challenge, why hadn't Joshua called to say everything was all fine and dandy with the challenge? Something along the lines of "Found the promised prize money right where he told me to find it. No need to worry. Everything's all fine and dandy with the challenge."

What if Joshua wasn't the Clark Kent type after all? What if all along he was actually the Lex Luthor type? For all Sophia knew he could have taken the quarter million and split town hours ago. Sure, he'd been all too happy to take *her* phone number. But had he offered Sophia *his* number? No.

So see? She had no choice but to return.

After getting her car towed yesterday afternoon, Trusty Rusty, who never missed an opportunity to spout off a good movie quote, informed her the car was only mostly dead. "And mostly dead is slightly alive," he'd said in his best impression of Miracle Max from *The Princess Bride*.

Maybe she ought to start calling him Miracle Rusty. Ever since she'd picked up her car this morning, it purred like a kitten. Good thing, too, since she was in the middle of a covert operation here.

Sophia dimmed the headlights as she approached the hidden driveway entrance. Then wished she hadn't when she nearly ran over Joshua and his dog.

"Oh my!" She jerked the steering wheel hard. Too hard. She crashed into the mailbox. Wood splintered and glass shattered before she finally remembered how to use the brakes.

"Oh my," she whimpered again, really hoping Rusty didn't have tomorrow off. From the sounds of it, she was going to need another miracle. This time for her left headlight.

On a positive note, Joshua hadn't fled town. He was still here. And still very cute. But again, probably not the best time to be noticing things like that. Maybe later. After she received confirmation of the prize money. And fixed her car again.

Rolling down her window, Sophia draped a casual elbow over the door as if she were placing an order at the drive-through. "Sorry about that. Any word on the money for the challenge?"

Joshua snagged D'Artagnan's collar to keep him from stepping on glass. "Does your mechanic's shop hand out punch cards or something?"

"If only. I'm sure I'd be due for a free car by now. For the record, you really shouldn't go for walks in the middle of the night."

He pulled D'Artagnan a few more steps back as he glanced at his watch. "It's not even nine-thirty. And I was checking the mail. I forgot earlier."

She didn't want to be rude, but it looked like he'd forgotten to change clothes again too. He was still wearing the vintage Superman shirt. Obviously he was still caught in the "I'm a little overwhelmed" stage. Crashing into the mailbox probably didn't help matters for him.

"Look, I'm sorry to be a nuisance," Sophia said, climbing out of the car so D'Artagnan would stop trying to get to her. She made sure to avoid the broken glass as she joined Joshua on the narrow path. "But you said you'd call soon, and it's been over twenty-four hours. Can you blame me if I wanted to make sure you hadn't taken the money and run?"

She crouched down to pet D'Artagnan the same moment Joshua did. When he sighed, his soft breath fanned her cheek, and a pleasant shiver rippled down her spine. "Sorry to disappoint you," he said, "but I'm not nearly as exciting as that."

Continuing to pet D'Artagnan, she leaned closer for another cheek tickle. "You kidding? You've been the most exciting thing to happen to me in years. All the thrilling stuff usually happens to my siblings. Prison. Broken engagements. Contests."

He cracked a quick smile and straightened. "I'm sorry I don't have an answer for you yet about the contest money. But I promise I'll let you know soon."

"Soon, like in the next twenty-four hours? Or soon like 'I have no intentions of ever calling you again, but at this point I'll say anything just to make you leave'?"

"Soon, as in I won't rest until I find it." This time a full-fledged smile broke through, leaving Sophia no choice but to back away with a nod before she said something silly. Like "Man, you're so stinking cute."

Which might have snuck past her lips anyway based on the quiet chuckle she heard chasing her back to the car.

32

As crazy as it sounded, Charlotte might be adjusting to this bicycling gig. Maybe she *had* gotten into shape. Maybe cardio *was* her thing. Or maybe snoozing all day yesterday, then not having to pedal the majority of today made her feel like she'd gotten into shape and cardio was her thing.

Despite Charlotte's assurances that her foot was fine, Zach had insisted on taking yesterday off. Granted, he didn't have to work that hard to convince her once she popped the two Benadryl tabs the ER nurse had suggested to help keep the poison ivy rash at bay.

Then today, despite more reassurances that her foot was fine, Zach insisted on doing all the pedaling on the right side to keep her from putting pressure on her foot. Which would have been a great plan if she was coordinated enough to use her left leg and not her right. When she quickly proved she wasn't, he insisted she stop pedaling all together.

Then he insisted they take frequent breaks so she could elevate her foot—and no doubt so he could recover from lugging her weight in the midst of a heat advisory. Which is probably why he insisted they call it a day here, sixty miles down the road, at Davis Lake Campground.

Fine by Charlotte. That bicycle seat hadn't gotten any more comfortable. Even less comfortable, though, was the weird silence going on now between her and Zach.

She slid off the back seat of the bike and stretched for her toes. Ever since their argument after the ER, everything had felt awkward. Polite. Like they were tiptoeing around each other. But honestly, she'd prefer they were at war.

"Foot okay?"

"Yep."

"Getting enough water?"

"Yep."

And she was sick of it. Sick of the pleasantries. Sick of the small talk. And most definitely sick of the scenery. The cow pastures and hay bales held a certain level of tranquility the first couple dozen miles. The last couple dozen? As boring as their conversations this afternoon.

"Breeze feels nice."

"It does, doesn't it?"

"Not too hard, not too soft."

"Just the right level of breeziness. Foot doing okay?"

That's when she had started to wish for a fight. Something to stir things up. But every time she tried, Zach hadn't taken the bait. He shrugged. Or worse—agreed. No way she could survive the rest of the trip like this. She liked Zach better when he acted more like . . . well, *Zach*.

"That looks like a good spot to set up the tent for the night." Charlotte rose from stretching her legs and pointed toward the bottom of a hill at the campsite.

He followed her gaze, casting a quick glance to the sky filled with pregnant rain clouds, and shrugged. "Sure. We can set up camp down there if that's what you want. Foot doing okay?"

See? Setting up a tent at the bottom of a hill when an oncoming storm was brewing was a horrible idea. And he knew it. And for the love of Pete, would he stop asking about her blasted foot already?

But if that's how he wanted to play the game, fine. She smiled and grabbed her set of handlebars. "Foot's great. Lead the way."

"Lead the way," he said with a fainthearted laugh. "Good one." Then he grabbed his handlebars and pushed the tandem bike down the hill as she suggested.

She could throttle him.

Thunder rumbled in the distance. She watched the back of his head and waited for him to acknowledge it. Nothing. He kept leading the way.

When another rumble sounded shortly after they'd reached the bottom of the hill, louder and closer, and the skies darkened to gray, she glanced at him out of the corner of her eye. He continued securing the tent with the pegs and said nothing. Unbelievable.

They ate the sub sandwiches they'd bought earlier at a gas station in silence. When the wind swept their sandwich bags off the picnic table, Zach jumped up from the bench to snag them with his foot.

"Getting awful windy, isn't it?" Charlotte said.

He squinted up at the sky. "Yeah. Hmm." Then lifted a shoulder in a *don't really know what to make of that* gesture before taking another crunch of his apple.

Charlotte inhaled a deep breath, searching for patience. Or at the very least, less homicidal thoughts. "Gee, you don't think it'll rain, do you?" She met his eyes straight on. He stared back at her for a beat, then stood and threw his apple core into the surrounding trees.

"Who can say?" he answered with another shrug, wiping his fingers on the black shorts he always changed into once they were done riding for the day. He stepped over to the bike and rummaged through one of the side bags and found his toothbrush. He brushed his teeth, rinsed with his bottle of water, spit, wiped his arm across his mouth, returned the toothbrush, zipped up the bag, and pulled out his sleeping bag.

By now the wind had whipped the tent into a frenzy. The opening flap vibrated with the storm's energy. Charlotte didn't know how they'd manage to get it zipped once they unzipped it.

But it appeared that was going to be her issue to deal with, seeing as Zach tossed his sleeping bag onto the ground, holding it in place with one foot until he could climb into it.

"You're sleeping there?" Lightning flashed across the sky. It was dumb enough to sleep in a tent at the bottom of a hill on a rainy night. What kind of idiot slept *outside* a tent at the bottom of a hill on a rainy night?

He folded his arms behind his head as if the next apocalypse weren't about to break loose any second. "I don't want to bother your foot. I'll be fine."

"Don't want to bother my foot," she repeated as a crack of thunder split the sky. The next moment a bucket of water poured from the heavens, dousing the ground around them. "That's it," Charlotte yelled. "I can't take it anymore."

"Then get inside the tent, where you won't get wet."

"I'm not talking about the weather. I'm talking about you. What's your problem?"

He continued to lie there with his arms folded behind his head, pretending he wasn't getting waterboarded by nature. "I don't have a problem." He turned his head to the side to spit out the stream of water that had invaded his mouth just from saying that sentence.

"Stop it. Of course you have a problem." Her hair plastered against her neck. Her T-shirt weighed down her shoulders with water weight. "Look at us. We both have a problem. We're standing in the middle of a torrential downpour."

"Then get in the tent."

"The tent is already flooded. What did you think would happen pitching the tent at the bottom of a mudslide?"

"Then why did you choose this location?"

"Because I wanted you to tell me it was a stupid idea."

Zach wrestled his way out of his sleeping bag and kicked it aside. He swiped a palm down his face, flinging water away as he marched forward until he was inches away from her face. "You want me to tell you it was a stupid idea? Fine. It was a stupid idea. The worst. Never heard anything dumber in all my life. Happy?"

He started to turn. She grabbed his arm. Her hand slipped from the slickness of rainwater, but she adjusted her grip and tugged him to face her. "Why are you being so mean to me?"

His eyes widened. "You're the one who told me to tell you it was a stupid idea."

"I'm not talking about that. I'm talking about yesterday and today. You being all polite and nice. It's mean. What's your problem?"

Somehow his eyes widened even more. "I don't know what you want from me."

"I want you to stop pretending."

"Pretending what?" His voice grew to a shout. Finally, they were getting somewhere. "That you're not losing your mind?"

Lightning cracked the sky apart and a blast of thunder shattered through the opening. Charlotte's shoulders hunched, but she forced her feet to remain where they were in the rapidly growing swamp. "You've been acting different ever since . . ."

"Ever since what? I saw you half naked? I thought we weren't supposed to talk about that."

Charlotte stared at him, uncertain if his face blurred because of the rainwater assaulting her face or tears. "I just want things to go back to how they were at the start of the trip. Otherwise I don't know if I can survive this."

He swiped water out of his eyes. "Maybe I'm just doing what I can to survive the rest of this trip with you. Ever think of that?"

"What does that mean?"

A bolt of lightning sliced through the sky. Zach flinched the same moment Charlotte heard the horrific crack. He grabbed Charlotte's hand and pulled her after him, dragging her as fast as he could in the mud before he tackled her to the ground and covered her body. The ground shook with a heavy thud.

Charlotte buried her face in Zach's neck, his weight covering the length of her.

After a moment, he lifted his face and started running his fingers over the back of her head, his fingers tangling in her wet hair. "You okay? You didn't hit your head, did you? Can you breathe? Did I knock the wind out of you?"

Oh, he'd knocked the wind out of her all right. She and Ben had dated for years, planned to marry. And she couldn't think of a single time they argued the way she and Zach did. Not even when Ben had called off their wedding.

Why did the thought of arguing with Zach thrill her more than keeping the peace with Ben ever had? She dipped her gaze to his mouth. Maybe because the thought of making up with Zach after every argument lit a blaze in her stomach faster than the lightning bolt in the sky.

"Charlotte, you okay?" Zach's thumb brushed her cheek. "Say something."

"What was that?" she managed to squeeze out.

"Lightning must have hit one of the trees. You sure you're okay?" He leaned up on his elbows, his hands braced on each side of her face as he looked the length of her body over as well as he could with their legs entangled. "You don't look okay. You look—"

"Kiss me."

Zach's head snapped up, his eyes locked on hers.

Charlotte slipped one hand around his neck and gripped the front of his wet shirt with her other. "You promised me one kiss if I asked. I'm asking."

His lips parted and his arms began to shake. She lifted her face closer to his.

"Charlotte, I'm not so sure—"

She closed the distance between them and silenced his words.

His lips were cold and tasted like rain. "Charlotte, what—"

She chased his lips a second time. This time they were warmer. Softer. Slower to pull away. "Charlotte, are you—"

She silenced him a third time. He balanced on his elbows, not touching her except for his lips, which scalded her skin as they moved from her mouth to her jaw, her neck, back to her lips. Then his arms were beneath her, rolling them over so she was on top of him.

They remained that way a long time. Long enough for the storm to pass. The rain to slow. Charlotte didn't know how long they might have continued if a beam of light hadn't hit them. If a throat hadn't cleared.

Charlotte startled, falling off Zach. He caught her with an arm and leaned forward on his other elbow, breathing hard and squinting against the harsh beam of light.

Whoever held the flashlight appeared to be shuffling back and forth on his feet, probably not sure what to say to a couple of people who got their kicks making out in mud piles. "Um, I just came down to check . . . It looked like a tree might have . . . Some other campers said they saw you two come down this way . . . so just wanted to . . ." He cleared his throat again. "Everybody doing okay?"

Zach climbed to his feet and offered Charlotte a hand up. "We're doing okay. Right, Charlotte? We're doing okay?"

They were both coated head to toe in muck, their tent flattened into a muddy pancake. "Yep. Doing okay."

The park ranger cleared his throat. "Okay, well . . ." His flashlight grazed over their campsite. "Hopefully the worst of the storm is over. Even so, you, uh, might want to consider moving to higher ground or . . ." He sighed. "Aw, you guys don't stand a chance of getting dried out tonight. And we don't have any open cabins. Tell you what, why don't you come stay with me? I live with my mom. She won't mind. Except—" He aimed his flashlight to the ground where they'd been rolling around like a couple of pigs on their honeymoon. "You can't be doing any of that."

Charlotte giggled and slapped a muddy palm over her mouth. She couldn't help it. It was either that or start crying. What had her life become? Covered in mud, kissing her ex-fiancé's brother like a crazed hormonal teenager, about to stay the night with a stranger and his mother.

What would Sophia think? What would her parents think? What would her entire town think? Oh, she knew exactly what they'd think. They'd think canoodling was her thing, not cardio.

Charlotte collapsed to the ground in hysterics.

33

Zach appreciated the hospitality, he did. It's not every day a stranger takes you into their home and provides you with food and dry clothes. He just wished the food were something other than pork and sauerkraut and the clothes something other than costumes from a stage production of *A Christmas Carol*.

Zach tugged at the collar of his Ebenezer Scrooge nightgown. He'd politely declined the matching nightcap. Charlotte had enough to giggle about from across the kitchen table as it was. In fact, she hadn't stopped giggling since the park ranger had discovered them at the campgrounds together.

For a minute, Zach thought she was having some sort of weird laughing panic attack when she'd collapsed in a muddy puddle, cackling her head off for a solid five minutes before Zach managed to get her back on her feet again.

Now, clean and dressed in black sweatpants and a cut-off sweatshirt, she looked slightly saner. Is that what their kiss had been for her? Temporary insanity?

"Sorry again about the clothes, Zach." Mary Lou, the ranger's mother, entered the kitchen. "I got rid of all my husband's clothes last summer since they weren't doing anything but collecting moth holes. Doubt any of them would have fit you anyway. He was built just like my son. Never could fatten either of them up with my cooking. More sauerkraut?"

Zach held up his hand. "I'm stuffed. Thank you."

Charlotte's cheeks flushed with repressed humor. She was just having the time of her life, wasn't she? "I'll take some more." She would too. Apparently she loved sauerkraut the same way she loved cheesecake.

He glanced past her shoulder to the mudroom, where the washer and dryer hummed with the task of cleaning their clothes. "So how long have you and your son lived here?" Hopefully a little conversation would distract Charlotte from his ridiculous getup. And distract himself from wanting to lean across the table and kiss her again, sauerkraut breath and all.

She might not be the only one suffering from temporary insanity.

What had happened back there? Every time he had tried leaning away from her to ask, she kept pressing forward to kiss him. He finally gave up and let her. Then might have taken over and done a little pressing and kissing himself.

He half listened to their host talk about the history of the house. He tried nodding his head at the right moments to show he was listening, but his eyes wouldn't stop wandering to Charlotte. Her lips.

Why had she kissed him?

He gripped the edge of the table. Probably just caught up in the moment. The storm. The yelling.

But that was another thing. What had she been going on about? Almost like she'd wanted to start a fight. Why get mad at him for trying to keep things neutral between them? Didn't she know it was killing him to live in close proximity to her day after day and pretend he wasn't a frog slowly cooking in a pot of boiling water as his feelings for her continued heating up?

He looked up from the scars on the table to find both women staring at him. Charlotte nudged him with her foot under the table, raising her brows. He stared back, slightly shaking his head. "Uh . . ." They were clearly waiting for him to say something, but he had no idea what.

Mary Lou smiled. "I think we caught him zoning out."

"It's been a couple of very long days." Charlotte met his gaze with an almost panicked expression. "She asked if we don't mind sharing a bed since she only has the one extra bedroom."

"Oh." Zach swallowed. Sharing a tent was one thing. Sharing a bed? Rain pattered against the windows.

"I figured Russel could sleep on the couch in the living room," Mary Lou said, clearing the dishes from the table. "Of course, if you're not comfortable with that arrangement, Zach and Russel can share the bed, and Charlotte could sleep on the couch. Have to warn you though, Russel's a snorer. I have to sleep with a sound machine just to drown him out from my bedroom."

"We'll be fine with the arrangement." No way was Zach sharing a bed with Russel. And no way were he and Charlotte going back out in that storm just to get all muddy again. He'd eat a plate full of sauerkraut before that happened.

No, they were staying the night here. Beneath a roof. Warm. Dry. Clean. And together.

"Well, good." Mary Lou stood and excused herself for bed. "Russel usually gets home sometime after ten. I already told him to plan on taking the couch. Your clothes should be done drying soon. I can't promise a fancy breakfast tomorrow, but you're welcome to help yourself to the bananas and whatever you find in the fridge."

Zach nodded with gratitude. "Thank you. And we'll try to be out of your hair first thing in the morning." Tomorrow was day five. Halfway point. They needed to do at least sixty miles, hopefully more.

"We can't tell you how much we appreciate this," Charlotte added. "Thank you so much."

"Not a problem. Don't mind in the least." Their host patted her thigh and four corgis shot up from their spots on the ground, scampering behind her as she disappeared down the hallway to her bedroom.

Charlotte scraped her thumb against the surface of the kitchen table. "I can wait down here until the clothes are done drying and get them folded and packed for tomorrow." They'd dragged their tent and belongings into the mudroom, trying to dry them out as best as they could.

"We can get it in the morning. You've got to be as wiped out as I am. Let's just call it a night."

She sighed, staring down at where her nail scratched. "Zach, I don't think I can share a bed with you."

Not after the way they'd kissed, they couldn't. "Don't worry. I was planning to sleep on the floor."

"That's still too close. I don't think I can sleep in the same room with you at all." She lifted her gaze, a smirk dancing on the edges of her lips. "Not with you looking so sexy in that Ebenezer nightgown. You might have to sleep with Russel."

He dipped his head to hit her with his most lethal glare. "I'm not sleeping anywhere near a snoring Russel. You're stuck with me and the sexy gown."

She giggled. "Then I guess you're stuck with me and my sauerkraut breath. Because I have no idea where my toothbrush is, and I don't even care."

"You're really embracing this troubadour lifestyle, aren't you?"

"I'm too far gone to stop now, baby."

Her hair hung in damp ringlets around her face and all he could do was stare. Man, she was beautiful. He motioned his head to the stairs.

"Go on up. I'll see to the clothes. I still need to load the sleeping bags into the dryer anyway."

She chewed on the corner of her lip. "You know, you don't have to sleep on the floor. We could—"

"Nope." The word fired fast from his mouth. He smiled to soften it. "Go on to bed, Charlotte." He didn't know what that kiss had meant. But anything more would mean *mistake*. She wasn't the only one too far gone, baby. Only Zach was making sure he put a stop to it now.

Because as much as he hated to admit it, her stupid brother was right. If he wasn't careful, he was going to hurt her.

He needed to remember why they were doing this challenge in the first place. So Charlotte could help out her mom. So Charlotte could start a music program in the town she loved. Not so Zach could break her heart when he moved to California, ending a relationship they never should have started.

Man, canoodling really did complicate things, didn't it?

34

Sophia stared at her phone, willing it to buzz with a text message. An emoji. A GIF. A poorly constructed sentence. Anything.

For two days she'd stared at her phone, waiting. For two days, nothing. Not since nearly running Joshua over with her car. At least this time he'd given her his number before she drove away. And he did say she could call him if she needed anything.

Well, technically Sophia did need something. She needed an answer.

Charlotte and Zach should've reached the halfway point by now. The further they biked, the more painful it was going to be if there wasn't any money. What was taking Joshua so long to give her a stinking answer? If he was still feeling overwhelmed, all he had to do was ask for help. Sophia would be there in a flash. Especially since Trusty Rusty had already gotten her car patched up again.

She tapped the screen, intending to send Joshua a friendly but strongly worded message, and bumped the call button instead. "Whoops." Before she could cancel the call, he answered. Oh wow. Maybe he'd been about to call her. Maybe he was ready to ask for help. "Hey, it's me."

She waited for his audible sigh of relief or heartfelt exclamation along the lines of "Praise be to God! I've been fasting and praying these past two days in hopes you would call."

What she got was a stretch of silence and, "I'm sorry, who?"

She cleared her throat. "Me. Sophia. Remember?" He had entered her contact information into his phone. She watched him. Had he forgotten to add her name? Or listed her as *Strange Woman with Car Troubles*?

"Oh. Sophia. Hi. Sorry. Yeah. Haven't slept. Mind's not firing on all cymbals."

Or cylinders, apparently. "How long have you not slept? Surely not since Hopkins died."

"No, I . . ." She thought they'd lost their connection until she heard a tiny snort. "Sorry, what?" he mumbled.

"Joshua, I'm coming over. Have you eaten supper yet?"

He said something she couldn't decipher since it was delivered in the midst of a jaw-cracking yawn. She'd bring some food with her. "I'm on my way."

Thirty minutes later, she found the small entrance to the driveway leading to the side of the property and made it to the house without needing a tow or breaking any headlights. Things were looking up already.

The setting sun painted the property in golden light with a backdrop of pinks and oranges. Juggling a paper grocery sack in one arm and a carton of drinks and takeout in the other, she kicked her car door shut, then took a moment to admire the stone fence. It really did add an extra layer of charm to the property.

D'Artagnan's collar jingled as he danced around her, barking out a throaty greeting. "Hey, boy. How you doing? Did you miss me? Oh, you're so handsome. Did you know you were handsome? I'll bet you did. Sorry, I can't pet you right now. But don't worry. I brought you a treat. Do you like hamburgers? Of course you do."

They carried on their conversation all the way to the front screen door, where she kicked the bottom of it a few times. "Hey, Joshua, you mind opening the door for me?" she shouted, looking inside for any signs of life in the dark entryway. "Joshua?"

She waited a minute, then used her chin to secure one of the grocery sacks against her body as she twisted the door handle. On her way to the kitchen, she glanced around. Notebooks and papers were spread all over the dining room table. Boxes of books and manila files flooded the floor. A narrow path snaked between cardboard boxes from room to room.

The house smelled like a used bookstore. If the disarray of belongings and boxes held any resemblance to Hopkins's financial situation, it wasn't any wonder Joshua had been losing sleep trying to sort it all out.

After finding some space on the kitchen table, she set down the food, then followed a narrow path back down the hallway, peeking into each room. Maybe Joshua was outside in that garagey-workshop building.

Nope, she found him. He was sitting in an upright chair next to a large wooden desk in what might be an office or library. His chin rested against his chest and a pile of papers blanketed his lap.

"Joshua?" Sophia whispered, not wanting to startle him. But she might as well have shouted, the way he jumped from the chair, scattering papers into a tornado as he darted glances around the room like he'd never seen it before. When his gaze landed on Sophia, he stared as if he'd never seen her before.

"I brought food," she said, lifting her hands in surrender.

"Food," he mumbled, rubbing his bloodshot eyes. His hair stood on end. He wore a sock on one foot, a shoe on the other. And based on the flash of ankle she saw beneath his wrinkled pant leg, he'd lost the sock for that foot. "Food," he said again.

"Yeah, food." Sophia glanced to D'Artagnan as if to ask *Is he okay?* D'Artagnan stared back as if to say *About that hamburger . . .*

"Joshua, don't take this the wrong way, but you're a mess. Let's get you something to eat." D'Artagnan scampered to the kitchen in full agreement. Joshua, not so much.

"I can't. I'm still trying to find it."

She really hoped the *it* in that statement referred to his missing sock and not the money.

"Well, you need to eat and sleep or you're never going to find anything." They'd address the *it* later. She marched to the kitchen and returned with a milkshake. Pressing the straw to his lips, she said, "Drink this."

He sucked down half the container. "Good job," she said in the same tone she might use with a toddler. Joshua must have noticed. He frowned. But at least a little spark had returned to his eyes.

"Eat this." She shoved three fries into his mouth.

"Why are you feeding me?" he mumbled around the food.

"Because french fries help everything. Eat some more." But he was already falling asleep midchew. Maybe she should stop force-feeding him. Maybe she should just get him to bed. Especially when she noticed the bottle of pills perched on the edge of the desk.

"Melatonin? Isn't that to help you sleep? Did you take one of these?" No wonder he was so out of it.

He nodded like a drunken sailor in turbulent seas. "Meant to grab the caffeine pill bottle." He swung his arm toward the hallway bathroom, nearly smacking himself in the face with his own hand.

"Okay. My initial statement stands. You're a mess." Thankfully sharing a dorm room last semester with a roommate who had tried making that old John Belushi movie *Animal House* her own personal college experience had given Sophia plenty of experience leading a half-conscious person to bed.

Swinging one of Joshua's arms around her shoulder, she wrapped an arm around his waist. "Okay, soldier. Lift those feet. Hup, two, three, four. Hup, two, three, four." Unfortunately Joshua carried a few more pounds than her petite roommate had. His weight sagged further against her with each *hup*.

"Dude, unless you want to sleep on the floor, you'll pick up those feet." She grunted. "Joshua, I'm serious." She groaned. "You're turning into dead weight." She dropped him.

Oomph. His body thudded against the hardwood floor at the bottom of the staircase. She braced her hands on her knees, catching her breath. "Did you just die? Because I do have a knack for being with people as they take their final breath." If only she'd been with Hopkins before his final breath, maybe they wouldn't be in this mess.

She nudged Joshua's foot. He snorted. Well, not dead at least. Just exhausted and slightly comatose.

Arching her back, she looked around for something to prop his head on. "Don't move."

He answered with a garbled response and another snort.

A quick glance in the kitchen told her D'Artagnan had located the hamburgers on his own. Great. She'd deal with cleanup in a minute. Climbing over Joshua, she took the creaky stairs to the top and searched for his bedroom. The rumpled sheets and unmade bed in the bedroom next to the hallway bathroom suggested that's where Joshua had been sleeping. Or rather, not sleeping.

She grabbed a pillow and a blanket, then creaked her way back down the wooden stairs and tucked in Joshua as best she could. He was already drooling, so she didn't think he was going to complain about whether his pillow was fluffed or not. She started to rise, then noticed his glasses smooshed against his nose.

She tried sliding them off gently. When they refused to let go of one ear, she became less gentle. "What'd you do? Superglue these on?" She managed to free the glasses, but not without losing her balance and sailing backwards. D'Artagnan appeared the next instant, licking her face with his hot hamburger breath.

Well, at least she had an excuse to continue missing her parents' phone calls. Because she wasn't going home until she got an answer about that money first. And based on the snores, that answer wasn't coming soon.

35

The following morning, settled on the porch swing, Sophia still didn't have an answer about the money. But the fact Joshua was finally awake made her think she might be a step closer.

"Good morning," she said as he stood in the doorway, blinking. "How are you feeling?" She steadied the porch swing. D'Artagnan rose from his spot next to her feet and trotted over to Joshua.

Patting the dog's side, Joshua squinted against the late morning sunlight. His hair stood up on one end. A crease ran down one cheek, disappearing into his unshaven scruff. And he wore the same rumpled shirt and jeans from last night. The same rumpled shirt and jeans from the first day they'd met, to be specific.

Hopefully they'd reached a level of friendship by now where she could start making personal hygiene suggestions, because she certainly had a few thoughts on the matter.

"How long have you been here?" He straightened from petting D'Artagnan.

Sophia glanced at her watch and pressed her foot to the floorboards to resume her gentle swing. "A little over fourteen and a half hours."

"Where are my glasses?"

Sophia grabbed them from the porch rail and held them out. "I didn't want to lose them."

He put them on, blinking a few more times. "I don't remember falling asleep on the couch."

"You didn't. You fell asleep at the bottom of the staircase. But I didn't want to just leave you there, so I started tapping your forehead nonstop the way my brother used to do to me when he would pin me down and annoy me like crazy. Well, I guess it annoyed you too. You woke up long enough to growl at me, then climb onto the couch because I told you that was the only way I was going to stop."

Joshua stared at her for a solid minute, just blinking. "I think I need a shower," he finally said.

"Oh, there's no doubt about that." He gave her a look. "What? I force-fed you french fries and tapped your forehead for at least five minutes last night. Surely that means we've reached a level of friendship where we can be honest and open about one another's hygiene."

He gave her another one of those looks. The kind that made her think he still wasn't fully awake. Which is why she hadn't hit him with any questions about the competition money yet.

"How about I whip up some omelets?" That seemed a safer topic than hygiene or finances.

For the first time since she'd arrived yesterday, he cracked one of his smiles. A smile that reminded her once again how cute he was, before he nodded and disappeared inside.

Sophia reached down and scratched behind D'Artagnan's ears. "Why do I have a much better feeling about my friendship with Joshua than I do about that money?"

36

Day five hadn't gone as either of them had hoped. Another surge of thunderstorms had kept Charlotte and Zach stranded at Mary Lou's until noon. Not wanting to wear out their welcome, they'd declined her offer of lunch. They were going to need to pedal into town and stock up on more food anyway.

But as soon as they made it back on the trail, the bike chain fell off. Which turned out to be a recurring problem every mile for the next five miles. By the time Zach figured out the problem and fixed it for good, another tsunami of rain hit.

One bright spot in the day was when a woman drove past and noticed them huddled together beneath a covering of trees at a rest area, waiting out the storm. She pulled up next to them, hopped out of her car, and handed them an umbrella with a Southern-twanged "You poor babies," then immediately drove off again.

Charlotte couldn't help but notice the kindness of strangers on this trip. First Mary Lou, then the umbrella lady. And later, after the storms finally cleared off and the sun broke through, a man in a pickup had slowed down next to them to make sure everything was okay. Charlotte had accidentally dropped her water bottle and they'd pulled over so she could walk back to retrieve it.

"Just checking," he'd said with a friendly wave before speeding off again.

Charlotte wasn't going to lie. In that moment she'd been awful tempted to ask the nice stranger if they could toss their bike in the back of his truck and hitch a ride the rest of the way to Kosciusko. Or maybe even the end of the Trace.

But they'd made it that far without cheating. They couldn't blow their chances now. Not with so much money on the line.

Which is why they'd made do stopping last night at a campsite for bikers called Witch Dance. Twenty miles was better than nothing.

Now it was day six, and thankfully the skies remained crystal clear, allowing them to cover the seventy-mile distance to a small camping area outside of Kosciusko without major incident.

So if they'd done the math right at lunch, they had four days left to finish 216 miles, which meant a little over fifty miles a day. Just like when they'd started. But for the first time, the finish line was starting to feel in sight. And Charlotte couldn't wait any longer to power up her phone, so she could tell Sophia all about it.

Lifting her phone, Charlotte searched for a signal. "I might need to try further up this path. I'm not getting a very strong signal. Zach, did you hear me?"

"Yep. I'm gonna go take care of business." He pecked her cheek, then brushed past, apparently in search of a bathroom. Or in his case, a decent-sized bush. That seemed to be his preference even when there were perfectly good restrooms available. Guys were so weird.

Except he'd been acting especially weird lately. Ever since the night of the storm. And not the same weird he'd been acting like before the storm. That weird had been passive and nice. This weird was more like his usual demeanor, only . . . *weird.*

She couldn't put her finger on it. He acted like they were a couple, without being a couple. But they were a couple, right? A real couple? They'd yelled at each other. They'd kissed. Surely that meant they were a real couple now. A real couple who would last more than ten days.

Charlotte rubbed her sweaty forehead. Maybe she was the one being weird. Especially since she was the one who made the rule about only being a couple for the sake of the challenge. All the more reason she needed to talk to Sophia. Not because Sophia would shed any light on Charlotte's situation, but hearing Sophia's goofy life philosophies always made Charlotte feel better.

After moaning and groaning her way up the path—cardio might be her new thing, but that didn't erase the fact that her body ached from head to toe—she found a clearing at the top of the trail surrounded by conifer trees. Charlotte walked to the open shelter covering a group of picnic tables and lifted her phone. Slightly better signal. Two bars. Maybe even enough to do a video call.

She tapped her screen and waited. Sophia's face appeared, then froze. "Sophia? Can you hear me?"

Poor connection her phone informed her right before it dropped the call. "Yeah, I can see that."

She needed to be higher. She looked around for a better option. The tables and benches were bolted to a concrete slab beneath a wooden shelter. Her eyes landed on a round metal trash can. If she could turn it over and climb up on it, then maybe . . .

But it was filled to the rim with trash. She wrinkled her nose at the thought of having to pick up the spoiled garbage afterward. The trash can was close to one of the outer support beams. She might be able to hold onto the beam and balance on the outer rim or something. It was worth a shot.

A minute later, clutching the support beam with one arm, both feet balanced on the edges of the trash can, she lifted her cell phone like the Statue of Liberty's torch.

Poor connection.

What if she climbed up onto the roof? Granted, that would require more upper body strength than she currently possessed. And probably more bravery than she currently possessed, since the spiderwebs in the corner beams were giving her a bad case of the willies.

But dang it, sometimes a girl just needs to talk to her sister.

Tucking her phone into her waistband and not giving herself time to think about spiders or broken legs, Charlotte grabbed the edge of the roof with one hand and a corner beam with the other, then jumped from the lip of the trash can with all her might.

After pulling at least three muscles in her thighs and turning her arms into noodles, she made it. "I did it, I did it, I did it," she panted. She rolled onto her back and stared at the violet sky fading quickly to dark indigo.

"I am woman, hear me roar. I'm the conquering hero, hahaha, yes I am. I—" She felt her shorts. Her shirt. The tiles on the roof. Then peeked over the edge of the roof and whimpered.

"I'm the idiot who dropped my phone and got herself stuck." Beneath her, next to the tipped-over trash can, in a pile of fast-food wrappers, lay her phone.

"Zach?" Charlotte called out. "Having a slight little issue here." She waited several beats. "Can you hear me?"

The hoot of an owl answered. Tugging her legs to her chest, she wrapped her arms around herself. No need to worry. Zach would find her. Soon. Once he finished using the bathroom. Probably on his way now.

She peeked again at her phone on the ground. It sat dark and quiet. She couldn't tell if the screen had shattered or if liquid from the trash had splattered on it. Either way, it would be okay. She'd just use Zach's phone. Because Zach would bring it when he appeared on that trail any second. So what if she thought Zach had mentioned something about his phone already being dead? He'd probably just been making small talk.

Nice weather we're having, don't you think?

Yep. Makes me want to recharge my phone even if I don't need to.

"Zach!" she screamed again.

. . . ✦ . . .

Zach meandered down the trail under the pretense of finding a bathroom. Charlotte probably thought that entailed finding a bush. He didn't want to burst her bubble, but so far on this trip he had never used Mother Nature as a restroom. So far he'd always been able to locate an actual toilet. But it was fun letting Charlotte think he was some type of Survivorman.

He followed the trail to a blacktop road. The entrance to the park had a map carved into a giant wooden sign, and if he recalled correctly, the road circled a small lake with trails shooting outward along the entire route.

Twisting side to side, he cracked his back. Survivorman, ha. It was going to take more than peeing behind a bush to survive this trip. He didn't know how long he could keep up the casual pretense that all was well between them without raising Charlotte's suspicions that there could never be anything between them. Period.

The last thing they needed was some big emotional talk that led to hurt feelings when they still had over two hundred miles left to cover. Which was why his main method of attack today had been to kiss her on the cheek. So far it was working. It conveyed that *hey, everything is great between us* vibe without allowing anything deeper to develop between them.

Unfortunately, he didn't know how much longer his lips would continue obeying the order to stick to her cheek.

Which is why his other method of attack was to go on pretend searches for bathrooms so he could buy as much time as possible away from her. Then act busy setting up the tent, rummaging through the bags to make sure they had everything ready for the next morning, eating supper, using the bathroom, preparing for bed, using the bathroom again, checking the flashlight, and saying goodnight.

Stay busy, avoid close contact, deflect meaningful conversations. That was the plan.

He glanced at his watch. He could probably head back. By the time he finished his evening ritual, it should be time for bed.

A sign across the road announced a mile-long trail that started and ended at the same point. He glanced at his watch again. Maybe a quick walk around the trail first. Charlotte had mentioned something about washing up after she finished talking to her sister. Goodness knows he didn't need to risk another repeat of the shower fiasco. One more glimpse of her like that and he'd never make it through the next few days.

Maybe he'd walk the trail twice.

37

What on earth could Zach possibly be doing? There were bushes galore. He should have found a bathroom by now. Several bathrooms.

Darkness encroached on Charlotte. Something grazed the skin on her shoulder. She slapped her palm at it. Better have not been a spider. She scooted closer to the edge of the roof. Maybe the ground wasn't as far away as she thought. Maybe she could drop and not break her ankle. Or mess up the sutures on her heel. Or die.

"Zach!"

She just couldn't risk it. Not when they'd made it this far. Not when they were over halfway to the finish. Not when she had a propensity for spraining her ankle just walking across a well-manicured golf course.

Where. Was. Zach?

Charlotte hugged her knees against her chest and forced herself to take a few slow, easy breaths. What did she always tell Sophia? *Have faith. Things will work out. Even bad things. Scary things. Embarrassing things. Things like that night in the barn.*

No. She scrunched her eyes shut, not wanting to think about that night in the barn. Even though it had worked out. Technically. She might have wet her pants first, but it had worked out.

Even so, she'd rather not think about it.

Except thinking about *that* night might take her mind off thinking about *this* night.

She lifted her head. It had started off as a game with her brother and his friend. She'd thought she was impressing them. No matter how hard they tied the knots, she could always get free. Like magic. It had been a game. Just a silly game. Until it wasn't.

Until the ropes had been too tight. The barn too dark. Too scary. And Will never came back for her.

Tears splattered against her knees.

Why hadn't Will come back? He was her brother. He knew she was stuck. He should have come back. He shouldn't have left her alone. In the dark. Struggling. Not when they'd always been so close.

She fell to her side, hugging her knees against her chest. If her own brother hadn't come back to save her, if her own fiancé hadn't shown up to marry her, could she really expect Zach to come find her tonight?

. . . ♦ . . .

Zach stumbled over a root. Where on earth could she be? After taking two laps around the trail earlier, he'd set up their tent, eaten a snack, and waited for her to show up. When she didn't, he'd checked the bathrooms and tried calling her on his phone—only to remember his battery had died the night of the Uber ride when he forgot to turn it off afterward.

He checked the bathrooms again, then started up the trail she'd taken earlier to call her sister.

"Charlotte," he called out. He stopped when he thought he heard his name. He shouted again and listened.

Yep, definitely heard his name. Or at least something that resembled his name. He cleared the top of the trail and caught the sound of a sob.

His heart stuttered. "Charlotte?" His eyes searched the darkness. Had she hurt herself? His mind didn't even want to consider the possibility that someone else had hurt her. "Charlotte, where are you?"

A trash can lay tipped over on its side, wrappers, napkins, and bottles scattered around it. Had she been attacked?

"You came looking for me," she said in a choked-up voice from somewhere above his head.

Well, of course he came looking for her. What did she think he would do? Just shrug his shoulders and go to bed?

"What are you doing up there?" he said, once he'd located her on top of the shelter. Then he sent a quick glance around him. Whatever had sent her to safety on top of a roof might still be around. "It wasn't a bear, was it?"

Wait. The Natchez Trace didn't have any bears. Or did it?

He reached for his pocket. Shoot. He'd left his knife with the bike. Not that a knife would do much against a bear. Charlotte had the right idea in climbing. Unless it was a brown bear. Couldn't brown bears climb? Or was that black bears? Why couldn't he remember a single thing about anything survival related?

Because Charlotte was crying. Why was she crying? It had to be a bear.

"What are you doing?" Charlotte asked, her sniffling drawing his attention to the issue at hand.

"Searching for bears."

"Why?"

"I don't know. Isn't that why you're on top of the shelter?"

"I dropped my phone."

"Okay." He waited for more. "So you climbed up on the roof?"

"I was trying to get a better signal on the roof. But I dropped my phone. And knocked over the trash can. Now I'm stuck."

And crying. But now didn't seem the time to point that out. He'd point it out later, once his heart rate dropped back to a reasonable level. Hopefully sometime this century.

"So would you like some help getting down?"

"Well, I mean, unless you're busy with other plans tonight."

"Sarcasm? Is that how we're going to handle this?"

"Sorry. I'm rattled and embarrassed and . . . yes, I would really like some help getting down."

Zach stepped to the edge of the shelter and held up his hands. "Okay then. I'm ready."

The moonlight reflected off her shadowed shape. "Ready for what? I'm not a toddler. I can't just hop down into your arms."

"What's your suggestion?"

"Get closer. I'll . . . I don't know. Maybe I can slide over and drop my feet down on your shoulders."

"Okay." That might possibly work. He supposed. He stepped right beneath where her feet started to peek out over the edge.

"Get as close as you can."

He inched forward. "I'm right beneath you."

"Get closer." Her muffled words got lost inside a grunt as she scooted her feet further over the edge.

He straightened as tall as he could while bracing his feet apart to support her oncoming weight. "I can't exactly grow any taller."

"This hurts my stomach. Am I about there?"

Her knees were bent, so that her feet aimed for the sky. "You're not even pointed the right direction."

"I don't think I can do this."

"You can." His hands pawed at the air, not even close to touching her. "You're going to have to scoot closer to the edge."

A grunt reached his ears. The hair on Zach's neck rose higher than Charlotte's feet. "Charlotte, please tell me that was you."

She must have heard it too, because she froze and whispered, "That wasn't me."

Zach turned and caught a shadowed mound moving closer. "Charlotte," Zach whispered. "Don't panic, but there's some sort of . . . something." Not a raccoon. Not a possum. "A wild hog maybe." He had heard of campers coming across those in this territory before.

"A wild what?" she whispered in a shriek that sounded an awful lot like panic.

The hog snorted and ambled closer, his attention so far directed on the trash sprawled all over the ground. Zach could probably walk away without the hog having any interest in him. But he couldn't leave Charlotte up there alone.

With one eye on the hog, Zach edged his way to the other side of the shelter. If he could get Charlotte down, they could slip away. The small beast was too distracted with the trash to worry about them.

Then another grunt and snort sounded behind him. He turned to find two more shadowed bumps angling toward him. These two with tusks. And they were starting to charge.

Zach discovered something amazing in the next second. He discovered he had a vertical leap worthy of the NBA when his life depended on it.

He also discovered, whatever type of hogs these were, they weren't the type to easily move on. Not when they wanted to investigate every morsel and scrap of trash in the vicinity. Didn't look like he and Charlotte were going anywhere for a while.

So much for keeping his distance.

Zach nudged Charlotte's shoulder with his. "What was that you said before the trip about kissing a pig?"

38

The sound of birds twittering beckoned Charlotte awake the following morning. She cracked open an eye to a bronze-tinted canopy of early light.

Whoops.

She must have fallen asleep before her first watch. She and Zach had agreed to take turns letting each other doze while the other person stayed on guard to make sure neither of them rolled off the slanted roof into a mosh pit of wild hogs.

But sometime early on, probably when Zach suggested she lie down and use his shoulder as a pillow, she must have fallen asleep. Hard. And then snuggled into him as if the rest of his body were her own personal sleeping bag. But who could blame her? This wonderful man had come back for her. He hadn't left her alone in the dark. He'd made sure to find her because . . . well, they were a real couple, weren't they?

"Looks like we survived," his low voice rumbled next to her ear.

"Sorry."

His chest vibrated with soft laughter. "That we survived?"

"No. That I fell asleep right away. We were supposed to take turns."

"Sweetheart, if you think I was going to catch a wink of sleep last night a dozen feet in the air with wild animals roaming beneath us, you don't know me at all."

She shifted against him, trying not to revel too much in the warmth of his body heat wrapped around her. Or the fact that he called her sweetheart. But yeah. She smiled. They were definitely a real couple.

"And I suppose the fact you knew I wouldn't be able to stay awake after biking all day, no matter the situation, proves you know me all too well." Charlotte tilted her face, pressing her nose, her lips, against the angle beneath his stubbled jaw. "Sometimes I wonder if you might not know me better than anyone."

Zach sat up, gently but swiftly breaking their contact. He flashed a quick smile and dropped a kiss to her cheek. "We need to get moving. We've got a lot of miles to cover again today."

Or maybe they weren't a couple. Because the same feeling she'd had several times over the past twenty-four hours washed over her like the early-morning mist, pebbling her skin with goose bumps. That feeling Zach was keeping her at arm's length. Just like Ben had during the weeks leading up to the wedding.

"Why do you keep doing that?"

"Doing what?" Zach scooted to the edge of the roof and looked down.

"Pulling away from me."

"We can't stay up here forever."

"I'm not talking about the roof."

Zach glanced over his shoulder at her and scrubbed a palm over his unshaven face. "We've been riding a tandem bicycle together for hundreds of miles. I can't pull away from you. It's physically impossible."

"Why won't you let me get close?"

"You want to get close? Come here. We can get real close as we figure out how to climb down from this roof together."

"Just tell me what it is. There's obviously some sort of wall between us. What is it? My looks? My personality? My morning breath?"

"Charlotte, it's way too early for this type of conversation. I'm going to need some sort of energy drink before we start playing your therapy games."

"Well, maybe I'm tired of playing your games. Did you ever think of that?" Charlotte folded her arms, refusing to budge until he gave her some sort of explanation. Before the trip he was all but begging to kiss her. Now that they'd kissed, he acted as if he found the wild hogs more appealing than her. "Am I a bad kisser? Is that it?"

Zach lifted his hands in surrender. "I'm done." He disappeared over the edge. She heard a soft grunt as he landed on the ground. Part of her wished he had weak ankles. Would serve him right to sprain both.

"Are you coming or am I leaving you behind for the hogs?" he called up to her.

Her stomach growled worse than any hog.

"I take that to mean you're coming," Zach said.

Charlotte scooted to the edge of the roof. "We're not finished with this conversation. If there's anything I regret from my broken engagement to your brother, it's that I didn't push harder for answers." She rolled onto her stomach and lowered her legs down until Zach could grab them and guide them to his shoulders.

"If you're so bound and determined to talk, why don't you tell me why you were crying last night?"

She held on to the edge of the roof, her feet on his shoulders like a cheerleader. "I was about to be mauled to death by a pack of wild animals. Forgive me for getting a little emotional."

He shifted his weight, his voice straining a bit from the load on his shoulders. "Nice try, but you were sobbing before the boars even made an appearance."

"No, I wasn't." She grabbed onto his head and clutched a handful of hair for leverage.

"Can you please refrain from scalping me, and yes, you were. I could hear you."

Charlotte remembered clearly why she failed her cheerleading tryouts in high school as she latched one leg beneath his armpit and wrapped the other around his neck.

"What are you doing?" he wheezed.

"Trying to get down."

"Pretty sure this is an illegal wrestling move."

"I don't want to fall."

"We're both going to fall if you suffocate me to death. Why were you crying?"

"If my tears were such a concern, why didn't you ask me about them last night?"

"Because I was too busy trying not to cry over the pigs."

He swung her around his torso as if they were swing dancing, then clutched her against his chest like she was a mischievous toddler.

"Well, this is just awkward," Charlotte said, wiggling to break free.

He squeezed tighter. "Just tell me why you were crying, then I'll let go."

"I'll only tell you why I was crying if you tell me why you've put up this wall between us."

"I haven't put up a wall between us."

"Then I guess I wasn't crying." Charlotte shoved against his chest. He lost his grip on her, then fumbled to retrieve her again as if she were a football. This was ridiculous.

"Oh my goodness, you are seriously not going to let this go." Or let her go. He had wrapped his arms around her from behind, clutching her to his chest again. "Fine. Being up there on that roof last night reminded me of a time my brother and his friend who lived out on a farm tied me up and left me in an empty horse stall. There. Happy?"

He held her for several breaths, not saying a word. Finally, he loosened his grip, his voice quiet but fierce. "Your brother and his friend did what?"

"It wasn't like that. I mean, I let them tie me up. Up until then I could always get loose in a few minutes, like I was Houdini. That time, I don't know, they used smaller ropes. I . . . had a lot more trouble."

"How long did they leave you like that?"

Tears started to burn at the back of Charlotte's eyes. "I don't know. It was a long time ago. It doesn't matter. Eventually I got free." After she'd wet her pants, but she wasn't about to mention that.

"How old were you?"

"I think I've held up my end of the arrangement. It's your turn to start talking."

"How old were you?" he asked again.

She swiped her phone from the ground, then took off at a brisk pace to get away from him. She should have known better than to try and make him talk. He was too much like his brother. Good at asking questions. Even better at avoiding answers.

"How old, Charlotte?"

"Why does it matter?" she said over her shoulder. "Is there a certain age cutoff that would have made it acceptable?"

"No." His footsteps trailed after her. "I just want to know how hard to beat up your brother the next time I see him."

"Which is exactly why I'm not telling you. I think there's been enough black eyes between you and Will throughout the years."

"There's going to be at least one more. Tell me how old."

Charlotte spun around. "Not happening. You don't get to hear me talk about my stuff if you refuse to talk about your stuff."

"My stuff is gone."

"Oh, knock it off. You have stuff. Everybody has stuff."

"No. My stuff. *Our stuff.*" Zach pointed over her shoulder. "It's all gone."

Charlotte whipped around, tripping over a tree root, then finding her footing as Zach rushed past her. "Are you sure?" she yelled, chasing after him.

"Do you see our bike anywhere? Our bags? Our trailer? This can't be happening."

"I'm sure it'll be fine."

"How?" Zach spun in a circle, waving to the vacant camping site. "How is this going to be fine?"

"I don't know, but freaking out isn't going to help." It sure didn't help the night she was tied up in the barn. "Are you sure you left everything here?"

"Am I sure I left our tandem bicycle and trailer crammed full of all our camping gear and belongings next to this tree as opposed to *that* tree?" Zach feigned deep concentration. "Well, gee. Maybe you're right. Maybe it's hiding behind a different tree. One that has a twenty-foot circumference."

"Sarcasm? Is that how we're going to handle this?" she said, tossing his own words back at him.

"You have any other suggestions?"

"Just have a little faith, okay?"

Zach gouged his hands through his hair and stared at her. "What do you think is going to happen if we don't finish this challenge on time? What, you'll just pack up your guitar and find a governess position where you can sing to the von Trapp family children while your mother miraculously recovers? Sure. Sounds great. Can't believe I was ever worried. Let's just laugh our way back home, where we can buy a round of drinks for the entire town who thought we could actually finish this race."

"Are you done now?"

"No." Zach turned and kicked the tree closest to him. "Now I'm done."

"Good. Because I promise you—somehow, some way—this is going to work out. It always does. Did we not just survive a wild hog attack less than twelve hours ago? Trust me. Better yet, trust God."

Zach tipped his head back in a biting laugh. "Trust God. Sure. Because he never disappoints, does he? Look, babe," he said, not giving her a chance to respond, "if you want to host a revival here with the squirrels, go for it. Power to you. Me? I'm going to find a park ranger and figure out how to file a police report. With a little luck, maybe we'll get everything back in time to finish this race so you can keep your job and I can get to California."

Oof. Charlotte hugged her arms around her middle, his words a sucker punch straight to the gut.

He still planned on going to California.

Well, of course he still planned on going to California. What had made her think otherwise? Those kisses they'd shared? Those kisses *she*'d initiated? Those kisses he'd been going out of his way to avoid ever since? "We're never going to be a real couple, are we?"

He held her gaze, his dark eyes filling with something she couldn't quite name. Frustration? Remorse? Pain? He made a fist and tapped it against the rough bark of the tree next to him as he dipped his head. "And there you have it, Charlotte. The wall between us."

39

"Great news," Sophia hollered out the driver's side window as soon as she saw Joshua step onto the front porch. He shielded his eyes from the afternoon sun, squinting at her approach down the driveway. "I was able to get the rest of the week off from work. I told them it was a family emergency. I mean, technically it is. We're getting down to the wire here."

Sophia braked and turned off the car, then raced to the back seat, dragging out her luggage. "I figured it'd be easier for me to just move in for a bit. No point driving back and forth when you need my help here, right? I hope you don't mind I brought along my sister's cat."

She lifted the blue carrier, where a slew of pitiful meows had started the moment she left Charlotte's driveway, and plopped it in the yard. "You won't even know he's here."

Joshua might not, but D'Artagnan certainly did. He raced around the side of the house in full-on Kentucky Derby mode. "Uh-oh." Before

Charlotte could reach the carrier, a gray flash of fur escaped—little sneak must've been chiseling his way out the entire ride over—and darted for the nearest tree.

"D'Artagnan—stop!"

"Patches—no!"

Sophia and Joshua shouted and chased after both animals.

On the plus side, Patches made it up the tree before D'Artagnan caught him. On the downside, Sophia doubted Patches would ever set paws on this earth again so long as D'Artagnan was alive.

"Joshua?" Sophia stared up into the thick branches towering over them while D'Artagnan circled the tree, barking and searching. "Please tell me you've already found the two hundred fifty thousand dollars, so when I inform my sister that I lost her cat, I'll have some hope that maybe, just maybe, she won't kill me on the spot."

She waited for him to say something. "Joshua?" Sophia said a minute later when he still hadn't spoken a word. "I need you to say something encouraging here."

D'Artagnan sank to his stomach in the grass, focus still locked on the tree. But at least he'd stopped barking. Which is why Sophia had no trouble hearing the resignation in Joshua's somber tone.

"I'm starting to wonder if Hopkins promised that money because he figured they wouldn't be able to complete the challenge on time. And honestly, Sophia . . . I'm beginning to hope that too. Because I can't find it. I just can't find it. And I'm starting to lose faith that I ever will."

The branches blurred when Sophia lifted her teary gaze back to the tree. So much for something encouraging.

40

Faith. Zach shook his head at the grinding crunch of the ice machine struggling to do its job in the cheapest hotel they could find near Kosciusko.

Sure, Charlotte. All life's troubles could be solved with a little faith. That might've been a cute philosophy back when they had a solid chance of completing the challenge, but now that they'd lost another entire day of biking—*now that they'd lost their bike*—Zach failed to see how a little faith was going to get them across the finish line in time.

Which is why Zach had done exactly what he said he was going to do and filed a police report. Not that it would help. Officer Earl had seemed more concerned about whether the fish would be biting tomorrow than the case of the missing tandem.

Zach slapped his hand on the side of the grinding ice machine. Maybe Charlotte should add this stupid machine to her list of prayer concerns. An avalanche of ice cubes poured into his bucket the next second.

Without moving, Zach lifted his gaze to the ceiling as if he could see through the floor into her room. Maybe she already had.

It felt weird not being with her. All their time together, starting with Ben's wedding, had bonded her to him in a way he couldn't explain. Almost as if he couldn't imagine going back to their separate lives once this was over.

But they would. They had to. No way could he settle down in Bailey Springs. Bad enough growing up there. No way was he ever going to convince Charlotte to leave it either.

The scent of chlorine hung heavy in the air as he walked past the main lobby. A lanky college-aged guy with an ear full of piercings sat behind the desk. Apparently not a lot of action taking place tonight. He and Charlotte hadn't had any trouble getting two rooms.

Too bad they couldn't afford to stay more than one night. And not just because of their dwindling funds. They were running out of time.

Zach climbed the stairs up to the second floor, where he and Charlotte had rooms across from each other. He hadn't talked to her since dropping off the change of clothes he'd picked up for them at a thrift store close to the police station.

He paused outside her room, tempted to knock. But what would he say? *Sorry I don't see a future between us. But hey, no reason we can't still be friends and make out in mud piles when the situation arises, right?*

Yeah, he didn't think that'd go over too well.

He swiped his room card, the air conditioning chilling his skin as soon as he stepped inside. After adjusting the temperature, he settled on the bed and stared at the ceiling. Something told him he was in for another restless night. This time because Charlotte wasn't at his side.

41

Highway traffic competed with the soft twitter of birds as Charlotte stepped outside the hotel the following morning. The golden sun heated her skin and felt good after being inside the cold air conditioning all night.

Carrying the Styrofoam cup of coffee she'd helped herself to in the lobby, she meandered down a worn path to where a rugged bench sat next to a filmy green pond surrounded by overgrown grass.

For all her talk about faith, she couldn't deny the doubts that had circled in her mind in the dark of night. What if they didn't find their bike? No way they had enough money left to purchase another one. And even if they did, now they'd need to bike at least seventy-two miles a day to have any hope of finishing on time.

She sank to the bench, the thin shorts Zach had found for her at a Salvation Army thrift store providing little protection against the bench's splintered wood, and offered up the same prayer she'd prayed all night long. *God, just . . . please.*

At one point yesterday evening she'd thought about knocking on Zach's door. But what she would say, she didn't know. *Hey, I know we don't have a future, but I'm pretty sure I'm in love with you and could use a giant hug, maybe a marriage proposal, to help me feel better about this whole losing-a-bike situation, perhaps life in general.*

Yeah, she didn't imagine that would have gone over very well.

Heavy footsteps clomped down the path behind her. She turned, squinting against the cheery morning sunlight, to find Zach ambling her way. "Hey," he said, taking a seat next to her, coffee in hand.

"Hey." She scooched over to make room for him, the bench snagging her shorts in the process. "Any word yet?" she asked, gently unlatching the fabric from the bench's jaws.

He shook his head, staring straight ahead at the pond.

She hadn't figured there would be. They drank their coffee, making small talk about how they'd slept and the water pressure in the shower and the choice of vending machine snacks.

"We should probably come up with a plan B, don't you think?" Charlotte said after they'd covered at length the nautical decor of the rooms and the texture of the bath towels.

"Any suggestions on what this plan B should look like?"

"Not really, other than it should probably include a plan C, D, and E."

"I'll keep asking around. See if there's another tandem bicycle we can buy."

"With what money? We barely have enough for food."

Zach slugged back the rest of his coffee. "I don't know, Charlotte. I don't know. What do you want me to do here? I'm trying to fix this. I found us some clothes and a couple of cheap helmets, but Salvation Army wasn't exactly bursting with options." He immediately hung his head and crumpled his coffee cup. "Sorry. I slept awful last night and my coffee hasn't kicked in. I didn't mean to snap at you."

"You didn't snap. And I'm sorry too. I know you're trying to fix this as much as I am."

Zach stood and tossed his empty cup into a trash bin a couple feet from the bench. "What about this?" He motioned his hand back and forth between them. "Us? How do we fix that?"

Was he sure his coffee hadn't kicked in? This seemed like a pretty ambitious conversation to have first thing in the morning. "Zach, I . . . I don't know that there is anything to fix. We knew from the start a long-lasting relationship between us would never work. Why don't we—"

"I love you."

Charlotte held her breath, frozen in place, while Zach seemed to be experiencing the opposite effect from his declaration. He blew out a giant breath, nearly sinking to his knees as he clutched the top of his head and stumbled back several steps. Any further, he'd fall in the pond.

"I can't believe . . ."

"That you said that?" Charlotte gripped the edge of the bench. Splinters dug into her palms.

Zach stared at her, a devastating grin slowly spreading across his rugged face. "No. That it took me so long to say it."

"Are you sure this isn't the canoodling talking? We've literally been together for less than two weeks."

"No, this is me, Zach Bryant talking. And I love you, Charlotte Carter."

If she thought his smile was devastating before, the look of pure wonder radiating from the sparkle of his eyes all the way out to the creased laugh lines would have buckled her knees had she been standing.

"Wow," he said. "I get it now. This is what was missing with Shannon. I see the difference. I do. I love you. And you know what? Now that I've said it, I think I might have to keep saying it. A lot."

"Oh, I wish you wouldn't."

A bit of the light in his eyes flickered with doubt. "You don't love me?"

Charlotte dropped her gaze to her legs. The area below where her bicycle shorts ended had darkened from all the recent sun exposure. She clasped her hands over the severe tan line, wishing she could cover up her feelings as easily.

"Because I think you do," Zach continued, his shoes inching through the dew of the grass, closer and closer to her.

She stared at her hands, clutched together over her thighs, willing herself not to think or feel anything. He didn't mean it. He couldn't mean it. And now wasn't the time anyway. Not when they needed to focus on finishing the challenge.

When he dropped to his knees in front of her, she had no choice but to meet his gaze. "I know we've said there's a wall between us. But if love doesn't knock down walls, what does?"

"It's not that simple."

"So let's make it simple. Do you love me?"

"Zach . . ." She was sitting outside a dumpy hotel in secondhand clothes about to fail the biggest opportunity of her life. This was *not* the glorious moment she envisioned for ever confessing her love to a man.

"Yes or no, Charlotte. Forget about everything else for just one second and answer the question."

Charlotte closed her eyes and tried pressing her lips together, but her heart slipped out a whispered answer before she could stop it. "Of course I do. You think I would've made out with you in the mud if I wasn't crazy in love with you?"

Her eyes opened in time to catch Zach leaning forward, probably to start another make-out session based on the hungry look in his eyes. Charlotte palmed his chest. "But that doesn't fix this. If anything, it makes it worse."

"Why?"

"You know why." She lifted her gaze to a cloudless azure sky that offered no help in return. Which annoyed her. How dare the day act so bright and sunshiny when she faced nothing but troubles this morning, including this much-too-handsome man who had the audacity to fall in love with her.

"Why?" Zach pressed closer.

"We want different things. Different lives. I want to stay close to my family and build a music program in Bailey Springs. Can you honestly tell me that's what you want?"

"I . . ." He blew out a breath. "I want you by my side. That's what I want. That's all I could think about last night. It doesn't feel right thinking about us not being together after all of this."

"Well, I don't see how staying together is possible. Not if you're planning to go off to California once this is done. And you should. Really. I don't want to talk you out of it. The last thing I'd ever want is for you to resent me because I held you back from a great opportunity. I'm just trying to remind you why a real relationship between us isn't possible."

"Not possible isn't good enough. Aren't you the one always spouting off about keeping the faith?"

"Yeah, and weren't you the one scoffing about that faith only yesterday?"

Zach held her gaze a long couple of seconds, his breath fanning her lips, before he leaned back, rubbing his palm up and down his face. "Look. I'm not going to lie. God swiped the rug out from under my feet two years ago when he decided he had more important things to do than stop a driver from falling asleep at the wheel and colliding head-on with my dad."

"Zach, I—"

"No." He reached for her hands, brushing his thumbs across her knuckles. "I'm not looking for pity here. I'm just trying to get you to understand. All my life I've been taught God is good, but if you ask me, cutting a man's life short a few months before retirement is just downright cruel. At least that's how it feels. So I'll admit, I'm still working through some issues with God, okay? But I think we can agree I've been nothing but respectful about your faith."

He paused, squinting one eye shut. "Okay, yesterday I might have walked a fine line when I made that comment about hosting a revival with the squirrels."

Charlotte offered a sad smile. "Zach, I appreciate you being honest with me, but I don't think faith was ever the real barrier between us. It's more like . . . everything else. We're too different. I started to forget that, so you were right to put up a wall between us."

"No, I wasn't."

"See? This is my point. We're never on the same page when it comes to us."

"Then why don't we go back to the page where we love each other?"

"I'd rather go back to the page where our only focus was finishing this challenge on time. Please. Nothing else matters right now except that."

Zach's lips pressed together as he turned his head and wiped a bead of sweat from his brow. The heat of the day was already promising to be a killer. Just like this conversation if he continued to press it. Thankfully he didn't. He rose to his feet and held out a hand, almost like a truce, then tugged her up from the bench. "So back to coming up with a plan B then. Any suggestions?"

"Well," she said, dropping his hand so she could take a step away and hopefully clear her head a bit. "For starters, I think we definitely get back to enforcing the no-kissing clause."

Zach lifted his palms. "Hey, I've been on my best behavior. You were the one who started tackling me with your lips the other night."

"Stop."

"That's what I kept saying, but you just wouldn't listen."

Charlotte playfully punched him in the gut, glad they were somewhat back on familiar ground. "Second thing I think we do is pray for a miracle, because I honestly don't know what else we're going to do."

Before Zach could respond, a shout caught their attention from the parking lot next to the hotel, where a man stood next to a truck, waving his arms at them. "Do you know him?" Charlotte said, shielding her eyes.

Zach frowned. "No. Maybe. Kind of looks like the officer I talked to yesterday."

"You don't think . . ." Hope spurred Charlotte into action. She raced up the hill, waving her arms and shouting back at him. "Please tell me you found it. Oh please, please, please."

"Ta-da." The officer lowered the back of his truck bed and motioned as if he were Vanna White on *Wheel of Fortune* and their tandem bicycle a glorious prize.

"How did you find it?" Charlotte said, jumping up and down like an overexcited contestant.

"Well, that's a funny thing," the officer said, stroking his mustache. "You see, I headed out to the lake to do a little fishing this morning. But instead of going to my usual spot, I thought I'd give another spot a try. Don't know why. I like my usual spot. It's why I usually go there. But this morning, I thought, *No, Earl. Let's shake things up a bit. Let's try a different spot.* Good thing I listened to myself 'cuz soon as I got to the unusual spot, I saw something shining in the thicket. Which isn't usual."

"So you found it," Charlotte cut in, afraid they'd never make it to the finish line on time if she didn't.

"Afraid that's all I found though," Earl said, dragging the bike down from the truck. "No sign of your other belongings."

Zach had meandered up the path and now stood staring quietly at the tandem bike, almost like he couldn't believe it. Charlotte almost couldn't either.

Other than lots of mud splatters, the bike looked okay. No missing chains. No flat tires. Nothing missing but the bicycle horn. "Thank God," Charlotte whispered.

"Glory hallelujah be," Earl added good naturedly, slapping Zach on the back.

Zach rubbed his chin, apparently not ready to add any amens to this revival just yet. "We still don't have our trailer. Our tent. Our clothes. Water bottles. Food."

"That's okay. We only have a couple hundred miles left." Charlotte tried not to think about the words that had just come out of her mouth. *A couple hundred? Only?*

"We still need to eat," Zach pointed out. "We're down to nickels and dimes for the rest of the trip. Enough for a few protein bars, maybe one more packet of butt cream."

Earl snickered. "I don't even want to know what that means," he said, digging into his pocket and pulling out some folded cash. "But here. Take this. It ought to cover some grub."

"Oh, you don't have to do that," Charlotte said with little conviction since her stomach was already growling.

"Nah, take it." Earl shoved the cash into her hand, then spun to rummage through the back of his truck. "Should have a tent in here too. Nothing fancy, mind you. Used it back in my Boy Scout days. Now I mostly just use it to keep guts from mucking up the truck. Ah, here we go." He hauled out a crusty-looking pile of fabric. "Do a little taxidermy work on the side. But hey, better than nothing, right?"

Charlotte forced her lips into a smile and grabbed the stinky armload, quickly handing it off to Zach.

"Oh. Wow. Thanks." Zach tried handing the tent back to Earl. "But I really don't know how we would carry it since we don't have our trailer, so . . ."

A bag smacked Zach in the face.

"Sorry," Earl said with a laugh. "Just got excited I could provide that too. What an unusual morning this is turning out to be. If I discover what happened to the rest of your things, I'll figure out a way to let you know."

Slamming the bed of his truck shut, Earl offered a quick wave. "I better get back to the lake. And this time to my usual spot. Can't pass up a day like this when the fish are sure to be biting." He climbed into his truck, shooting another wave out the window.

Charlotte and Zach watched him drive away, neither saying anything for a minute. "Well," Charlotte said, eventually breaking the silence. "I guess we got our miracle, right?"

"Right." Zach cast a doubtful look first to the mangy tent in his arms, then to Charlotte. "You do realize how many miles we're going to need to bike today."

"Enough miles I'll hopefully be so exhausted I won't care that I'm sleeping in a blood-encrusted tent with nothing but the skunky stench of roadkill guts surrounding me."

Zach shoved the putrid contents into the worn Army-green canvas backpack Earl had also clearly used for decades, then swung the bag over his shoulders, sliding his arms through the straps. "Just making sure we're on the same page," he said with a wink.

42

Around noon they stopped at a sandwich shop connected to a gas station for some much-needed nourishment.

"We're making good time," Charlotte said, unclipping her helmet and lifting the smashed ponytail from the nape of her neck to allow some blessed relief. "The wind must be on our backs."

Or maybe Zach's confession of love had given her more energy than she wanted to admit. Especially when she was only supposed to be thinking about making it to the finish line.

Eighty miles today. Another eighty tomorrow. Then fifty. She could do it. She would do it. She'd save her music program and build a nest egg for her mom's health all in one cross of the finish line.

Then once that was settled, maybe she could figure out what to do about Zach. And his confession of love. And all her spiraling thoughts about wanting to kiss the lips that had offered that confession of love.

She scrunched her eyes shut. So much for not thinking about it.

"Here." Zach tapped her arm and handed her some of the money Earl had given them, thankfully focusing all her thoughts on her ravenous stomach. "Do you mind grabbing the sandwiches this time? I'll wait for you at the picnic bench across the road."

"Sounds good." Charlotte clutched the folded bill to her chest. "And God bless Earl."

"And God bless Earl," Zach echoed back, sounding downright reverent until he added, "I'm gonna take a leak behind one of those bushes so I can keep an eye on the bike. Don't forget the spicy pickles."

"Spicy pickles. Got it."

The air conditioning bathed Charlotte's overheated skin in divine bliss as soon as she stepped inside the gas station. She inhaled the delicious aroma of bread wafting from the connected sandwich shop.

But first, the bathroom.

Charlotte had just flushed the toilet and stepped out of the stall when a young woman with wild curls burst into the restroom, a baby in one arm, a whimpering toddler in the other.

"We're almost there," the young woman said to the little girl in a frantic shout. "Just keep holding it." Her gaze landed on Charlotte. "You mind?"

Before Charlotte could answer, the drooly baby was shoved into her arms. She didn't know who was more alarmed, the infant or herself. "I haven't washed my hands," Charlotte stammered.

"Don't care," the mother said, rushing the toddler into a stall.

But apparently the baby cared. His face instantly puckered up. *Oh no.* Charlotte didn't have much experience with babies, but she knew what was coming.

"Shh shh shh," she said, bouncing up and down at a rapid pace. It didn't help. The baby's high-pitched squeals pierced her ears the next second, bouncing off the walls and stall doors. "It's okay. You're okay. Everything's okay."

The baby obviously disagreed. And so did the toddler, because now her wails were adding to the orchestra of chaos.

Charlotte stepped over to make sure something awful hadn't happened, like the toddler's arms falling off, because she couldn't fathom what would cause such awful screams.

Both arms remained in place, but unfortunately, so did her pants, despite all the mom's efforts to pull them down quickly. A steady stream of urine soaked through them, running down each pant leg. How could such a tiny bladder hold so much fluid?

"It's okay, it's okay," the mom kept yelling over all the weeping and wailing.

If urine-soaked pants was this mom's definition of *okay*, Charlotte shuddered to think what a not-okay moment looked like. The poor lady continued tugging down the sopping pants until she could set the little girl on the toilet, where of course not a single drop of urine dripped into the bowl.

Both toddler and baby remained red-faced and shrieking, with tears dripping down their cheeks. And now—*uh-oh*—Mom had collapsed onto the floor and started sobbing too.

Probably not the time to mention the baby just had a major diaper blowout. Charlotte felt the warmth creeping past her fingers, and a glance in the mirror confirmed her suspicion.

Wow. Was this motherhood?

"Um . . . is there someone I can get to help you?" Charlotte shouted to be heard over the crying. Hopefully this woman wasn't traveling alone. Charlotte didn't have time to handle bodily-fluid crisis situations with complete strangers inside gas station bathrooms. Not today. Not when she and Zach needed to get back on the road as soon as possible.

The woman looked up from the floor, tears dripping down her cheeks. "We're driving to visit my parents. I'm by myself."

Shoot. Well, in that case, of course Charlotte would help. But she needed to help fast. "Did you happen to bring a diaper bag inside with you?" Maybe the poor lady had dropped it in her rush to get to the toilet.

"It's in the car. I think. I don't know. It could be in the trunk. Or maybe I left it on top of the roof after our last stop. Who knows."

"What's your car look like? I'll get it for you." Anything to get away from the ear-piercing noise. Standing two inches away from a tornado siren would be quieter. The woman described her vehicle. Charlotte caught the words *blue* and *stupid*. She could probably figure it out.

She dashed out the door, still carrying the squealing infant covered in a mixture of fluids, and quickly spotted the blue car. With its engine still running. Maybe that's what the lady had meant by the stupid part.

It took a few minutes, but Charlotte found the diaper bag in the trunk as well as a change of clothes for the toddler and an extra package of baby wipes. She turned off the car, locked the door, and spun with the supplies in one hand, the baby in the other, then bumped into Zach.

"What in the world are you doing?"

"Oh, good. Here." She thrust the baby into his hands. "Careful, his back is covered in poo."

He gripped the baby under the armpits. "Who is this?"

"No idea," Charlotte said, using the wipes to clean off her hands. "I always thought I wanted to have kids, but now I'm not so sure."

Zach lifted the baby up and down, making airplane noises. Charlotte couldn't believe how quickly the baby stopped crying. Not only that, started giggling. He tried handing the baby back to Charlotte, but she held up her hands. "No way. My ears are just recovering. That baby is yours until you hand him back to his mother."

"Where's his mom?"

"Having a mental breakdown on the bathroom floor. Can you take the baby and all this stuff in to her? I'll go watch the bike."

"I'm not walking into a woman's restroom with a baby covered in poop."

"Then take him into the men's restroom and change his diaper first."

"I don't know how to change diapers."

"How do you not know how to change diapers? You just made all those airplane noises."

"What does that have to do with changing diapers?"

"Everything. They go hand in hand. You're clearly better suited for this endeavor."

"Aw, well, would you look at this," a raspy voice cut in. A short elderly woman with long gray hair scooted her walker closer, then lifted a hand to play with the baby's fingers. "Aren't you just the cutest thing. And the spitting image of your papa, aren't you? Yes, you are. My my, he looks just like you," she said to Zach.

Zach sent Charlotte a look and it took everything in her not to laugh. A bald man with giant ears joined them. "Well, what do we have here, Margie?"

"Isn't he just the sweetest little guy, Ralph? Look at that handsome face."

Ralph ran a palm over his smooth scalp. "My wife always did have a thing for bald guys. Uh-oh." He pointed to the stain spreading up the baby's onesie. "Looks like this little fella done filled his britches and then some. Oh yeah. He sure did. Oh my, I remember those days."

"How old is he?" Margie asked Charlotte. "He looks about five months. Am I right?"

"Oh, I don't actually—"

"I'm betting she's right," Ralph cut in. "You know why? Her dad used to work down at the carnival. He guessed ages and weights. And he was good, too. Margie takes after him."

She blushed and batted a palm. "Not as good as my father, of course."

"Don't sell yourself short. You knew exactly how much that watermelon at the grocery store weighed last week."

"Yeah, but I was two ounces off on the cantaloupe."

Now Ralph batted his palm in the air. "It was a funny-shaped cantaloupe. Anybody would have had trouble with that one." Ralph tugged on his wife's elbow. "We better let these two young'uns take care of business."

Margie reluctantly unlatched herself from the baby's fingers and gripped her walker. After several singsongy goodbyes to the baby, they disappeared into the sub shop. Soon as the door closed behind them, Zach hit Charlotte with a serious look. "Why do we attract every strange person on this planet like bees to honey?"

Charlotte giggled and pointed at the baby's leaky diaper. "Don't you mean flies to poo?"

"Will you please take this baby back now? I'm not going into a woman's restroom."

"Fine." Charlotte settled the diaper bag on her shoulder and retrieved the infant back into her arms. She was actually a bit surprised the mom hadn't come out to see what the holdup was. "I'll grab the sandwiches once I'm done. We've delayed long enough as it is, so be prepared to eat fast." Zach started to follow her. "What are you doing? You're supposed to be guarding the bike."

"I need to wash my hands first. The bike will be fine."

"It better be. We can't handle any more delays."

They both entered the gas station and headed quicky for the bathrooms. Charlotte pushed open the women's door, ready to apologize for taking so long.

But she didn't have to apologize at all. The mother had disappeared. And there on the toilet, still crying, sat the toddler.

43

Zach had never held a baby this long in all his life. He had to admit, it felt kind of nice—once the diaper situation had been resolved. He lifted the baby above his head, spinning and swerving while making airplane noises. It was the only trick he knew, but so far it seemed to be the only trick he needed. The baby drooled in delight.

Unlike Charlotte, who had been ranting and foaming at the mouth for the past fifteen minutes as she clung to the toddler's hand. "Where would she go? Do you think she was kidnapped? She had to have been, right? She didn't seem like the type of mother to abandon her children. Granted, she was sobbing on a dirty bathroom floor. Maybe she snapped. Do you think she snapped? Oh no, I bet she snapped. We need to alert the authorities."

"We did alert the authorities," Zach reminded her, afraid Charlotte was two seconds away from snapping. "It's going to be okay. They're on their way now."

"You know they're going to have tons of questions for us. I don't even remember what the mother looked like. What if they suspect us? What if they book us? What if we can't post bail? What if we can't finish the race because we've got to flee the country since we're now on America's Most Wanted list?"

Oh, she'd snapped, all right. "Charlotte, look at me. We *are* going to get arrested if you continue acting like a lunatic. Calm down. The police are pulling into the parking lot now. It's all going to be straightened out in no time. We don't have a thousand miles to bike. We have less than eighty. We'll make up those miles in no time. We've got this."

He hoped. Because yeah, this delay could definitely cause problems. Best-case scenario—they'd have to bike a little past dark. Worst-case scenario—everything Charlotte said.

A squad car parked in front of the gas station. Two uniformed officers climbed out, both eyeing Charlotte and Zach with frowns. "We got a call about a missing woman," the first officer said.

"Yes." Charlotte immediately started flailing her arms and babbling worse than the baby. "She was in the bathroom crying when I took the baby, and now she's gone. Just gone."

The first officer glanced at his partner, a woman with a reddish ponytail, who returned his glance with a meaningful look of her own. As if they were already communicating in silent cop-partner talk.

"You took her baby?" the female officer said.

"Yes." Charlotte pointed to the baby in Zach's arms. "He'd pooped all over. The baby, not Zach. So I took him while I went in search of the diaper bag. Well, I found the diaper bag, but then a couple of people started talking to us about cantaloupes, so I didn't get back right away. Then by the time I did get back, she was gone. And that's all I know. Honest."

The officers looked at each other again, then back to Charlotte and Zach. "We'll need you to come downtown and make an official statement," the first officer said.

"But everything I just said was official. I don't know anything else. And we really need to get going. We're doing this challenge, you see. My town's band program is depending on us. My mother's very life is depending on us."

The officers exchanged another look. And suddenly Zach saw Charlotte through their eyes. She sounded stark raving mad. Especially when she started adding words like *canoodle* into her explanation. The sooner they got out of here, the better. "Really, officers," Zach said in his most reasonable voice, "we don't know anything else. And we really do need to be on our way."

He propped the baby over his shoulder and patted his back. The woman officer motioned to the baby. "You're saying you don't know these children?"

"Never seen them before," Zach confirmed. Which might have been believable if the toddler hadn't chosen that moment to barrel into his leg and say a word muffled with tears. A word that sounded an awful lot like—

"Did he just call you Daddy?" the first officer said.

Zach angled a tight smile at Charlotte as the baby babbled contentedly against his shoulder and the toddler hugged his leg. "How about next time you watch the bike and I take care of getting the sandwiches?"

44

Charlotte didn't know how anybody could sit in a prison cell and act so calm. She paced like a caged lion, and Zach acted like he was merely sitting in a lawn chair waiting for a parade. "What if we never get out?" She continued pacing, cracking every knuckle in her hand. "What if we're locked up inside here forever?"

"That's not going to happen. We're innocent."

"So was the Count of Monte Cristo as I recall. Do you really want to have to play dead and escape here in a body bag after wasting away for a couple of decades? I don't."

"Calm down."

"Stop telling me to calm down. I will not calm down. I will anxiety up until I walk out of this cell a free woman."

"First off, we're not even in a cell. We're in the officers' break room. So do as they suggested, pour yourself a cup of coffee, and *calm down*."

Charlotte flopped into a chair next to the square table where Zach sat. "I don't get it. Why aren't you freaking out? Even if they release us this second, we're never going to make it the entire eighty miles today."

"That doesn't mean we won't have time to finish the challenge." He patted the baby on the rear end, looking like the sexiest father alive. And Charlotte so badly wanted to believe him. As if reading her thoughts, he nodded. "Trust me. We're going to win that money."

"I just don't see how."

"Have a little faith," he said with a wink.

Charlotte settled back in her seat. She couldn't tell if he was mocking her or rallying her. Either way, she supposed he was right. They could still get through this. Somehow. Right now it might feel like they were walking smack-dab into a closed door, but with a little faith, they might find that one open window just waiting to be squeezed through in the nick of time before it slammed shut on their fingers.

A woman wearing a long flowery dress and round glasses entered the room. "Hi, gang. I'm the social worker. I got a call about *the situation*," she said, making air quotes. "That's what everybody's calling it. *The situation.* Isn't that cute? The good news is we've located the mother. She was sobbing into a package of Pull-Ups at the Walmart just down the road. The bad news is her daughter still isn't potty trained." She smiled, pausing a beat, then clapped her hands together once. "Right. This is serious, obviously. Thank you for looking after the well-being of the children. We can take over from here."

Zach handed the baby into her outstretched arms. Once the social worker settled the baby in one arm, she reached her hand to the sleepy toddler who'd dozed off on the floor on top of Zach's shoes. "Come with me, honey. Your grandma is waiting for you out front."

"So we're free to go?" Charlotte said, feeling like she'd just received a governor's pardon in the eleventh hour. "Right now?"

The lady turned in the doorway. "Unless you'd like to confess to a crime. Then I'm sure they'd let you stay a while longer. Maybe take a mug shot. Get your fingers printed. Try on an orange suit. It's up to you."

"Orange isn't really our color." Zach grabbed Charlotte's hand and dragged her out of the police station straight to their tandem bicycle. "All right. First thing before anything, we eat lunch."

"How can you say that when we're hours behind schedule?"

"I'm starving. We never ate lunch."

Charlotte was starving too. But right now, she was feeding herself on pure panic and adrenaline. "I thought you wanted to win this challenge."

"I do," Zach said, shoving Charlotte's helmet into her hands. "But I want to live even more."

"Fine. But you better hope we don't have any more setbacks. In fact, *you* better start praying for a miracle."

Zach squeezed her hand. "Oh, trust me, darling. I already have. Which honestly, is a miracle all on its own."

45

"How do you feel about chicken fajitas for supper tonight?" Sophia gripped the doorframe and leaned into the office where Joshua had been holed up for hours.

Joshua stopped drumming his pen against the desk and looked up from a notebook covered in scribbles.

In the intense amount of time Sophia had spent with Joshua, she'd learned most of his habits. One of them was to take a good five seconds to unlatch his thoughts from whatever consumed him prior to her interruption and another five seconds to grab hold of her words after the interruption.

"What are my thoughts on chickens?" he said after the appropriate amount of ten seconds had passed.

Sometimes he didn't make the complete transition. She smiled and repeated herself.

"Oh. Sure." He dropped his gaze back to the notebook. "Any sign of the cat?"

Sophia offered another patient smile as she stepped around a pile of books to get to the desk. "Patches came down from the tree hours ago. I already told you that. Remember? He's tucked away in the bathroom." And D'Artagnan had been standing guard outside the bathroom ever since.

"Oh. Sure."

Sophia gently placed her palm on top of the notebook. "Joshua." She waited until he looked up at her. "I hate to say this, but if it's not here, then it's not here. There's nothing we can do."

He removed his glasses and massaged the bridge of his nose while he sank back in the chair. Dust motes danced above the desk in the last slice of daylight sneaking through the windows. "I just feel like I've got to be missing something. Hopkins wasn't a liar. Eccentric, sure. Full of riddles, always. But he wasn't a liar. If he told that nurse I'd find everything I need at home, then everything I need—including the challenge money—should be here at the house."

Sophia shoved some old newspapers aside so she could perch on the desk. "I don't think I've asked yet. How did you even know Hopkins? I sort of assumed nobody knew him. Not really. I mean, until his obituary came out, I'm pretty sure nobody around here knew he used to be a major-league baseball pitcher at one time."

Stretching his arms over his head, Joshua straightened and offered the first glimpse of a smile she'd seen all day. "Literally, one time. An injury ended his career his very first game. Also ended his marriage. His wife thought she was marrying the next Greg Maddux, then jumped ship as soon as she realized he was nothing but an out of work regular Joe."

"That'd probably mean a lot more to me if I knew who Greg Maddux was."

"Oh, Sophia." Joshua clutched his chest. "You hurt my heart. Greg

Maddux is one of the greatest baseball pitchers of all time. You should know this. Everybody should know this."

"Did Hopkins know this?" Sophia asked, hoping to get back to the main focus here.

"No, he didn't know this. He swore Pedro Martinez could outthrow Maddux any day. We spent a lot of late nights arguing the issue."

Sophia bounced her heels against the bottom drawer of the desk, waiting for him to elaborate. Then stopped banging her heels against the desk when she realized it was kind of annoying. "How did you and Hopkins meet?"

"We met a few summers ago at a church camp in Wisconsin. One of my old buddies from high school directs it every summer and is always desperate for volunteers. So I offered to help out at one of the sessions. Well, Hopkins had volunteered too. Knew the groundskeeper or something. Anyway, we got to talking that first night after all the campers had gone to bed. And, I don't know. We just connected. You know how sometimes you just feel like you *get* a person even though you don't really know all their details?"

Sophia met Joshua's gaze as her stomach did a pleasant little flip that made her want to start swinging her heels again. Yeah, she might know the feeling.

"Well, that's how it was for Hopkins and me. We spent a lot of late nights talking those two weeks. I mean sure, we talked about our lives. I told him all about how I wanted to go to seminary and how my dad convinced me to stay back and work at his furniture store instead. Hopkins told me all about his marriage. His divorce. How he eventually struck it rich later and ended up here in Illinois. But mostly," he said with one of his cute smiles, "we talked about baseball."

Joshua began drumming his pen on the desk as he stared out the window. "One of his dreams was to build a baseball diamond just like in that movie *Field of Dreams*. I actually came across a design he sketched of it somewhere here. Not sure why he never got around to doing it. He certainly had the money."

His attention returned to the desk. "Which is why I keep thinking the challenge money's got to be here. I know he had the funds. I just don't know what he did with the funds."

He adjusted his glasses and reached for the pile of manila folders on the desk. "Maybe I should—"

"Oh no you don't." Sophia swooped up the stack and marched for the hallway before he could touch them. "I'm not dragging you across the floor and spoon-feeding you back to health because you've gone catatonic from staring at a bunch of papers again. At least eat supper first."

She dumped the folders onto a chair in the living room, then grabbed the gramophone she'd spotted the night Joshua had been comatose. She knew it worked, because she'd listened her way through three records that night while waiting for him to revive.

"As my grandmother always used to say, sometimes when life gets tough, the best thing you can do is eat, not think, and—" she twirled into the kitchen with the gramophone in her arms—"dance."

Joshua's lips twitched with tired amusement as he reached for a water glass from the cupboard. "I'm with your grandmother on two of those suggestions. You gonna answer that?" He motioned to the kitchen table where her phone had started to ring.

"Probably just a spam call." Before Sophia could set down the gramophone, Joshua picked up her phone. She snatched it from his hand, but not quick enough to keep him from seeing her screen notification.

"It's your dad. Aren't you going to talk to him?" Joshua said when she immediately silenced the phone and shoved it into her back pocket.

"I will. Later. After dinner. But first a little music." Before Joshua could question her further, she started up the gramophone. Not giving him the option, Sophia grabbed his hands. "Ready to dance?"

"No. Never."

"I'll take that as a yes." She began forcing him into some sort of cha-cha. It seemed appropriate for whatever brassy Latin-sounding song was blaring from the speaker. "See, isn't this helping?"

"Helping what?"

"Helping us to not think about things." Or at least helping Sophia to not think about things. Like her parents. Or Joshua leaving soon to get back to his boring furniture job. Or Charlotte leaving simply to find a job if they didn't locate the money.

Nope. Sophia didn't want to think about anything. Except this moment. When she'd never witnessed worse dancing in all her life. Sophia couldn't stop laughing. "You're terrible."

"I tried telling you." But she noticed he couldn't stop smiling. And wow, did she like that smile. Wow, did she like him.

Somewhere in their dancing, they'd transitioned from the cha-cha to something that resembled ballroom dancing, which had them colliding into the kitchen counter, then the refrigerator.

"Maybe we should take this outside," Joshua said, nearly spinning her into the stove.

"Too bad Hopkins never got around to making that baseball diamond," Sophia said with a giggle when a kitchen chair toppled over. "We'd have a little more space. You could twirl me around home plate." She gripped Joshua's shoulders and stopped dancing.

"What? What's wrong? Did I step on your foot?" Joshua's hands slid to her waist, holding her with just the right amount of gentleness and firmness—just like the first day they met. And wow, did she really like his hands too. But now wasn't the time to think about that.

"Joshua." She shook his shoulders. "Did you hear what I said? Home plate."

"Yeah. What about it?"

"You said you saw a sketch for a baseball field, right? Well, what if Hopkins did start working on it? What if the money's not in the house? What if—"

"You'll find everything you need at home." He turned his head toward the window above the kitchen sink where twilight bathed the tall trees and rock fence in shadows. His breath stirred up the strands of hair that had come loose next to her ear while they danced. "You really think he could've meant out there?"

"Well, he's certainly buried treasure before, hasn't he? And it sounds like he loved baseball."

"He adored baseball," Joshua mumbled, then met her eyes with a new spark in his own. "Okay. I'll find that sketch again. It's worth a shot. Maybe tomorrow we'll find everything we need at home after all."

"I have a good feeling we will." Because she really didn't want to think about what her life would look like if they didn't.

46

Late the next evening, as the sun disappeared behind a row of towering conifer trees, Zach steered their tandem into one of the campground sites at Natchez State Park.

Unlike any of their previous stops, this campground was packed. RVs filled every lot, campers yacking in lawn chairs around their coolers and grills, lanterns strung up to take over where the sun was about to leave off.

"You care where we stay?" Zach asked over his shoulder, not that they had too many options. He spotted an area big enough to pitch their pathetic excuse of a tent next to a couple of Porta-Potties.

Charlotte mumbled something back. Something along the lines of being willing to sleep inside the Porta-Potties at this point. Poor girl. She had to be exhausted. Zach knew he was.

After the whole gas-station-missing-mother fiasco yesterday, they'd ended up biking their tails off to reach Jackson, Mississippi. But once they got there, Zach just didn't have the heart to make Charlotte sleep in that stinky tent. So thanks to the cash from Earl, they scraped together enough to afford a sketchy motel room that would've made the "snake-infested" picnic benches from their first night appear glamorous in Charlotte's eyes—if she'd kept them open longer than what it took to reach the bed and crash.

Today, needing to make up some ground, they'd left at the first glimmer of dawn and managed ninety miles, despite the ruthless heat index. Unfortunately, staying nourished and hydrated throughout that ruthless heat index had required using the rest of Earl's money. Which meant they were stuck with the stinky tent tonight.

But that wasn't what concerned Zach. What concerned Zach was how they were going to survive their last day tomorrow on a couple of bananas and granola bars—about all they'd have left after their supper tonight.

His stomach growled, Charlotte's answered back. They shared a weary smile.

"Hey, y'all," a woman's voice reached out to them.

Zach turned to see a plump woman waving her arms from across the paved road that circled the camping area. She cupped her hands around her mouth. "Don't mean to attack you as soon as you land, but we've got plenty of leftovers if you're hungry. You're welcome to join us." She waved to a picnic table parked next to her RV where a group of people were sprawled out, some sitting in lawn chairs, a few playing frisbee. "We're just dying to know where you've been and where you're going."

Charlotte's smile perked up as she glanced at Zach. She didn't even have to say it. An answer to prayer. And not just Charlotte's. Somewhere these past five hundred miles, Zach had started uttering quite a few himself.

"Thank you," Charlotte called back. "We'd be glad to join you."

"Wonderful," the woman replied with a friendly southern drawl. "My name's Faye. Head over whenever. No rush."

"You sure this is a good idea?" Zach pulled their crusty tent out of his backpack and flopped it onto the ground, giving Charlotte a wink. "They could be a bunch of crazies just waiting to slit our throats."

"I see a cooler. I see a grill. I see Tupperware containers. I don't care if they eat me for dinner afterward, so long as they feed me whatever I'm smelling first."

The delicious scent of barbecued meat and tangy spices wafted in their direction, and Zach's stomach agreed with Charlotte. "Look at that. We're on the same page again."

As soon as they'd finished cleaning up as best they could, Zach and Charlotte crossed the narrow paved road that circled the campground to join Faye and her family. Before they even made it through introductions, they were directed to a picnic table where two giant paper plates filled with ribs, baked beans, and coleslaw were shoved in front of their faces.

"Here's some chips."

"Don't forget the potato salad."

"Care for any watermelon?"

"Hope you like lemonade."

So this was what heaven tasted like. Zach groaned with gratitude while Charlotte's eyes leaked tears.

"Oh my." Faye patted Charlotte's shoulder. "You okay, honey?"

Charlotte shoveled in another bite. "These are the most glorious beans I've ever tasted."

Faye laughed. "Well, eat up. We've got plenty. And if you leave any room, we'll fill it with peach cobbler. Unless you'd rather have s'mores. That's what the kids like."

Zach gobbled down two more platefuls. Enough to replenish his energy from today and hopefully fuel it enough for tomorrow. All he could keep muttering between every bite was, "Thank you, thank you, thank you."

Faye peppered Charlotte with questions once she started slowing down after her second plate. Charlotte filled Faye in on the challenge, giving her the CliffsNotes version for why they were competing, namely her music program.

"A music teacher," Faye said. "How wonderful. What do you play?"

"I know enough to get students started on most any instrument, but my main ones are piano and guitar."

"Oh, you should play something for us." Faye motioned to one of the men gathered at a card table beneath the awning of their RV. "Mick, grab your guitar. Oh wait." Faye folded her hands together in apology. "Forgive me, you two must be exhausted. Sometimes I get carried away."

"It's okay," Charlotte said, cleaning her hands with a wet wipe. "It's the least I can do after this wonderful meal, which I'm pretty certain brought us back from the brink of death. Right, Zach?" She bumped her shoulder playfully against his.

He shoved another spoonful of potato salad into his mouth, nodding his head vigorously.

Faye grabbed the guitar from Mick with a laugh. "You two are so cute."

Zach winked at Charlotte, and she gave him another flirty shoulder bump. At least he thought it was flirty. With a full stomach, this whole night had suddenly become flirty and magical and full of twinkle stars.

"Any requests?" Charlotte asked as she moved to the top of the picnic table and settled the guitar over her knees.

"Surprise us," Faye said. "Or I know. Do you two have a special song?"

Without looking at Zach, Charlotte's lips lifted in a soft smile in the glow of the campfire. "We do, actually. I've never played it on the guitar, but we'll see how it goes."

Wiping his mouth clean, Zach handed his empty plate to Faye with a grateful nod then rested his elbows on the table as the beginning strains to a slow song floated into the night.

It took him a moment to recognize it. The moment he did, he

couldn't stop the dopiest grin from taking over his entire face. Faye smiled back at him, obviously taking note this was a special song indeed.

"The Nearness of You." That little rascal.

Faye palmed her heart, swaying to Charlotte's melodic voice. Faye's son wrapped his arms around his wife from behind her, resting his chin on her shoulder, while one of Faye's daughters swayed with her toddler son in her arms. The four men beneath the awning paused in their game of cards, some propping their cheeks on one hand, others leaning back into their chairs with a smile. All while a posse of children licked gooey marshmallows off their fingers with giggles and chocolate-smeared lips.

And Zach had never been more content to be a part of something in all his life. Because Charlotte was part of it too.

Once the final notes of the song faded into silence, Charlotte paused a beat, then lifted her shoulders into a shrug. "Sorry. That wasn't really much of a campfire song, was it?"

"It was perfect," Faye said. "Just perfect. It certainly earned you dessert. Ready for some cobbler?"

Charlotte returned the guitar to Mick. "Absolutely."

After they ate their fill of cobbler, Charlotte looked like she was about to fall asleep face-first in her empty plate. Zach reached for her hand. "We should call it a night."

"Goodness, you two must be exhausted," Faye said. "How far did you say you still had to go?"

"Just fifty miles," Charlotte said, keeping hold of Zach's hand.

"Just fifty miles." Faye laughed. "Did you hear that, Mick? *Just* fifty miles. Pretty sure five miles would kill us. Well, best of luck tomorrow. I'm sure you'll do fine. What an accomplishment. And what a fun story to tell your future kids someday. I hope you've been taking plenty of pictures."

"Oh. Well . . ." Charlotte stumbled to find words, and Zach wasn't sure if it was because of the pictures comment or the mention of future kids. "We've, uh—"

"Had issues with our phones," Zach finished for her. "You know, keeping them charged."

"Oh no. Well, that's no good." Faye reached toward her husband. "Here, Mick. Hand me your phone. You've got to have at least one photo. I mean, you know what they say. If you don't post it on social media, did it even happen?" She winked and took Mick's phone. "I'll get your number and text it to you later. Now scooch together and look cute."

Charlotte dropped Zach's hand and inched closer to him.

Faye frowned at her phone, then frowned at them. "I said look cute, not like you're recreating the American Gothic pose. I mean, at least look like you like each other," she added with a good-natured laugh.

"Better just lay one on her, Jack," Mick called out. "That's what Faye's after."

"It's Zach," Faye said over her shoulder.

"Well, Zach can kiss her too. Just nobody tell Jack," Mick said, elbowing the man next to him. They all started laughing.

"Oh hush," Faye said, twisting to scold the men before facing Charlotte and Zach again. "Sorry. Getting carried away again. You don't have to kiss—though that would make an awful sweet picture," she murmured from the side of her mouth as she lifted the phone again.

Zach couldn't agree more. Too bad they'd gone back to the no-kissing clause.

"Zach," Charlotte whispered, probably wanting to remind him. He'd no sooner turned his head than her lips were on his.

Charlotte certainly had a hard time following her own rules, didn't she?

"Oh," he heard Faye say. "There we go. Hold on. Let me get back to the camera. Where is it? Keep kissing. Mick—"

Zach slid his hands around Charlotte's waist, enjoying the soft press of her lips, the soft press of *everything* molded against him. Part of him hoped it took Faye the rest of the night to find the camera button again.

"What happened?" he heard Faye muttering. "Oh shoot. Mick, what's your code?"

Charlotte's lips smiled against his, and he couldn't stop from smiling back. Which made it kind of hard to keep kissing.

"Oh, now why'd it just take a picture of me?"

And it was definitely hard to keep kissing once they both started laughing.

47

The next morning after their feast straight from heaven, Zach and Charlotte pedaled away from the campsite before any of the other campers had awakened. A faint glow of light bathed the sky as they reached the main trail. Other than taking care of bathroom necessities, eating a quick breakfast, and making sure their water bottles were filled, they hadn't wasted any time getting started.

Zach wondered if Charlotte's desire to get up and get moving partly stemmed from not wanting to face their newest and biggest fans again. Fans who might ask for another kiss.

He smiled despite the fatigue of a restless night. He had a feeling replaying that kiss in his mind would fuel him better than the banana and protein bar they'd split for breakfast this morning. Though if he had to guess, her thoughts were more consumed with completing the challenge today.

He shot a quick glance at Charlotte over his shoulder. "You okay?"

"Yeah. Why?"

"You're being awful quiet. Thought maybe something was on your mind."

"No. Why? Something on your mind?"

He shrugged. "Nothing we need to talk about right now while you're grumpy."

"I'm not grumpy. I'm just . . ."

"What?"

"Hungry. I want pancakes."

"Well, why didn't you say something? Faye offered to make us some if we were willing to stick around."

"We don't have time to stick around. Not today. We can't afford any more distractions."

"Hmm . . . by distractions, do you mean photo opportunities?"

She smacked his back. "Stop stirring up trouble."

"No trouble here. In fact, I'm the one trying to stick to the ground rules we established."

"Can we not talk about ground rules or anything until I've had a chance to wake up a little more? Like maybe in fifty miles after we cross the finish line?"

"Sure." Zach gave it a good minute before he angled his head her direction. "I just thought we'd agreed no more kissing." Zach noticed Charlotte pedaled harder whenever she was annoyed. If he kept bugging her, they'd have fifty miles under their belt by noon.

"Don't act like that was my fault."

"I'm not placing any blame. I'm just saying I'd appreciate it if you'd learn to keep your hands and lips to yourself." She smacked him harder. "You're already not doing a very good job."

"You kissed me back."

"I was being polite. We were guests. Somebody had to show some manners. I guess I should just be relieved you didn't try breaking the no-nudity clause again." Cold water washed down his neck and back. "And now you're definitely breaking the no-wasting-resources clause."

"You are in some mood today."

"Must have been that kiss."

He didn't have to turn around to know she was trying not to smile.

Maybe he'd been wrong. Maybe she pedaled hardest when she was happy.

He just wished he felt nearly as happy as she did to be approaching the end of their time together.

The afternoon sun beat down on Sophia's head as she stared at the blisters on her hands. The dirt covering her clothes. The muddy sweat on her arms. "Are you sure you're looking at that sketch right?"

Joshua held the paper in one hand as he lifted his other arm toward the rock wall. "I don't know how else to look at it. Right field should be somewhere in that direction. Which means home plate should be somewhere around here."

Those words would instill a lot more confidence if they weren't the same words he'd been uttering ever since they loaded a cooler and shovels into the back of an old truck to begin their search several hours ago.

Sophia glanced around Hopkins's property. She hadn't seen this many holes since digging up her parents' backyard in search of one of Hopkins's other promised treasures years ago. In a weird way, it felt like things were coming full circle for her. Lots of holes, zero treasure.

"Is there any place we haven't looked yet that would make sense for home plate?" So far they'd dug up the entire garden, the perimeter of the gazebo, and one giant circumference around a funny-shaped tree—that last one at Sophia's insistence. But so far the only treasure they'd discovered was soil and worms.

"Maybe that's the problem," Joshua said, folding the sketch and shoving it into his back pocket. "We're assuming Hopkins would have chosen a place for home plate that makes sense. Knowing him, left field is right field. Or the dugout is the bleachers. Or—" He stopped waving his arms around like a crazy orchestra conductor and froze. "Is it me, or does that one rock look out of place?"

Sophia twisted to follow his gaze. "Yeah. Remember, I pointed that one out the first day I was here. It looks bigger and darker and all . . . pentagony-ish." She gasped. "Do you see what I'm seeing? It looks like home plate. Did we find it?"

"Maybe," Joshua said, digging the map back out of his pocket. "Okay. Yeah. I think I'm starting to see it. Maybe that wall wasn't supposed to be outfield. Maybe—"

She couldn't stick around for more maybes. She had to know.

Sophia sprinted, reaching the stone wall several steps before Joshua did. She dropped to her knees, struggling to move the giant stone on her own. Thankfully with Joshua's hands next to hers, they shoved it aside easily. And both saw it at the same time.

The treasure.

Or at least . . . something. A letter, from the looks of it. Sitting inside an airtight ziplock bag. *Oh please be the treasure.* "Here," Sophia said, shoving it into his hands. "You read it. I'm too nervous."

She jumped to her feet and began pacing. "Well?" she said after he'd had enough time to memorize the letter, let alone read it. "What does it say? Does it explain how to get the money or what?"

"It certainly explains things." Joshua held out the letter without saying another word. Sophia finally gave in. She snatched the letter from his hand and began reading.

Then she slowly sank to the ground once the words started to penetrate.

> *I know you'll be disappointed, perhaps devastated, when I tell you I have no earthly riches to give you for completing the bicycle challenge. But I promise I wasn't lying when I said you'd receive a prize of great value should you complete it.*
>
> *It's a prize I myself never received. A prize I would have treasured more than a lengthy baseball career or any amount of money. And that is the prize of a long and successful marriage.*
>
> *Funny the things you stew over when you know you're reaching the end of your life. Me, I couldn't stop stewing over a challenge that might help a couple land at a better place than my ex-wife and I did. A challenge that offered a taste of "for better, for worse, for richer, for poorer" before making those vows.*
>
> *I imagine biking together five hundred miles offered a sampling of for better or worse. And now that you know there isn't any money, perhaps you have an inkling of the for richer or poorer.*

Sophia had read enough. She crumpled the paper, not sure whether she wanted to punch someone or . . . cry.

Probably cry. Because thing was, Zach and Charlotte were never a couple. Not really. So how could she get mad over the unfairness of it all when every one of them had been stretching the rules from the start?

Well, every one of them except Joshua. Sweet, cute Joshua, who'd worked so hard to help. Sweet, cute Joshua who would no longer have a reason to stay.

Ignoring the building pressure behind her eyes, Sophia marched back to where their digging supplies were sprawled next to the truck and hurled the wadded paper into the truck bed.

D'Artagnan panted from the shade of a tree. Joshua picked up one of the shovels and jammed the tip into the ground. "I'm sorry," he said.

"You have nothing to be sorry for."

"I feel like I should have figured this out sooner. Especially now when I remember how many times he mentioned wishing he and his wife had been tested more before they got married. I should have seen this coming." Joshua pushed away from the shovel. After handing her a water bottle, he opened another one to pour into an empty Cool Whip container for D'Artagnan.

When Joshua plopped to the ground, resting his back against the tree, Sophia joined him. After a minute or so of silence, she rested her head against his shoulder. After another minute, she worked up the courage to ask the question she didn't want to hear the answer to. "So what will you do now?"

"Hmm?" He'd lightly dropped his head against hers before lifting it again.

"Your job? You don't like it."

He straightened further away from her. "I never said I didn't like my job."

"Yes, you did. You basically said your dad pressured you into it when you wanted to be a preacher or something. Plus, the night I dragged you across the floor, you said selling furniture was boring and you hated it." He may have been delirious with exhaustion, but he'd said it.

He stood and swiped the dirt from his hands. D'Artagnan, having apparently revived from lapping his water bowl dry, trotted over to press against Joshua's legs for affection. Which Joshua obliged. "Okay, so maybe I don't love my career. But it doesn't change the fact it's my job. I have to get back to Wisconsin."

"You could stay."

"Sophia . . ." She knew by his tone he was trying not to make his next words sting. "I've wasted too much time here as it is."

For not wanting his words to sting, they sure packed a wallop. "Why can't you do what you want?"

"It's not as simple as that."

"Sure it is." She stood, petting D'Artagnan so she had something to do with her hands other than grab onto Joshua and beg him to stay. "Go back to school. Begin a new chapter. Do something you enjoy."

He grabbed his hair, working it into a poorly shaped mohawk as he avoided her gaze. "I have commitments. You wouldn't understand."

"What's that supposed to mean? I'm not a child, you know." All right. Maybe she was acting like one at the moment.

Joshua hefted the cooler next to his shovel. "All I'm saying is eventually you have to realize not all of life's troubles can be solved with eating and dancing. Sometimes you have to . . . well, get back to work. Whether you want to or not."

"And sometimes you just have to walk away because it never mattered all that much to you in the first place. Sure, I get it."

"Sophia, c'mon." Joshua started to reach for her when her phone began ringing next to the cooler in the truck bed. Before she could tell him to ignore it, he grabbed the phone and held it out to her. "It's your dad again."

She took a step back as if he were trying to hand her a snake. "I'll call him back later."

Joshua stared at her, concern etched in his eyes. "I feel like he's been calling you a lot."

"Well, in case you haven't noticed, I've been kind of busy trying to save my sister's future." She jammed the tip of her shovel into the ground, not even sure why. Their little treasure hunt was over.

Her phone dinged with a text. "He sent you a message. Says it's important. I really think you should call him."

"Just set it back in the truck." She shouldn't have even brought it out here. "I'll call him as soon as I finish."

"Finish what? There's no money, Sophia."

"I know. You don't have to keep telling me." The phone started ringing again. With a groan, Sophia yanked her shovel out of the ground in search of a different spot. Somewhere further away from that evil phone.

"Hello?" she heard Joshua say.

Sophia whipped around. He did *not* just answer her phone.

"Hi, Mr. Carter, my name is Joshua. I'm a friend of Sophia's." Oh my word, he just answered her phone. "Yeah, she's okay. She's here with me now. Just a second."

He held out the phone. Sophia backed away with her palms raised. He took a step closer. She backed away further. Joshua shot her a confused look, then pressed the phone back to his ear. "Um, sorry. She's . . . No, she's safe. I promise she's okay."

Joshua locked gazes with Sophia as he continued to explain to her father who he was and what he was doing with Sophia's phone and why Sophia had been out of touch lately. Then he listened. For several minutes he listened, never taking his eyes off Sophia.

A trickle of sweat slid down her back. The sun beat on her hair. She should have worn a hat. Should have put on sunscreen. Should have left her phone locked up in a vault inside a bank.

Joshua's eyes softened as he continued to listen, adding in the occasional "I see" and "I understand" to whatever her father was telling him. What was her father telling him?

"Yes, sir," Joshua said, then cleared a huskiness out of his throat. "I'll be sure to tell her. And I'm very sorry."

No. Sophia didn't want to hear whatever made Joshua sorry. Not when her heart was already pounding. Her hands shaking. Her vision blurring.

Joshua slid her phone into his back pocket. He opened his mouth to say something, but she didn't need to hear what he had to say.

She already knew. Her parents were never having marital issues. They were never getting a divorce. No. No matter how hard she had tried to distract herself and not think, all along she had known.

Her mother was dying.

49

Charlotte couldn't believe it. The finish line was within sight. Well, maybe not within sight. She couldn't actually see anything other than some trees surrounding the rest area where they'd stopped to refill their water bottles.

But after biking nearly five hundred miles over the past week, less than ten miles felt within sight.

She arched her back with a giant stretch. First thing she planned to do once she made it home was get a massage. Her fingers snagged on her tangled hair. Okay, maybe a long bubble bath first, then a massage.

Birds twittered in the trees and a heavenly glow of sunlight filtered through the branches, making everything feel glorious. Because they had done it. Finished the race.

Okay, yes. That whole ten-mile issue. But aside from that, they had done it. Finished the race.

Charlotte glanced at the men's restroom. Zach was sure taking his sweet time. He had to be as anxious to cross the finish line as she was. Though what he planned to do after they crossed, Charlotte had no idea. But she doubted his plans had anything to do with a massage or a bubble bath. And she was starting to doubt his plans had anything to do with her.

So far today, once he'd finished teasing her about that kiss, he'd hardly strung more than three sentences together, let alone spouted the *L* word again.

Granted, she hadn't done a lot of talking either. Hard to carry on a conversation when you feel like a major league pitcher in the ninth inning of a no-hitter, not wanting to jinx it.

Because so far everything today had gone perfectly. The weather. The low traffic. Faye sneaking a card with fifty bucks into their bag as an "early wedding gift," which allowed them to fill up on those pancakes Charlotte had been craving for breakfast. And now the fact they were only ten miles from the finish.

Ten miles. Charlotte reached toward the sky in another long stretch, imagining another tower of pancakes waiting for her at the end. Why not?

She'd saved the town's music program. Saved her job. Her mom. And to think she'd done it all by spending a ridiculous amount of time outdoors. Crazy.

Even crazier—this budding hope that maybe she and Zach could figure out a way to make their relationship work. Maybe with his half of the two hundred fifty thousand dollars, he'd consider staying in Illinois with her. Anything was possible on a glorious day like today.

"Zach?" Charlotte called out. If he took any longer, she'd be due to use the restroom again. Maybe she could pop a squat behind one of those bushes just to add on to her impressive list of accomplishments. Though making it through the trip without resorting to those means probably deserved more recognition. At the very least an extra pancake.

Okay, since Zach was taking forever, she would use the bathroom one more time. Sure it reeked of urine and was overrun with spiders, but who cared on a glorious day like today?

She started into the restroom, then backtracked for the bicycle. Losing the bike again at this point would *not* be glorious.

After taking care of business, she returned to find Zach waiting for her out front.

Dark shadows hung beneath his eyes when he looked at her with a sigh of relief. "I know women don't like to go to the bathroom alone, but did you really have to take the bike with you?"

"I didn't want it to get stolen again. We're too close. If anything stops us now, I'll die. Literally drop to the ground dead. Not exaggerating. And by the way, you took forever. Everything okay?"

Zach ran a hand over his disheveled hair, then his bearded face, looking rather dead himself as he nodded.

"You ready then?" Charlotte asked.

He nodded again as he reached for the stinky backpack containing the stinky tent. "I'm ready. You ready? Got everything?"

Charlotte made a show of patting herself down. "Let's see, got my feet, my knees." She flapped her elbows. "Arms are attached, that's good. Yep, think I've got everything."

"You're really hilarious this afternoon."

"Well, that's 'cuz I made sure to pack my sense of humor first thing." She patted the back of her shorts as if it had a pocket.

Swinging the bag around his back and sliding his arms through the straps, he looked at her with a blend of annoyance and affection. Man, she loved that look. She pointed to the bike, needing to keep her focus on these last ten miles. Once they crossed the finish line, she'd dwell on that look and what to do about it. "Shall we?"

"After you."

She settled onto the back seat and clipped her helmet in place as Zach got situated on his seat.

"Actually . . ." He slid the bag off his back and tossed it onto the sidewalk in front of the restrooms. "I don't think we need that anymore. But maybe the next person who comes along will."

"Wow," Charlotte said as they began pedaling. "We're finishing this challenge with nothing but the clothes on our backs, aren't we? I can't believe it."

"What? You, not believe? Where's your faith?" Zach said with mock astonishment.

Charlotte playfully smacked him on the back. "Don't give me a hard time or I might just stop pedaling."

"And that would be different . . . how?"

She smacked him harder, and he turned his head enough for her to catch his smirk beneath his grizzled scruff.

Glorious. Everything, glorious.

50

Horrible. Everything, horrible. Two miles was all that separated them from the finish.

Zach could feel Charlotte urging the bicycle faster, probably wondering why they weren't clipping along. The roads were flat. The weather perfect. Not an ill wind blowing anywhere. They should be able to cover these two miles in a snap.

But he just couldn't bring himself to speed up.

"Everything okay?" Charlotte asked for the dozenth time after they had plodded another mile slower than an elderly snail with a walker.

He lifted a shoulder, shaking his head noncommittally. "Right knee. It bothers me sometimes." This wasn't one of those times, but Charlotte didn't ask for details.

"Oh. Well, we can take another break, I guess. I mean, I know we're both anxious to finish, but we don't have to kill ourselves to get there."

Anxious to finish. Yeah, that was the thing. Zach wasn't anxious to finish. He was the exact opposite of anxious to finish. He was . . . relaxed to finish? That didn't sound right either. All he knew was for the first time in his life, he wanted to stay put. Stick around. Place roots. With Charlotte.

But what would that look like? How was he supposed to place roots and make a life with her if he didn't know how to make a living in Bailey Springs? Illinois wasn't exactly booming with employment opportunities for outdoor travel guides. Would she ever consider making a life with him somewhere else? Like Northern California?

Because the more he thought about it, the more he knew he couldn't turn down that job. It was too perfect. Well, too perfect except for one thing. It didn't include Charlotte.

He'd lost count of how many times he'd opened his mouth earlier, trying to find the right words to ask her to come with him. Then closed his mouth when the right words never came. Because what was he supposed to say?

Hey, do you mind leaving behind your music program? Your dream? Your family—your sick mom? For me?

No way could he do that. But the thought of leaving without her . . .

No way could he do that either, he thought with a groan.

"You okay up there?" Charlotte asked.

"You know what?" Zach cleared the tightness out of his throat. "A break might be good. Sorry. I know we're almost there, but my knee's acting out of sorts." And by *knee*, he meant his brain. His heart.

"No problem. We can pull over here if you want."

He bit back another groan. What was he doing? Being stupid, obviously. Dragging this out wasn't fair to Charlotte. They needed to cross the finish line. He owed her that much. He'd figure out what to say after they reached the end. "Actually, I'm okay. Let's keep going."

"You sure?"

"It's only two miles. Let's just get there."

And after two miles, they did.

They took the exit, following a short road that led them into Jackson, Louisiana. They cruised to a stop at the first gas station parking lot they saw. Then they both climbed off the bike. Stood there. And stared at each other.

The scent of gasoline and fast food permeated the air. A man in a sleeveless shirt walked past, side-eying their bike on his way into the gas station. Another guy slurped from his giant slushy drink, ignoring them completely.

"Did we just do it?" Charlotte slowly reached up and unsnapped her helmet. "Because I have to admit, this feels anticlimactic. I thought there'd be a parade or something. Are we sure we're done?"

"We're done. We did it. We finished, Charlotte." Zach propped his own helmet over one of the handlebars, wishing he could give her the celebratory finish she deserved. At the very least, her own giant slushy "Do you have any idea how proud I am of you? Come here." He pulled her into a tight hug.

She squeezed back, then gave him a playful shove. "Do you have any idea how bad we both smell? Maybe it's a good thing there isn't a parade here to welcome us."

With a grin, she motioned to the gas station. "I'm going to refill my bottle and try calling my sister. Hopefully there's enough battery left in my phone to get through. I wonder if we can start getting some of that prize money now. I'm starving for a meal that isn't a sub sandwich."

As soon as she shot inside, Zach pushed the bike around to the back of the station to think. Or cry. Whichever came first. Because they'd done it. Finished the race.

He leaned against the back wall, his shoulder pressing into the bricks as he rubbed the ache building in his chest.

"Get a grip," he whispered. It wasn't as if this was the last moment they'd ever be together. Sure, Charlotte would want to get back to Illinois, and he'd need to get out to California ASAP—they wouldn't keep holding that job for him forever—but maybe the two of them could use a tiny amount of that prize money to relax for a few days. Press pause. Figure things out.

No need to part ways so quickly.

Except . . . what was left to figure out? Being a couple and falling in love on the trail was one thing. But being a couple and making a relationship work in reality . . . Well, it just wasn't a reality, was it? Not for them.

Not unless Zach gave up California. Committed to carving out a life back in Bailey Springs. Could he do that?

Zach pushed off the wall. He was going to have to do *something*. They'd gone through too much to part ways now. There had to be a solution. This couldn't be the end. With two hundred fifty thousand dollars there had to be a way for Charlotte to leave her mom in good hands and at least consider the possibility of coming to California with him.

He rounded the corner and spotted her with her cellphone hanging limply at her side. "Did you get ahold of Sophia?"

She looked at the phone in her hand as if she had no idea how it had gotten there. Then she met Zach's gaze with the same hopeless expression, the same pained words she'd said the night he'd found her inside an empty church sanctuary two years ago after his brother had called off the wedding. "It's over, Zach. Everything. It's all over."

51

"It's going to be okay."

Charlotte shook her head. Zach had been murmuring that phrase as he held her for the past five minutes. Right after he'd led her to the back of the gas station, away from truckers and bikers and nosey snackers. But he was wrong. Dead wrong. It wasn't going to be okay.

"Tell me again what Sophia said."

Charlotte pushed out of Zach's arms and paced next to the brick wall. "I don't know. She was crying too hard to make everything out in her voice mail. But I caught enough to know my mom isn't doing well. Sophia said something about her having to go to the hospital. I had a text message from my dad saying she's fine and not to worry, but I know he's just saying that so I won't freak out. But I am freaking out. I need to get to North Carolina, and I don't know how because—" Her voice hitched. "There's no money. Sophia said Hopkins never planned to hand over twenty-five thousand dollars, let alone two hundred fifty thousand dollars. There's no prize. None. This whole thing was a mistake."

Of all the things Sophia had told her, Charlotte was ashamed to say that was what had punched her in the gut more than anything. *No money.* How could there not be any money? The whole point of this bike ride had been to win that money. How could it have never existed in the first place? "I don't understand any of this."

Zach reached for her, but Charlotte pushed him away. She needed space. She needed answers. She needed to get away from this stupid gas station. She kicked an empty, greasy fast-food sack onto a patch of dried grass separating the back parking lot from the drive-through. "How did I get this so wrong?"

"You didn't get anything wrong."

"No? Then tell me what I'm doing at a gas station in Louisiana right now. Tell me why I spent two thousand dollars on a tandem bicycle I never wanted." More tears rolled down her cheeks. "Tell me how these past ten days weren't a complete waste of time for me—or you. Which I'm honestly really sorry about. I never should have dragged you into this."

"Aw, Charlotte, don't talk like that." He reached for her hand. "We'll figure something out. Keep the faith, right?"

She folded her arms across her chest and backed away from his touch. "My mom's in the hospital and I can't even afford a plane ticket to get to her right now. So you can save the rah-rah speech about keeping the faith. I'm done with that. You're not the only one tired of having God yank the rug out from under your feet."

Zach gripped her shoulders, forcing her to stand still and face him. "Listen, I know it feels awful right now. Trust me. I get it. I've been there. In fact, up until this bike trip, I'd say I was still there. But . . . I was wrong."

"Great. Wonderful. Now you can be the one to start hosting revivals with the squirrels."

"I'm serious, Charlotte."

"Sure you are. Until next week when you change your mind again."

She tried stepping around him, but he blocked her path. "What's that supposed to mean?"

"Oh c'mon, Zach. You never see anything through, and you know it." Now really wasn't the time to be picking fights with Zach, but seriously, couldn't they just be on the same page for once?

"Name an example."

He asked for it. She lifted her voice to be heard over a classic rock song blaring from a car radio in the drive-through behind them. "Okay. Does dropping out of college after one semester ring a bell?"

"That was years ago. Name another example."

"Zach, in the past five years, you've changed jobs more often than you've changed underwear."

"I change my underwear every day, so you know that's not true."

"Fine. How about asking Shannon to elope with you, then apparently realizing later you never loved her."

"That's . . . sort of true."

"Two days ago you said you loved me."

"That's absolutely true."

"Is it? Because so far I haven't heard you mention a single word about changing your plans from going to California so you can move back to Illinois with me." And honestly, she didn't blame him one bit. He *shouldn't* change his plans. Not when he had such a great opportunity waiting for him. Better than any opportunities he'd find waiting for him back in Bailey Springs, that was for sure.

The music faded as the car drove away, Zach staring at her with his lips pressed together, the only sound between them an empty plastic bottle skittering across the pavement. His shoulders sank as he exhaled a deep breath. "I'll admit it's complicated. I have the perfect job opportunity in California, but no you. In Illinois I have you and . . . well, that's about it. So yeah. I might need some time to figure things out."

Charlotte trapped another roaming trash bag with her foot, then smashed it into the overflowing trash bin that smelled about as good as her life right now. "There's nothing to figure out. Don't you see? We're finally on the same page. You need to go to California. You know you'll never be happy stuck in Bailey Springs with me. Because that's exactly what I am, Zach. I don't know what's going on with my mom, but . . . I'm stuck."

The last word cracked and a rush of tears fell down her face. Zach tugged her into his arms. And this time he didn't try telling her it was going to be okay.

52

ONE WEEK LATER

Sophia cleared her throat and stared at the lump buried beneath a quilt covered in blue seashells and yellow starfish. "I don't want to put my nose where it doesn't belong, but I am your sister, and as your sister, I think one of my job requirements is to put my nose where it doesn't belong."

The lump—formerly known as Charlotte—didn't budge. Sophia didn't think the lump had budged in close to a week. How long could a human being survive in the form of an immobile lump? She leaned against the doorframe and took a sip of her hot chocolate. "What happened between you and Zach?"

"Nothing," a muffled voice responded.

The lump speaks! Cradling her mug, Sophia moved to the edge of the bed and perched next to the lump. "Then how come you've been acting like you're the one dying instead of Mom?"

"That's not funny."

"I'm not trying to be funny," Sophia insisted. All right, maybe she was trying to be a little bit funny. Cracking bad jokes seemed to be the only frayed thread that had kept her from unraveling ever since she'd rushed down to North Carolina. Ever since she'd refused to hear anything her parents had to say until she could see them face to face. Ever since she'd left Charlotte a panicked voice mail to meet her in North Carolina as soon as possible, knowing she wouldn't be able to handle anything her parents had to say without her sister beside her. Only to discover . . .

"Mom's pregnant." No matter how many times Sophia whispered the words out loud, she still couldn't completely grasp the idea that their mother—their going-gray, post-cancer, so-sick-she-could-have-died-five-years-ago, never-imagined-she-and-dad-were-still-having-sex-at-their-age *mother*—was pregnant.

No wonder her parents had been acting strange. They weren't thinking about divorce or death. They were thinking about another baby. A baby they thought they were going to lose last week, which was what Dad had been trying to call her about. Thankfully the scare that had sent Mom into the hospital turned out to be a false alarm. But the doctors still warned that the pregnancy was extremely high risk due to her age and health history. She'd need to take it easy.

Sophia set her mug on the white wicker table next to the bed, then dropped her hand onto the quilt tugged over Charlotte's shoulder. "What happened out there, Charlotte? I know this can't be about Mom. She looks amazing. She's glowing. You're the only one around here that looks miserable."

Charlotte met Sophia's gaze with puffy eyes and a reddened nose. "I'm just tired," she said, yanking the covers back over her head.

"Oh no you don't." Sophia jerked the blanket down. "You're not going back into a coma until you tell me what's going on with you and Zach, because I know that's what this is about. Mom's okay. Your music program is okay. Or at least still alive. I know not getting that two hundred fifty thousand dollars was a big blow, but thanks to Ben's donation and his company's new grant, you're better off than you have been in years. So stop trying to hide, and tell me what's going on."

Charlotte tugged the blanket. "I don't want to talk about it."

Sophia tugged it right back. "Yeah well, I tried that whole avoid-painful-conversations approach, and guess what—it didn't work. So we're going to talk about it. Are you in love with Zach?"

Charlotte scrambled for the blankets, but Sophia was quicker. She yanked everything off the bed and flung the quilt and sheets into the corner of the bedroom, leaving Charlotte covered in nothing but striped pajama pants and a gray V-necked shirt. Charlotte huffed out a breath, then collapsed back onto the bed as she folded her arms and glared at the ceiling.

"Did something happen on the trip? Did he hurt you?"

A little flicker of emotion flared in Charlotte's eyes. She shook her head side to side.

"Well, then, what is it? What's the problem? I can't stand seeing you like this. Do you want me to get some ice cream? Scrounge up those Beach Party movies you love? What?"

Good grief, being the encouraging cheerleader was exhausting. Sophia didn't know how Charlotte had done it for so many years. With what little moves she remembered from her two years of tap dance in early grade school, Sophia began dancing. "Is this helping?" she asked, toe-and-heel clicking side to side at the bottom of the bed. "Are you feeling better yet?"

The doorbell rang, saving her sister from answering. Not that Charlotte would have said anything. The girl hadn't cracked a joke in days.

Sophia planted her hands on her hips. She'd never seen Charlotte like this. Not even after her broken engagement with Ben.

So far Mom kept saying to let her rest. Hadn't she rested enough by now?

The doorbell rang again. Sophia glanced to the hallway. She should probably go answer it, though she had no idea who in the world would be ringing their bell at a sea cottage in North Carolina.

She thought about returning the wadded pile of blankets to Charlotte, then shook her head. Let Charlotte get them herself. Sophia jogged down the stairs and flung open the front door, not sure who she expected to see.

But certainly not expecting to see him.

53

A FEW DAYS LATER

Zach used his forearm to wipe off the perspiration building along his forehead, then readjusted his backpack over his shoulders. Another mile, then he'd take a break. Maybe. Part of him preferred to keep moving. Taking breaks gave a man too much time to think.

One of the reasons he'd risen long before the sun this morning was so he wouldn't have to stay in his bed and pretend to sleep when all he could do was think.

So far everything at Pinehaven Resort exceeded his expectations. He loved the owner. He loved the pay. He loved the job. Six days a week he'd be in charge of escorting guests along sections of the Lost Coast Trail, maintaining the resort's hiking and kayaking equipment, and offering wilderness tips, training, or directions to those who preferred to venture off on their own.

Zach couldn't have found a job better suited to his skills. He knew that.

Anyone who knew him knew that. The whole world probably knew that. And yet he couldn't stop thinking this whole thing had been a mistake.

Boarding the plane to fly out here, mistake. Saying goodbye to Charlotte outside a swanky hotel in Baton Rouge, mistake. Not that he'd had much of a choice. He'd pretty much been forced to say goodbye, since she had to run to catch her flight to North Carolina the following morning.

Zach reached for his water bottle. Soon as he got his first paycheck, he planned to reimburse Ben for covering Charlotte's plane ticket. The swanky hotel. The cab ride that had gotten them from the gas station down the interstate to the swanky hotel. Oh, and let's not forget shipping the bike back to Illinois.

Yeah, it might take more than Zach's first paycheck. Good grief, would there ever come a time he didn't feel like a failure compared to his brother?

Zach paused long enough to squirt a stream of water into his mouth, then shoved the bottle back into the side pocket of his backpack. Beneath a gray misty sky, the Pacific Ocean crashed into white foamy sprays against the rocky shoreline flanking his left.

Would there ever be a time Zach got things right? He picked up the pace as the voice in his head started to answer with a resounding 'No.' Then another voice drew his attention.

"Oh, praise God from whom all blessings flow, there you are."

Zach stopped so suddenly the weight of his backpack nearly tipped him forward. He had to be seeing things. But the closer the man came, panting and mopping sweat off his bald head, the more Zach believed it must be real. "Rick? What in the world are you doing here?"

Rick propped his hands on his waist. "I came to see you. Make sure you're doing okay. Goodness, that's a view, isn't it?" He swung a hand toward the shoreline. "All those waves and water and whatever."

"That's pure poetry."

"Isn't it?" Rick cracked a smile as he wiped off his head with a bandana. "So how are you? You okay? I can't stick around. Kate, you know . . ." He propped both his hands way out in front of his stomach.

"She's reaching beached-whale pregnancy size. Starting to have those fake contractions and everything. I keep telling her it's all that salsa. Either way, the baby's getting close. I figured I better make sure you were okay before things got crazy. So are you? Okay?"

Waves smacked against the shoreline, filling the silence, as Rick continued to mop his sweat and Zach continued to stare. "Are you telling me you seriously flew all the way out to California, hiked two miles—"

"Ah jeez Louise, that was only two miles?"

"—just to ask me if I'm okay?"

"Well, you don't have to make it sound like this is some sort of *Fatal Attraction* scenario. I'm your best friend. And it's sort of in my pastoral job description, that whole being a shepherd and all. Plus you aren't answering your phone. Why aren't you answering your phone?"

"I guess I didn't think it would matter if I fell off the radar for a bit."

"Of course it matters. I got worried. Everybody got worried. Okay, fine. Mostly just your mom and me got worried, but isn't that enough?" Rick pointed to Zach's backpack. "You got any snacks in there or is that just for looks?"

Zach shrugged the pack off his shoulders and dug out a bag of trail mix. "You've never been worried before."

"Well, nothing like this has ever happened before. The challenge turning out to be some sort of weird premarital counseling sham. Mrs. Carter turning out to be *pregnant.* Charlotte going into some sort of coma according to Sophia, who tends to exaggerate, so I'm sure Charlotte's not actually in a coma. But even so, I hear she's not doing good. Which makes me wonder why she's not doing good and what happened on that trail and are you doing good."

"I can't believe Mrs. Carter is pregnant."

"Believe it."

"I can't believe you flew here just to check on me."

"Believe it."

"I can't believe you already inhaled that entire bag of trail mix."

"Hey, the altitude makes me hungry. I'm not used to it."

"We're literally level with the sea."

"Well, I'm not used to that either. Now can we get back to the real issue. Are you okay? Like I said, I don't have much time. Kate's probably got Nita at gunpoint this very second forcing her to make another bucketful of salsa, and believe me, I wish I was kidding. So start talking. Did something happen on that trail?"

If Rick had flown across the country on his tiny preacher's salary with a pregnant wife due any day just to see if Zach was okay, the least Zach could do was be completely honest with him. "Something happened on the trail. I fell in love with Charlotte. Charlotte fell in love with me. I found my faith. Charlotte lost hers."

Rick lifted his finger, as if pointing to each of Zach's sentences on an invisible chalkboard to make sure he followed all of it, then dropped his hand with a groan. "Ah, crud. So you're saying I went after the wrong lost sheep? I tell you, this shepherding gig never gets easier."

Then Rick tugged Zach into a tight hug and pounded him on his backpack. "But man, is it worth it. Now tell me the *War and Peace* version of what you just said."

They hiked back to the resort and Zach spent the rest of the day telling Rick everything from the trip. Everything from before the trip. Everything from before they roomed together in college. Everything from his life he could think of.

By the time Zach dropped Rick off at the airport to make his red-eye flight back to Illinois that night, Zach knew two things. One, he had the greatest best friend in the world. Two, Rick wasn't the only one who could fly across the country just to make sure someone was okay.

But something, a whisper deep in his soul, told him that wasn't the move he should make. Not this time. Charlotte didn't need a grand gesture. Charlotte needed Zach to stay put until she figured things out.

And this time Zach was going to get things right.

Cool water washed over Charlotte's feet, softening the grainy sand to mush between her toes before the tide pulled the foamy spray back to the ocean. She'd been walking the shoreline all afternoon, same as she had every day since her brother Will had arrived.

Will. Her brother. *Here.* She couldn't believe it.

As happy as she was to see him, she had to admit that there had been a brief moment when she'd hoped it was somebody else at the door a few days ago. Somebody who'd changed his mind about California.

Charlotte dug the balls of her feet into the wet sand. A couple of seagulls landed close to the shoreline. Charlotte watched them, the breeze stirring up the ends of her hair. When they scuttled off, Charlotte almost envied them.

Which was stupid. And not like herself at all. Charlotte didn't envy birds. Because Charlotte didn't scuttle. Charlotte stayed put. Charlotte saw things through. Which is why she would *of course* stay in Bailey

Springs, continue on with the music program, and help her parents out with the new baby.

Charlotte glanced at the cottage, where Mom was probably still napping. Sophia was right. Their mom had a new glow and happiness about her. But Charlotte thought that had more to do with having all her children under one roof again, rather than growing another baby inside her body. That part was definitely making her tired. Hence the naps.

When Mom wasn't napping, they'd gotten into a routine of playing games and drinking tea. Well, Charlotte drank tea. Mom pretended to drink the probiotic, natural energy tea Charlotte had found a recipe for online, then dumped it down the sink when she thought nobody was looking. To be fair, the tea did taste like metal.

Every evening Sophia would fix supper, and afterward they'd gather outside by the fire pit, talking about everything and nothing. Sophia had found a guitar somewhere and presented it to Charlotte. "Didn't I tell you playing the guitar by campfires was totally your thing?"

Charlotte knew it wasn't possible to make up for lost years, but boy did they come awful close this past week. Finally, the vacation her parents deserved. All five of them. Together.

Everything Charlotte could have hoped for at the beginning of this summer was working out. Her job. Her mom's health. Even seeing her brother again.

So why did Charlotte feel like she'd never stood on shakier ground in all her life?

Motion drew her attention away from the shoreline. She shielded her gaze from the sun. The slight limp, wiry shoulders, and hands in the pockets quickly told her it was Will.

Charlotte turned to face the ocean. When he reached her side, he did the same. "She's still sleeping," he said.

Charlotte nodded because she didn't know what else to say. The wind tugged a strand of hair loose from her ponytail. She tried replacing it behind her ear a few times before giving up. They stood together in silence, letting the ocean do all the talking.

Her brother buried his hands deeper into his pockets. She gave him a sidelong look as the wind pressed his shirt against his torso. He looked fit. Healthy. Better than she'd ever seen him before. Which begged the question. "Why'd you avoid me for so long?"

Mingled in those conversations about everything and nothing the past couple of nights, she'd learned Will hadn't been avoiding his family after his prison release. No, he'd just been avoiding her.

His head dipped toward the ground where he dug his bare feet in the sand next to hers. "Because . . ." He must have shrugged at least five times before finally saying, "Remember that night in the barn?"

Of course she remembered that night in the barn.

"You ever wonder why I didn't come back?"

Only all the time. She nodded.

He lifted his face, one eye squinting shut in the bright sunlight as he glanced at the cottage, then focused on Charlotte. "Because I didn't think you needed me. And by the time I realized maybe you did . . . I guess I figured I'd hurt you too much to come back."

She didn't know whether to slug him or hug him. Because yeah, he'd definitely hurt her. But he was her brother. All she'd ever wanted was for him to come back. Then and now.

Flicking a tear from the corner of her eye before he could spot it and clam up because he thought she was about to get all emotional, she bumped her shoulder against his. "Well, I'm glad you're back now."

Even if he was too late to loosen the ropes holding her in place. Because that was the problem, wasn't it? The real problem she couldn't explain to Sophia. Yes, something had happened on the trail. She'd finally gotten a little taste of adventure. And yes, she'd fallen in love with Zach. But none of that mattered. Not when she couldn't break free from the responsibilities wrapped around her, tying her down to her hometown.

Responsibilities that up until the bike trip, she'd been glad to have wrapped around her, securing her in place. Because up until now, she'd never realized that one day she'd have trouble breaking free.

Lost in her thoughts, it took her a moment to realize her brother was clearing his throat and twitching his shoulders as if he were about to start another marathon shrugging session. "You okay?" Charlotte asked.

"Not really. I can't figure out how to say this without sounding like an idiot."

"Well, then maybe you should just say it."

"I met someone." He dipped his head toward the sand, but not quick enough to hide the dopey grin spreading across his lips. "Her dad's the one who's been helping me out with getting my plumbing license. And . . . well, she's amazing. I love her."

Was her brother blushing? Charlotte angled her face toward the tide, so he wouldn't see her mouth gaping open. "And does this amazing someone have a name?"

"Hannah." He cleared his throat, digging his hands into his pockets probably to give his shoulders a break. "She's been wanting to meet you guys for a while now. I couldn't hold her off any longer. She's coming later this week." He cleared his throat again, sounding like a boy asking a girl out on his very first date. "She has a daughter too."

"What?" Charlotte didn't even attempt to hide her surprise this time. "And how old is she?"

"Four. She's really smart. I think she's smarter than me."

"Well, that's not saying much."

He grinned. "She's cute. She looks just like her mom."

Charlotte couldn't help it. She stared at her brother. Who was this man? He looked so . . . domesticated. "You really feel like you're up for all that?"

"Some days, no. Some days I'm pretty sure I'll screw it up. But sometimes it's not about feeling ready. It's about finding something you don't want to lose, then vowing to never stop going after it no matter how many setbacks you have along the way." He offered Charlotte an amazed look. "I sing Sunday school songs with a four-year-old now. And you want to know the craziest part? I couldn't be happier."

Who was this man? "That's great, Will."

What? She could do better than that. This man was her brother. *Her brother.* "Will Carter is in love and singing Sunday school songs with a four-year-old," she shouted, then threw her arms around him with a laugh. "Never dreamed I'd see the day."

"Sure you did," he whispered, his voice rough and broken next to her ear. "Heck, you were probably the only one who never lost faith in me."

Moisture sheened in his eyes when he pulled away and dug a hand in his pocket. "I'm going to ask her to marry me. After she meets Mom and Dad this weekend." He pulled out a box and opened the lid. A simple ring with a small solitaire diamond winked back from the velvet lining. "Think she'll like it?"

"She'll love it," Charlotte said, relieved he'd moved on from the faith talk.

Sure, everything had turned out fine for her this summer. Her job. Her parents. Even her brother. But what if it hadn't? One voice mail message had given her a glimpse of where her faith really stood. And it was no firmer beneath her feet than the sand surrounding her toes.

Will replaced the ring, then pulled something from his other pocket. "I bought this for Hannah's daughter. I wanted to give her something too, you know." He handed it to Charlotte. "Think that'll work?"

Charlotte forced a laugh past the tightness in her throat. It was a sucker ring. "What four-year-old wouldn't adore this?"

"I have a necklace to give her at some point, but considering she can't even make it through the day without losing one of her socks, I thought I'd wait to give her the necklace until the wedding day. Assuming Hannah says yes."

Charlotte handed the packaged sucker ring back to him. "I have a feeling she will."

Will exhaled a breath of relief. "Good." His voice relaxed and turned playful. "Hey, do you know anything about Sophia's mystery man?"

"What are you talking about?"

"She's been texting a lot, trying to act nonchalant. But she's always smiling like an idiot. I caught a glimpse of her phone once. Looked like the caller ID said Clark Kent Hottie." He shoved the rings back in his pockets, then jutted his chin toward the cottage. "I'm going to see if Mom's awake yet."

"Sure. Be there in a few minutes."

He started to turn, then swiveled back, gently grabbing her elbow. "Hey. Almost forgot the real reason I came out here to talk to you. I'm long overdue giving you an apology. I know I should have reached out to you way sooner, but . . . I don't know. For some reason it was different with you. Harder. I think because at one time we used to be the closest. Anyway, I'm sorry. And I want you to know that whatever happens with Mom and this baby, it's not on you this time. Looking after them, I mean. Hannah and me, we've been talking, and we both agree it's my turn. For sticking around. Helping out. Whatever Mom and Dad need, I've got this. I'm not going anywhere."

"Well, neither am I." She cleared the tightness from her throat. High-risk pregnancy aside, why would she leave just when her music program had a chance to take off? Thanks to Ben, her dream was finally coming true.

Thanks to Ben. Had she really just thought that? What happened to *Take that, Benjamin Bryant*? And why did a thriving music program feel less and less like a dream come true? And more and more like ropes tying her down?

Will released her elbow to dig his hands into his pockets. The lines around his eyes creased as he squinted out toward the water. "I'm just saying you have options. You know, in case there's someone, maybe a guy you just biked a whole bunch of miles with through thick and thin, that you wanted to pursue instead of your music program."

Charlotte clutched her stomach. Talk about a sucker punch. She inhaled a deep breath, then slowly released it. "I thought you and Zach hated each other."

Will offered a pained smile. "There might be a punch or two we still need to get out of the way. But that's only because we both care about you."

Guys were so weird. She watched him start making his way up the sandy hill back to the cottage. Man, had he changed. Or maybe finally gotten back to himself.

Charlotte looked out to the ocean for several minutes before she closed her eyes with a sigh. Maybe it was time for Charlotte to get back to herself too. The Charlotte who long ago used to dream of possibilities outside her own little world. Who didn't let her own vision of what her life had to look like tie her down.

"Hey Will," she hollered over her shoulder.

He paused to look back.

"I *do* need you, you know."

He dipped his head in acknowledgment. "Like I said, you don't need to worry about Mom and Dad. I've got this."

"I'm not talking about them. I'm talking about the plumbing at my house. If I'm ever going to put my house on the market, I'm going to need you to fix it. Soon. At family discount price."

His dimpled grin reminded her of the brother she knew so well growing up. "I think that can be arranged."

Charlotte tilted her face back toward the sky and held her arms out wide. Without any ropes holding her down, who knows? Maybe Charlotte Carter could finally scuttle off.

55

Sophia's fingers shook as she braided her hair over her shoulder. What if he didn't come? She paced back and forth at the train station. What if he *shouldn't* come? What if she was rushing things? What if this was too much?

It was one thing to text back and forth. But meeting her parents? Her brother and sister? Her brother's new fiancée as of last night? Yeah, this might be too much.

The train screeched to an ear-piercing halt. She undid the braid. And why had she asked him to come in a text message? It was too hard to decipher his tone in a text message. Had he been happy about it? Resigned? All he'd messaged back was **I'll be there**.

Was it an *I'll be there* with a long-suffering sigh? Or was it an *I'll be there* to the tune of the Jackson 5 classic? Was this a step forward in their relationship, or was this the weekend she'd forever mark on her mental calendar as the time everything had turned awkward and fallen apart?

She rapidly braided her hair again, sending a quick prayer skyward. *Please let this not be one of my stupid decisions. Please let this be a blessing for my mom. My family. My heart. Oh Lord please—*

Joshua stepped down from the train, a duffel bag over his shoulder. His eyes landed on her and he smiled. A Jackson Five kind of smile.

Thank you, Lord.

Sophia stepped forward with a wave. "Hi."

He walked until he was right in front of her, his gaze never leaving her face. "Hi."

They both stood there, grinning like idiots. "You look taller," Sophia finally said.

"Really? Must be all the weight that's off my shoulders from finally telling my dad what I want to do with my life." He'd texted Sophia about his decision to go back to school and start working toward his master of divinity degree.

"I'm proud of you. And thank you so much for coming. I know you're super busy, so trust me, I would have understood if you didn't have time to come down here."

"I didn't really have a choice."

"You didn't?" Oh no. She'd bullied him into coming, hadn't she? Pushed too hard. And since he was such a nice guy, he'd of course responded with a long-suffering *I'll be there.*

"I missed you too much to stay away."

"Oh." She reached for her braid. "Is that so?"

He nodded, intercepting her hand with the perfect level of gentleness and firmness. "I was trying to come up with a reasonable excuse to show up uninvited when you thankfully saved me the trouble." He pressed a kiss to her palm, his eyes never leaving hers. "I missed you."

"I think you already said that." She stepped closer, erasing the small distance between them. "But it's okay if you want to say it again."

He let his duffel bag slide from his shoulder and drop to the ground. "I really, really missed you."

"Yeah?"

"Oh yeah." He leaned closer, his warm breath tickling her lips. "But you know who's missed you even more?"

She fisted his T-shirt. "D'Artagnan?"

His eyes crinkled in a smile as his fingers found her braid and played with the strands. "No. Trusty Rusty. He says business has been so boring without all your car troubles keeping him busy."

Then his lips dropped against hers, and Sophia couldn't believe she'd ever been worried.

56

A FEW WEEKS LATER

Zach smoothed the tie choking his neck like a noose and willed his hands not to shake as he met the dozen gazes peering back at him from their seats around a rectangular table. Clearing his throat, he said, "I once stumbled upon a momma grizzly and her two cubs during one of my hikes in Alaska. And I'm pretty sure I didn't feel half as scared as I do right now, knowing I need to convince sixteen people in suits to hand over money."

The group all chuckled, and Zach exhaled some of his nerves. "I won't lie. I've always been more comfortable out in the wild than I have been within four walls. But I'm also more comfortable with food in my belly than not. So when my boss asked me to give this presentation, I said, 'Nothing would make me happier.'"

Chairs creaked as the executive board members smiled and settled into their seats. Zach clicked to the first slide on the PowerPoint presentation and whispered a prayer he wouldn't bungle it.

An hour and a half later, Zach had shed his tie and was on the road back to the resort with a grin on his face. "See? Didn't I say you'd do great?" his boss said through the Bluetooth in the resort's SUV. "I knew once you got going, your love and passion for everything nature would be contagious and spread like—"

"Wildfire?"

"I was going to say poison ivy."

The sun broke through a patch of white clouds. Zach flipped down the visor with a laugh, thinking of Charlotte and her little run-in with poison ivy.

Then again, everything made him think of Charlotte. Halfway through his presentation, one of the board members had brushed her hair behind her ear and his mind flashed to Charlotte. Why? Because Charlotte had hair and an ear? He didn't know. He only knew Charlotte was never far from his thoughts. Ever.

Which is why these past six weeks had been torture.

"Well, I'm glad to hear it went okay, even though I had no doubt it would. We'll talk more when you get back. Good job. Oh and hey," his boss said before ending the call, "I meant to tell you sooner. Even though I think you're doing a great job, I'm interviewing a potential new employee today to take some of the load off those presentations. You mind sitting in on the interview when you get back? This person would be working pretty closely with you, so I want to make sure you think it's a good fit."

"Oh." Had his boss mentioned hiring someone? Not that Zach couldn't use the help. Especially if his boss expected him to continue giving presentations to possible investors, like he had this morning. That had never been Zach's forte. "Sounds good. Yeah. I should be back in about an hour, so I'll just head straight to your office."

"Perfect. See you then."

The wind through the open windows rustled through his hair, which was long overdue for a trim. He blasted the radio and drummed his thumbs on the steering wheel, but then shut it off after a few minutes. *Not that I'm not grateful for everything you've been doing here, God . . .*

All the pieces of his life were slowly fitting together. His job. His faith. His relationship with his brother. They'd talked more in the past six weeks than they'd talked in years.

But there's still that one little matter you know I'd like to resolve. It's been six weeks. Pretty soon it will have been two months. Then once her school year starts, I'm afraid it's going to turn into a year. How long do I need to wait? I only bring this up because I've been reading my Bible, which ought to earn me some extra points, not that you're keeping track of points, but I'm a little concerned because there's this whole wandering around in the desert for forty years section, and that's kind of a long time. Maybe not to you, but it sure is to me. And I know I've promised to do things right this time, but waiting forty years for things to work out between Charlotte and me doesn't feel right. I don't think it's right. Oh God, please don't let that be right.

After another hour of praying and pleading, Zach reached the turn-off to the resort. He climbed out of the SUV and slid off his tie, ready to get out of the stiff clothes, when he remembered the interview. Oh, right. Better pop in and see if they'd started yet.

He jogged up the stairs to the large log cabin that housed the main welcoming center and offices. Jamie, his boss's college-aged daughter, was manning the front desk. She tilted her head toward the back office with a smile. "He said to head on back."

Zach nodded and kept moving. After a quick knock, he opened the door. "Okay to come in?"

His boss, seated behind his desk, motioned toward a chair. "Yes. Perfect timing. We were just going over Charlotte's qualifications."

Charlotte?

Zach clung to the door handle, his gaze landing on the beauty seated in a chair across from the desk. She swiped a loose strand of hair behind her ear. *Charlotte.*

"So, let's see." His boss peered down his glasses at the paper on his desk. "Looks like you definitely know a thing or two about fundraising. That's good. I see your qualifications also include playing the guitar next to campfires."

"You might say that's my thing."

"Wonderful. Well, I see no reason why you shouldn't join our team. But I'll leave the final decision up to Zach." He stood and offered Charlotte a warm smile and handshake. "It's nice to finally meet you—especially after hearing so much about you these past several weeks. Let me know how the interview turns out," he said, punching Zach's shoulder on his way out of the office.

The door closed and Zach still hadn't stopped staring at Charlotte. *Charlotte.* "You're here."

"I'm here." She rose from her seat. "I hope that's okay."

Okay? Zach scraped his hand across his jaw, glancing to the door, the trees past the open window blinds, the walls, then to Charlotte. She was here. Really here. "I didn't expect you for another forty years."

"Oh." Her brow wrinkled.

"That's not . . . I mean, I was willing to wait forty years if that's what it took. But I'm really glad that's not what it took. Because you're here. Now. And it's only been six weeks. Even if it has felt like forty years."

The lines on her forehead smoothed and a smile danced on the edge of her mouth. "So shall we continue on with the interview?"

He'd rather kiss that smile dancing on the edge of her mouth. But he supposed there were a few questions to be answered first. "How do you feel about kayaking?"

"Oh, about the same way I feel about canoeing."

"How comfortable are you with hiking?"

"Very. As long as I don't encounter any wildlife. Especially bees."

"Reasonable." Zach smiled, then held her gaze as he took a step closer. Now for the real question. "What are you doing here?"

"Other than interviewing for a job I'm obviously way overqualified for?" She played with the zipper on her light blue hoodie, suddenly looking unsure.

"What about the music program?" He edged forward another step.

She ran the zipper up and down the bottom of her sweatshirt a few times, then let go with a sigh. "I've started seeing someone."

Zach's feet froze. "What?"

"No. Sorry. That didn't come out right. A counselor. I meant I've started seeing a counselor."

Zach released a shaky breath. "Good clarification."

"Rick connected me with someone he knows. And it's been good. Turns out there's been a lot of tough issues in my life I've never talked through. With anyone. Including God. No wonder my faith crumbled, right?"

"Your faith didn't crumble, Charlotte. It just stumbled a bit. Believe me when I say I know a thing or two about that. But I'm guessing you regained your footing a lot quicker than I did."

She offered a soft hopeful smile, playing with her hoodie zipper again. "Rick says you two have been talking a lot lately."

"Yeah, turns out there's a few issues I've been needing to talk through too. Issues I've been avoiding for years because . . . I don't know. I guess I never felt ready."

"Sometimes it's not about feeling ready. It's about finding something you don't want to lose, then vowing to never stop going after it no matter how many setbacks you have along the way."

"Those sound like some pretty wise words."

"I thought so too, when Will said them the other week."

Zach groaned. "That punk. He really has changed, hasn't he? And here I was planning to pummel him next time we met."

"Well, if our little bike trip taught me anything, it's that our plans don't always play out like we think they will. And thank God for that."

Zach wanted nothing more than to erase the space between them with a crushing embrace, but he forced himself to remain still. He could do that. Not for forty years, but maybe forty more seconds. Long enough for Charlotte to answer his initial question. "And your music program? What about that?"

"Maybe I was just meant to plant the seeds for a music program. Maybe I was never meant to do the growing. Ty's already found a couple of great candidates interested in the job. I know without a doubt the program will be in good hands."

Zach slid a step closer and tipped up his hands. "And your mom?"

Charlotte slipped her hands into his like he'd hoped she would. "Oh, she's an emotional wreck. No doubt about that. But she's a happy emotional wreck. She was more excited than anyone, I think, when I said I was ready to move on with my life. I think part of her was just so relieved knowing my social life wouldn't revolve around watching Frankie Avalon movies anymore."

"Well, I can guarantee you my mother will be equally as thrilled. But I do have to ask. Do you really see yourself being happy? Here? Outdoors? With me?"

"If you can see yourself being happy doing the occasional presentation and fundraiser indoors with me." She released his hands and circled her arms around his waist. "Truth is . . . well, I love you. And I don't want to ride tandem through this life with anybody but you. For better or worse. Richer or poorer. Shoot, Zach. We don't always have to be on the same page. Just as long as we're on the same bike, right? And we both promise to keep pedaling no matter how many setbacks we have along the way?"

She reached up, running a hand through his hair down to where it ended past his ear. He smiled, pressing his cheek into her palm. "I can promise to keep pedaling. But I can't make any promises about never encountering wildlife—especially bees."

"Well, I've already worked out a plan for that. One of my former students helped me come up with the idea. Ever heard of circular breathing?"

Zach smoothed a loose lock of hair past her ear and ran his hands down her back. "No, but it sounds like something we're going to need in two seconds."

"Why two seconds?"

Zach pressed her close to him. Close enough to feel Charlotte's breath fan his lips. "Because I'm two seconds away from kissing you senseless. And honey, I don't plan to come up for air for at least forty years."

EPILOGUE

THREE MONTHS LATER

"Is this crazy? This is crazy, isn't it? You can say it. It's crazy. We're moving too fast." Charlotte paced back and forth in front of the full-length mirror, her white dress swishing around her ankles with each turn.

"It's not crazy. Waiting any longer would be crazy. What do you need to do? Climb Mount Everest to prove you and Zach are compatible? If you haven't killed each other by now, I think it's true love. Wasn't that sort of the point of Hopkins's ridiculous challenge?" Sophia trailed behind her with a veil. "Now, would you stop moving so I can pin this to your head? We need to see the full effect."

"I already told you I don't want a veil."

"And I already told *you*," Sophia said with a grunt as she wrestled Charlotte's head far enough down to poke her scalp with something pointy, "I don't care what you say you don't want because most of the time what you say you don't want, you end up wanting, so you'd be better off just letting me do what I want."

Charlotte spun to fend off her sister and caught a glimpse of her veil-clad head in the bridal shop mirror. "Oh wowzer," she whispered, clasping her hands together in front of her chest. "Do you know who I look like?"

Sophia nodded, her eyes shining with happy tears. "Mom. It's her veil."

Charlotte touched the ends of the veil with reverence. "I think I want a veil."

"Hmm, imagine that." Sophia folded her arms with a knowing smirk. "Now that the veil issue is resolved, you need to pick out a dress. Something prettier than that one."

Charlotte lifted the folds of the skirt. "What's wrong with this one?"

"Nothing, if we'd time-traveled back to 1994."

"Everything comes back in style at some point."

"I don't think we're at that point. Try on something else. Or actually—" Sophia ducked behind a rack of dresses and returned with a familiar pink garment bag. "Try on this."

Well, wasn't she just full of surprises? "Sophia. I cannot wear the dress I was supposed to wear in my wedding to Ben."

"Why not? Nobody ever got the chance to see you in this dress. And you loved this dress. Remember how much you loved this dress?"

"I remember getting rid of this dress, that's what I remember."

"Yeah, well, Mom and I bought it back from the consignment shop as soon as you left. It's been hiding in the back of Mom and Dad's closet ever since."

"Why would you do that?"

Sophia gave her a look like she should know better. "Because nothing was ever wrong with the dress. The dress was perfect. The problem was with the guy. You know the old saying, don't throw out the dress with the bathwater. Now try it on. I'll bet it looks even more amazing on you this time."

"Because I finally got the right guy?"

"I was going to say because all that time outdoors has helped you tone up and slim down." Sophia winked. "But yeah, sure. What you said."

Charlotte and Sophia teased and laughed as she tried on the dress. And of course, Sophia was right. Nothing was wrong with the dress. The dress was perfect. Last time just hadn't been the right time to wear it.

"So we're not rushing things?" Charlotte asked when they left the wedding shop a little later. She'd bought a new pair of expensive shoes since she felt bad about not buying anything else from the boutique.

"Technically you and Zach have been in a committed canoodling relationship since before the bike trip."

"Well, when you put it that way." Charlotte adjusted her grip on the garment bag, glancing at the sparkly diamond on her ring finger. "I feel kind of bad dress shopping without Mom though. I mean, that was one of the main reasons we flew back for the weekend." But yesterday the doctors had put her mom on strict bed rest until the baby arrived.

Sophia bumped her shoulder. "Don't worry. She already knew you were going to choose the dress from the back of their closet. But hey, if it makes you feel any better, Mom will get another chance to go wedding-dress shopping with me."

"What?" Charlotte froze, then gasped at the sparkle shining from Sophia's ring finger. She slugged her sister on the shoulder. "Where did you get that? And why didn't you say something? When did this happen?"

"I didn't want to make this day about me. And it only happened last night. Besides, we're not even thinking about picking a date until at least one of us graduates. A lot of it also depends on how Mom does this next year with the baby." Sophia grabbed Charlotte's wrist. "But oh Charlotte, he was so cute. I've never seen a man so nervous. Which made me nervous. I thought he was either going to break up with me or tell me he was dying. But once I figured out he wanted to marry me, well . . . We both recovered quickly from our nerves."

"I'll be sure to keep Mom's veil spick-and-span for you."

Sophia wrapped her arm through Charlotte's as they continued down the sidewalk. "Thanks. And who knows? Maybe our little sister can wear it someday."

"Maybe by the time she's of marrying age, that dress back at the store will be in fashion again."

"Let's not bring this party down. We're trying to enjoy ourselves."

They rounded the corner and both sisters were greeted with the happiest of visions. Joshua holding a leash connected to a tongue-lolling, tail-wagging D'Artagnan. And Zach, holding a helmet next to the tandem bicycle they'd been keeping in Mom and Dad's garage ever since their bike trip.

Charlotte handed her dress, veil, and shoes off to Sophia, exchanging them for the helmet.

"I can't believe you two are going for a bike ride," Sophia said, leaning into Joshua's side for a hug. "Anybody tell you two you might be obsessed?"

Charlotte clipped her helmet into place and reached for the rear handlebars. "Well, it's certainly a healthier obsession than cheesecake."

"Got that right, pilgrim." Zach swooped in and kissed Charlotte long enough for Sophia to mutter something about getting a room. Long enough for Charlotte to lose her grip and her balance as the bike toppled sideways, carrying the weight of her and Zach with it.

They landed in a tangled pile next to the sidewalk, and all Charlotte could do was tip her head back and laugh and be grateful. Because this tandem ride was only getting started.

A NOTE FROM THE AUTHOR

Back in the spring of 2010, a guy I'd been dating and getting pretty serious with told me about a bike trip he took with a buddy, starting at the northern border of Minnesota and going down to New Orleans. "What would you think about doing a trip together like that? It wouldn't have to be as long. Maybe just along the Natchez Trace?"

I had no idea what the Natchez Trace was, and I think the furthest I'd ever ridden a bicycle in one day was maybe around fifteen miles. But what can I say? I was young and in love, so I said, "Sure! Let's do it!"

So late June into early July that summer we did it. We biked from Nashville, Tennessee, to Baton Rouge, Louisiana, on a tandem bicycle that a pair of good friends let us borrow for the trip. Neither of us had ridden a tandem before, but we got the hang of it pretty quickly. (Well, after we crashed into a bush at our very first stop, we got the hang of it pretty quickly.)

By the end of five hundred miles, after pedaling our way through heat advisories, downpours, flat tires, wrong directions, snack-hungry raccoons, and more peanut-butter-tortilla sandwiches than a person should ever eat in one week, we *definitely* had the hang of it. And we knew one thing for certain—we were ready to pedal through more of life's journeys together. (Hopefully on more comfortable seats, though.) We got married that December.

I've always known the important role that trip played in leading into my marriage. But what a joy it is to see now, close to fourteen years later, how God is using the stories and memories from that trip to create new stories and memories in my life as a writer—something I certainly never imagined back when I was panting and sweating my way up those Tennessee hills.

Which makes me wonder what other joys await from the hills I'm climbing today. I look forward to finding out. And I hope, dear reader friend, whatever hills you're facing today, you'll be encouraged to keep pedaling too.

ACKNOWLEDGMENTS

Well, it only seems fair to start off by thanking my husband. Dave, if you hadn't asked me to go on that bike trip with you, I don't think this story would have ever come about. I'm grateful for your encouragement when it comes to my writing. And I'm even more grateful you handled that raccoon situation during our bike trip, because we both know I'd still be curled up in the fetal position at the bottom of my sleeping bag to this very day if it hadn't been for you.

Maria and Charlie, thank you for being two of my biggest fans. (You know I'll always be one of yours!) I love how excited you are to celebrate my second book. Granted, I know that's partially because you just love any excuse to eat cake, but I'm grateful anyway.

To the rest of my family—whether you're just in it for the cake or not—thank you for all your encouragement and enthusiasm. I love you all!

To the entire team I get the pleasure of working with at Tyndale—from marketing, sales, PR, editing, and beyond—thank you! To Kathy Olson, my editor, I'm especially grateful for your kindness and insight. You've helped make this story better, and you've helped make me a better writer in the process. Maybe someday I'll even grasp how to use *might* and *may* appropriately. (Don't hold your breath, though.) Elizabeth Jackson, thank you for all your input, encouragement, and kindness while getting this book ready for publication. And Libby Dykstra, you know I adore your cover designs. Thank you for putting my stories in such cute packages.

To my agent, Rachelle Gardner, thank you for somehow seeing the potential in the earlier, far-less-polished drafts of this story. I'm so grateful for your guidance and feedback. And I'm especially grateful you don't hesitate to say, "You know, you might want to tone this down a bit," when things start getting a little too over-the-top.

Speaking of over-the-top . . . Katie, Toni, Alaina, and Megan—thank you. But seriously, you can calm down now. (Or maybe don't. Maybe I actually love seeing how excited you guys get over each of my stories, and maybe I think you are the best.)

Speaking of the best, a big thank you to my coworkers at Springfield Memorial Hospital, especially my fellow nurses and respiratory therapists on 2C. For years this writing gig felt like a secret little dream I had on the side. I never imagined how excited and supportive you would be when I finally brought my publishing dream out into the light. Thank you for being such awesome coworkers and friends!

Now that we're speaking of awesome friends, have I mentioned how blessed I am to be in a writing group with Becky Yauger, Becky DePaulis, Lynn Watson, CJ Myerly, Wendy Galinetti, and Denise Colby? Because I am. Thank you, ladies, for celebrating (and sometimes lamenting) this writing journey with me.

Also, a special shout-out to those who've invited me to their book clubs this past year. Alyssa Tusek, Lisa Dillon, Carrie Tucker, Debbie Turnbull, and Nora St. Laurent—thanks for helping get the word out about my books. And thank you to the retailers, bloggers, and reviewers who've given these stories a chance.

Finally, thank you, God, for giving me a reason to write and a story to write. And thank *you*, dear reader, for taking the time to read it.

ABOUT THE AUTHOR

BECCA KINZER lives in Springfield, Illinois, where she works as a critical care nurse. When she's not taking care of sick patients or reminding her husband and two kids that frozen chicken nuggets is a gourmet meal, she enjoys making up lighthearted stories with serious laughs. She is a 2018 ACFW First Impressions Contest winner, a 2019 Genesis Contest winner, a 2021 Cascade Award winner, and an all-around champion coffee drinker. *Love in Tandem* is her second novel. Visit Becca online at beccakinzer.com.

DISCUSSION QUESTIONS

1. Initially Zach and Charlotte don't seem to have a lot in common. Have you ever developed a deep friendship with someone who at first seemed like your complete opposite?
2. On the other hand, Sophia and Joshua seem to connect right away. Have you ever had that sort of friendship experience?
3. What's the most memorable trip you've ever taken?
4. When Charlotte and Zach reach their goal, they discover the results aren't what they expected. Have you ever reached a goal and found the results or maybe your reaction to reaching the goal wasn't what you expected?
5. How well did you relate to Sophia? Are you the type of person who prefers to handle bad news up front or do you tend to avoid it until you absolutely have to face it?
6. What did you think when you found out the real purpose of the couples challenge?
7. If you were to spend an afternoon on a tandem bicycle with one of the characters from this book, which character would you choose?

8. Zach and Charlotte both go through situations where they feel like God pulled the rug out from under their feet. Have you ever felt this way? How did you hold on to your faith?

9. Charlotte and Zach experienced the kindness of strangers multiple times on their trip. Do you have any stories of kind strangers helping you out? Or maybe a time when you were the kind stranger helping someone else out?

10. Is there anywhere in the world you wish you could spend ten days exploring? (Not necessarily on a tandem bike.)

CONNECT WITH BECCA ONLINE AT

beccakinzer.com

OR FOLLOW HER ON

@beccaannkinzer

@BeccaKinzer

@Becca_Kinzer

CP1812